JEROME MCGINN

Al Ana's Curse

I am truly grateful for the unwavering support and belief my Mom, Dad, all my children, my brother Joe and his family have shown me, even during the most challenging moments of my life. I am especially appreciative of my Mom's invaluable contributions to this book. Her dedication and hard work have been invaluable, and I am forever indebted to her for her efforts. Words cannot express the depth of my gratitude for the incredible people in my life who have made this accomplishment a reality.

"Do not be overcome by evil, but overcome
evil with good."

— Romans 12:21

"To live is the rarest thing in the world.
Most people exist, that is all."

— Oscar Wilde

Contents

Acknowledgement

I am truly grateful to Shawna Hampton, my editor, and proofreader whose invaluable guidance and support played a pivotal role in helping me bring my first book to fruition. Her expertise and dedication were instrumental in shaping my work. I would also like to extend my heartfelt appreciation to Kerry Ellis for her remarkable talent and artistic vision, which breathed life into the graphics, elevating the visual appeal of the book to new heights.

1

Banshee Screams

Aedan glanced down at his exam paper, the last few scribbles of ink marking the end of his battle with the American Revolutionary War and twelfth grade. It was over now. Done. No more high school. He let out a sigh of relief that seemed to carry the weight of every minute spent memorizing dates and names, which often jumbled together in his head like a deck of cards someone dropped.

A small smile crept across his face as he closed the exam booklet, a sense of accomplishment washing over him. He felt immense gratitude for the teachers who had guided him through his academic journey, their dedication and patience helping him navigate even the most challenging topics. The countless hours he spent poring over textbooks and study materials had finally paid off, and he couldn't help but feel a profound appreciation for the knowledge he had gained. As he glanced around the classroom, memories of late-night study sessions, spirited debates, and shared laughter with his classmates flooded his mind. These friendships, forged in the crucible of academic rigor, had become a cherished part of his high school experience.

His chest tightened as he thought about what came next. The security of the familiar hallways and classrooms he had known for years would soon be replaced by the great unknown of adulthood. He had spent so much time dreaming about this moment, desperate to leave behind the endless tests and homework, but now that it was here, a knot of anxiety twisted in his stomach. What if he failed at whatever he tried next? What if he made the wrong choices and ended up regretting everything? What if he didn't do well or acclimate to college life?

The future stretched out before him, vast and terrifying in its possibilities. He took a shaky breath, trying to calm all the fears racing through his mind. Maybe this was just the beginning of an even greater journey, one filled with new challenges and opportunities he couldn't even imagine yet. The thought did little to settle his nerves, but he knew he had to keep moving forward, one uncertain step at a time.

Aedan momentarily peered through the classroom window at a ribbon of water that carved its way past Northern Straits High School. "Chook River," Aedan mumbled under his breath; he always thought there was something sinister about it, even if most days it just sat there, as lazy as him on a Sunday afternoon. There were, of course, countless stories, despite the troubling reports of unsolved missing person cases featured on local news channels and in newspapers, but some thrill seekers remained undaunted, humbly continuing their explorations along the river.

Around Aedan, the rest of the history class was wrapping up too. Mary Thompson sat next to him, her red hair resting on her shoulders, and she had been done for ages, pen resting neatly atop her completed test, a small smile of satisfaction playing on her lips. Her calmness was like an anchor in the stormy sea of high school drama.

As Aedan observed Mary's composed demeanor, he couldn't help but feel a pang of envy. Her confidence and poise seemed effortless, a stark contrast to the swirling doubts and insecurities that often plagued his mind. Yet, there was something admirable about her tranquility, a quiet strength that appeared to radiate from within. At that moment, Aedan realized true confidence wasn't about pretending to have all the answers or projecting an air of superiority.

It was about embracing one's flaws and imperfections, while still maintaining a feeling of self-assurance. Mary's serenity stemmed from a deep acceptance of herself, flaws and all. As the final seconds ticked away, Aedan made a silent vow to cultivate that same inner peace. He knew it wouldn't be easy, but with determination and self-compassion, he could learn to navigate the turbulent waters of adolescence with the same grace and equanimity that Mary exuded so naturally.

Lindsey Merritt let out a little yawn and stretched her arms above her head like she was tired, her ironed-straight, jet-black hair falling in soft waves over her shoulders. She caught Aedan's eye and offered a warm, friendly smile that made him feel hypnotized as his stomach did backflips. Lindsey was kindness personified and Mary's best friend; she brightened up people's darkest days without even trying. Her personality and optimism were a source of inspiration for everyone around her. And yeah, maybe Aedan was crushing hard, but who among their peers wouldn't be?

As Lindsey's bright smile lingered, Aedan found himself reflecting on the remarkable qualities that made her so captivating. Beyond her outward beauty, there was a depth to her character that drew people in like moths to a light. She possessed a steady strength of spirit, facing life's challenges head-on with a resilience that was both humbling and awe-inspiring. Lindsey's compassion knew no bounds, and she extended warmth and understanding to all who crossed her path.

She had a way of making even the most guarded individuals feel seen and accepted, creating a sense of belonging that was rare and precious. Her laughter was infectious, filling the air with a joyous melody that uplifted those around her, if even only for a moment. Yet, beneath her sunny disposition lay a well of wisdom that belied her youth. Lindsey had a keen insight into the human condition, offering guidance and perspective that often left those older and more experienced in awe of her emotional intelligence. She was a true force of nature, a shining beacon of hope and positivity in a world that sometimes felt too dim.

Then there was Tim Spencer with his charismatic and easygoing nature, leaning back in his chair, cool as ever. He flashed a grin Aedan's way and gave a thumbs-up. The guy was unbreakable, calm, and relaxed even in stressful situations, living his best life, laughing in the face of any potential meltdown. He had a knack for making everyone feel like they were in on the joke, even when there wasn't one.

Tim's demeanor was infectious, spreading levity throughout the room. It was as if he possessed an innate ability to defuse tension, transforming even the most high-pressure scenarios into opportunities for camaraderie and lighthearted banter. His mere presence seemed to remind everyone that, despite the challenges they faced, there was always room for a bit of humor and perspective. Aedan couldn't help but admire Tim's unflappable spirit. It was a refreshing oasis of calm amidst negativeness. There was something profoundly reassuring about Tim's nonchalant attitude, a subtle reminder that even the most daunting obstacles could be overcome with a positive mindset and a touch of levity.

"Alright, pencils down and just a reminder for those of you graduating, the ceremony will be in two weeks...Check the schedule posted by the front office on your way out," Mr. Henderson called from the front of the room, snapping Aedan out of his thoughts. He straightened his papers, suddenly self-conscious about his scrawling handwriting, and took a deep breath.

"Time to face the music, Aedan," he whispered to himself as he stood up, ready to turn in the test that felt more like a declaration of independence from high school than anything else.

Aedan clutched the paper to his chest like a shield, his heart thumping in anticipation. It was just a short walk from the back of the classroom to Mr. Henderson's desk, but with every pair of eyes on him, it felt like crossing a battlefield. Aedan took a step forward, his sneakers squeaking against the linoleum floor, doing his best to seem unfazed.

"Watch your step, O'Clumsy," Henry Gills's drawling voice cut through the air, just as his foot casually extended into Aedan's path.

There was no time to react. One moment Aedan was upright, the next his feet betrayed him, and the world tilted sideways. In what seemed like slow motion, his elbow smashed into the cold surface of a nearby desk, sending a shockwave up his arm. Papers scattered like fallen soldiers around him, fluttering to the ground in a cascade of defeat.

Laughter erupted from all corners of the room, a harsh discordant mixture of sounds of mockery that seemed to bounce off the walls and drill into his ears. Aedan tried to gather the strewn pages, his cheeks burning hotter than a forge melting metal.

"Nice one, Aedan," Henry jeered from above, looming over him like some overconfident general surveying the aftermath of a battle he'd orchestrated without lifting a sword. "You just revolutionized the art of face-planting."

Aedan pushed himself up, trying to recover what little dignity he could muster, feeling the weight of Henry's words like a yoke around his neck. Henry's smirk was a flag planted on the territory he claimed with each taunt, reminding Aedan that in the high school hierarchy, he was a mere foot soldier under his command.

"Next time, try not to dive headfirst into history, huh?" Henry's chuckle was laced with scorn as he stepped back, granting Aedan space to rise—a courtesy wrapped in humiliation.

The laughter around Aedan began to die down, but the echo of it remained, etched into the back of his mind. And there, in the thick of his embarrassment, Aedan made a silent vow to himself. Someday, he'd march out of this town, out of Henry Gills's shadow, and onto a field where he wasn't just the clumsy kid at the butt of every joke. Someday. But for now, he just had to stand up and face the embarrassment.

With knees that felt like they were made from the same rubber as Gumby, Aedan forced himself off the floor. The laughter had quieted, but the stares...they weren't so kind. They clung to Aedan, and he saw a mix of amusement and pity in his classmates' eyes.

"Yikes," Aedan heard Tim say out loud from his desk, his concerned face peeking over the stack of textbooks standing like a fort between them. Mary's lips pressed together, a thin line of disapproval aimed not at Aedan, but at Henry's retreating. She was always one for justice, or at least some semblance of it in these halls.

But it was Lindsey's glare that halted the scramble of Aedan's hands collecting his papers. Her eyes, usually so bright with laughter, now flickered with something else—*concern*. It was tough for Aedan to read those eyes through the red fog of embarrassment that clouded his vision.

"Here, let me help you," Lindsey said, approaching with a grace that seemed to mute the snickers still bubbling around them. She offered her hand, fingers delicate but steady, a lifeline amidst the choppy seas of high school ridicule.

"Thanks," Aedan mumbled, accepting the help. Her touch was light, yet it anchored him enough to find his feet. "I guess I'm more of a physical learner when it comes to history."

"Looks like you've got the 'fall' of the British down pretty well," she joked softly, a warm smile dancing on her lips. It was the kind of humor that didn't sting, a shared joke rather than a pointed barb.

"Revolutionary War humor." Aedan managed a weak chuckle.

"You're full of surprises, Lindsey."

"Only the best for my favorite history buff." Her tone was teasing, but there was an undercurrent of sincerity that did funny things to his stomach.

"Favorite, huh?" Aedan tried to sound coy, but the heat in his cheeks probably gave away the game.

"Of course," she replied, her hand slipping away as Aedan steadied himself. "But maybe stick to conquering exams instead of desks next time?"

"Deal," Aedan said, his voice steadier now, though inside his heart he was drumming out a rhythm fit for a battlefield charge.

As Lindsey walked back to her seat, the rest of the class began to dissolve into a low chatter of post-exam relief. Aedan straightened his papers, tucked his pride away, and resolved to survive another day in Northern Straits High—clumsy, sure, but never alone.

The bell had rung and the school emptied, leaving behind nothing but the echo of the day's chaos. Lindsey and Aedan walked side by side toward the river in comfortable silence, the kind you only find with someone who doesn't need words to fill the spaces between heartbeats. It was a path they'd taken time and time again, yet today, it felt like stepping into a new chapter.

"Chook River's looking lively today," Aedan commented, as he and Lindsey approached the gentle gurgle that accompanied their stroll home. The winding ribbon of water caught the afternoon sun, casting dark shadows onto the overhanging branches.

"It's always been here, watching over them," Lindsey mused, her view lingering on the undulating surface. "Kind of like a guardian, don't you think?"

"Or a sentinel," Aedan added, kicking a pebble into the river. It plopped, sending ripples across the otherwise undisturbed water. As the ripples dissipated, the murky water seemed to come alive with movement and color. The images shifted and swirled, revealing glimpses of a life once lived. A couple strolling through a sun-dappled park, their faces aglow with joy and love. Memories etched in time, captured in the depths of the water's reflection.

Each ripple brought forth a new scene, a fleeting moment frozen in the present. It was as if the very existence had been painted white onto the liquid canvas, inviting the observer to ponder the momentary nature of life itself. What stories lay beneath the surface, waiting to be uncovered? What moments had been cherished, only to fade into the mists of time? The water's stillness returned, but the images lingered, a poignant reminder of the beauty and fragility of the human experience.

"Maybe both." Lindsey's smile flickered with a hint of mystery. "But there's an eeriness to it too. Like it knows things—things we're not supposed to understand."

Aedan nodded. Everyone in Cheboygan respected the river. Some said it was a symbol of life, flowing endlessly as generations came and went, while others avoided it after dusk, swearing they'd heard strange voices or seen disturbing shadows flitting just beneath the surface. To Aedan, Chook River was a reminder that even in a peaceful place like this, darkness could lurk just below the calm exterior.

"Remember when we were kids? We dared each other to touch the water at midnight," Lindsey said with a laugh, though it didn't quite reach her eyes.

"Never took you for superstitious." Aedan grinned, trying to lighten the mood.

"Who says I am?" she shot back playfully. "But you have to admit, there's something about this place that makes you believe in the possibility of...more."

"More?" Aedan echoed, the word hanging between them. More than just a river, more than just a town. It was the "more" that made your skin prickle and your pulse quicken; the "more" that called out to the part of you that hungered for answers to questions you hadn't even asked.

"Like stories waiting to be told," Lindsey replied, her voice carried away by the breeze. "Stories," Aedan repeated softly, his imagination already weaving tales of what might be hidden within the waters of Chook River. And somewhere deep inside, he knew that his curiosity wouldn't let this go.

They kept walking along the riverbank as the sun dipped below the horizon, casting a warm glow over the water. "Want me to walk you home?" Aedan asked in a concerned voice.

"Sure, I'd like that," Lindsey said, eagerly accepting his offer, touched by his thoughtfulness. They turned to head home when at the corner of the tree line, an ominous, dark image emerged from the shadows, its piercing stare fixed upon them like a predator stalking its prey.

The figure, a banshee, stood upright like a human, with long streaming hair that she incessantly combed, sending both Aedan and Lindsey into a panic. The banshee was wearing a gray cloak draped over a green dress, almost mocking in its normalcy, while her eyes, blacked out, hinted at her tormented existence. She had a ghastly complexion—as if death itself had taken on a carnal form.

Aedan, terrified, shouted, "Banshee!"

"What have we stumbled upon?" Lindsey replied, accompanied by heavy, labored breathing, as if she had just finished sprinting around a track. The strained, ragged quality of her voice hinted at an underlying expression of distress or exertion.

A chill ran down Aedan's spine as the menacing banshee stepped into view, its features obscured by the fading light. Lindsey instinctively moved closer to Aedan. They stood frozen, and Aedan was unsure of what to do or say. The banshee let out a low high-pitched scream, her eyes glinting with a pang of primal hunger and still glowing bloodshot red. *"You'll lose your soul,"* the banshee warned in a disembodied voice.

"Get behind me," Aedan said, his protective instincts kicking in, and he slowly positioned himself in front of Lindsey, shielding her from potential harm.

The tension was obvious, the air thick with fear and uncertainty. As the banshee inched closer, Aedan braced himself for the worst, his mind racing with possibilities. Was this a mirage, or something more sinister? The unknown was often more terrifying than any known threat. In that moment, time seemed to slow down, each breath he took was a brawl against the weight of doom that encompassed them. He knew their lives could change forever in the blink of an eye, and all he could do was face the danger head-on, united with Lindsey in the determination to survive.

The fear that gripped his heart was undeniable, but he found solace in the knowledge that he was not alone in this ordeal. Aedan hoped Lindsey drew strength from his uniform amount of courage, while he found purpose in shielding the one he held dear.

As the creature drew nearer, its movements deliberate and calculated, he readied himself for the unknown. His mind raced, contemplating every possible outcome, yet he remained grounded in the present moment as his senses heightened and instincts sharpened.

Suddenly, the banshee let out another horrifying bellow as Aedan and Lindsey backed up quickly. Their retreat was far enough that the creature stopped screaming and disappeared into the river. A deafening silence fell over the area, but his apprehension lingered. Aedan and Lindsey remained frozen, and his heart pounded in his chest.

The creature's bellow echoed in his mind, a chilling reminder of the unknown dangers that lurked in the river. Aedan and Lindsey exchanged a wordless glance, their eyes wide with fear and uncertainty. Then they turned and ran away, Aedan's awareness alert to any sound or movement that might signal the creature's return.

With every step back to Lindsey's house, the weight of their foolish-ness grew heavier on him, and the urgency to reach safety became more pressing.

"Thank you, Aedan!" Lindsey exclaimed with a beaming smile as they arrived at her front door.

"No problem, Lindsey!" Aedan responded cheerfully, his eyes sparkling as he watched her enter her house. Feeling elated, Aedan pivoted on his heel and ran back home, eager to get to work.

* * *

O'Connor's Market was the kind of place where everyone knew your name, like on that *Cheers* show—or at least they pretended to. The aisles were narrow, the lights a bit too fluorescent, and every product seemed to be fighting for attention. Aedan slipped behind the counter and started ringing up and bagging groceries, trying to keep up with the never-ending conveyor belt of items. Tim ventured into the depths of Stocker Land, a mythical realm where boxes lurked around every corner waiting to be stacked in rows with other items of their kind.

"Hey, Aedan," Mrs. Whitaker greeted him as she always did, placing her items down one by one, with precision.

"Hi, Mrs. Whitaker," Aedan replied, a little distracted. It wasn't just the monotony of cans and boxes that had his attention divided; something was off with the customers today. Their movements seemed sluggish, their expressions distant. Mr. Jenkins, the usher from the Calumet Theatre who usually had a joke ready, just mumbled thanks and shuffled out the door. Even the kids seemed unusually quiet, clutching their mothers' skirts rather than begging for candy.

"Are you okay?" Aedan asked Mrs. Whitaker, noticing her tired eyes.

"Just haven't been sleeping well, dear," she confessed with a weary smile. "Strange dreams."

Aedan nodded, placing her bags of groceries into her cart. "Hope you get some rest tonight."

"Thank you, Aedan," she said before heading toward the exit, her steps slow and measured. As Aedan watched her go, a chill ran down his spine. Was it all just a coincidence? Or was there something else at play here, maybe something was hidden beneath the surface, much like the secrets Aedan imagined Chook River held. One thing was certain: his curiosity was piqued, and the stories waiting to be told called out to him, louder than ever.

The bell above the door jingled, and Aedan glanced up from the end of the conveyor belt with curiosity. Just then, his dad slapped a CLOSED sign on the register next to Aedan's line, and he did it with a flourish that was so quintessentially Eddie O'Connor. Eddie caught the eye of Mrs. Henderson, who was next in line, and gave her a playful wink that just added to the fun and lively atmosphere.

"Sorry, Diane, this machine's swallowed enough cash for one day," he joked, pointing to the ancient cash register with mock severity. "But I'll personally make sure you're taken care of over here." He gestured grandly to the only open checkout lane—Aedan's.

Mrs. Henderson chuckled, her earlier impatience melting away like snow on a sunny March afternoon. "Only if you double-bag those eggs, Eddie. Last time Aedan packed 'em, I made scrambled eggs just by driving home."

"Hey," Aedan protested, but there was no heat behind it. It was hard to be mad when his dad could turn a complaint into a communal laugh.

"Consider it done, Diane. My boy will treat your groceries like fine china," Dad assured her, sending Aedan a conspiratorial grin.

Mrs. Henderson smiled back, appreciating his knack for smoothing things over, a trait Aedan wished he'd inherited more of, especially when—

"Hey, Aedan," came a voice that spun his heart on its axis.

There she was: Lindsey Merritt, with her parents, Billim and Joy, waiting in line.

Her dad's hands were hidden in his pocket as her mom's fingers rapped a silent beat against her purse, probably already thinking of some witty remark to brighten the mood.

"Hi," Aedan managed, feeling the heat rise to his cheeks as Lindsey's eyes met his. Her smile did funny things to Aedan's stomach, like he'd swallowed a bunch of butterflies on a dare.

"Nice job on the history exam," Lindsey said, her eyes crinkling at the edges. Then Aedan realized the sarcasm behind the comment, because she had seen the fiasco that ensued when he handed in his paper earlier today.

"Thanks," Aedan stammered, hoping he didn't look as red as the tomatoes he started bagging. "You too."

"Always a scholar, our Aedan," his dad chimed in, not missing a beat as he handed Mrs. Henderson's double-bagged eggs to her with a bow. "Takes after his old man, minus the rugged good looks."

"Very funny, Dad," Aedan shot back, but any further banter was lost as he focused on the Merritts' groceries, making sure he handled them with extra care. His dad's laughter mingled with the chatter of customers, creating a brief warmth that filled the market.

Aedan risked another glance at Lindsey. She was watching him, amusement dancing in her eyes, and he thought—just maybe—there was something more to her smile than mere friendliness.

As Aedan shuffled the Merritts' groceries into bags, his fingers betrayed him, slipping on a carton of eggs. With a fumble and a save, they landed softly among the loaves of bread like a nestling finding its place in a birds' nest. Aedan let out a breath that he hadn't realized he was holding. "Close one," he said to himself.

Tim was mopping the floor two aisles over, staring at Aedan like a birdwatcher on safari. He shot Aedan a glance that screamed "comedy gold," making a face that reminded Aedan just how much of a clown he could be. *I mean, come on, I must have been a real riot for Tim to look at me like that, especially since every time Lindsey got near me I acted like a clumsy fool that had just seen a celebrity,* Aedan thought. He rolled his eyes and went back to work, determined to finish his work with diligence and be done before Lindsey noticed how clumsy she could make him.

"Careful there, Aedan," Joy Merritt teased with her characteristic lightheartedness. "Wouldn't want a one-egg omelet for breakfast," Billim added, his voice oiled with the easy humor of someone used to life's little mishaps.

"Got it under control," Aedan assured them, his cheeks burning. It wasn't like him to be clumsy—well, not this clumsy anyway—but Lindsey's presence had his usual dexterity doing somersaults. "It doesn't add up," Aedan said to himself. It wasn't like it was hard walking her home or walking with her in a hallway at school, but sometimes Aedan got nervous when she got anywhere near him outside of those places.

Next came the cans: beans, corn, and peaches, all lined up like soldiers on parade. Aedan stacked them with precision this time, determined to regain some semblance of competence.

That's when Lindsey leaned in closer, her eyes glinting with mischief. "Need a hand?" she offered, her voice teasing.

"Uh, no, I'm—" Aedan's response was cut short as their hands brushed while they reached for the same can of tomato soup. Her touch sparked a jolt that raced up Aedan's arm, and in an instant, the can slipped from his grasp, clattering onto the floor with a sound that echoed his internal mortification.

"Oops," she said, her lips curving into a flirty smile that sent Aedan's heart into overdrive.

"Smooth, O'Connor," Aedan chastised himself silently, bending to pick up the can. As he stood back up, he caught the tail end of a giggle from Lindsey, and despite the embarrassment, he couldn't help but grin. His cheeks were as red as the tomato soup.

"Guess that one wanted to escape," Aedan joked weakly, hoping his attempt at humor would cover up how much he wished the ground would swallow him whole.

Lindsey's laughter still hovered in the air as Aedan watched her and her family make their way to the exit. She threw one last glance over her shoulder, her eyes meeting Aedan's, and his heart somersaulted like he was a member of the US Olympic Gymnastics team competing for the gold medal. Aedan's fingers tentatively lifted in a shy wave, which Lindsey returned with a bright smile that could light up the dimmest corners of O'Connor's Market.

Aedan let out a sigh, partly of relief, and turned back to the conveyor belt, ready to tackle the next pile of groceries. But before he could even reach for the loaf of bread that was inching its way toward him, a shadow fell across the counter.

"Evening, Aedan." The voice was gravelly, like stones tumbling down a mountain. Aedan looked up to find Old Man Harry looming before him. A creepy older man in his sixties, he was also grumpy. Aedan assumed he'd seen a lot in his long life and had become jaded and cynical, and he wasn't afraid to speak his mind, even if it meant offending others. His hunched figure was more pronounced than ever, a silhouette cut from the past, and his piercing, menacing look seemed to see right through Aedan. The store's fluorescent lights radiated eerie highlights on his thick glasses and deepened the wrinkles etched into his face. "Hey, Mr. Harry," Aedan replied, forcing a polite smile. "How's it going?"

"Same old, same old," he grumbled, leaning heavily on his cane. "These bones don't like the cold much, but they keep carrying me around."

"Let me help you with your stuff," Aedan offered, noticing the sparse items in his basket—bread, milk, and a few cans of soup. *Not tomato, thankfully*, Aedan thought.

"Appreciate it, young man," Harry said, though his tone suggested he'd seen enough years not to need anyone's help. "You know, you remind me of myself at your age, all elbows and two left feet."

"Guess I'm still working on the whole coordination thing," Aedan admitted, trying to laugh it off. It wasn't often someone struck up a conversation with him without some agenda. With Harry, though, you never knew what to expect.

"Take your time, lad. Life's a long lesson," he said, a cryptic twinkle in his eye. "And speaking of lessons, I've got stories that could fill a book thicker than the can you dropped earlier."

Aedan blinked, momentarily caught off guard. Had Harry seen that? Aedan didn't get the chance to wonder; as the man leaned in closer, he got quiet.

"Stories about this town...things you won't find in any history book." Aedan's curiosity was piqued despite himself, and he glanced around to ensure no one was ear-hustling. "Really? Like what kind of stories?"

"Ah, but that would be telling," Harry teased, straightening up with a creak of his joints. "Maybe another time, when there aren't so many prying ears around."

"Sure, Mr. Harry," Aedan said, bagging his groceries with a renewed interest. Who knew what secrets this strange old man held? Aedan handed him his bag, wondering if he would ever get a chance to hear those tales.

"Thanks, Aedan," Harry said, offering a nod that felt like an acknowl-edgment of some unspoken understanding between them. Then, with a final glance that seemed to say "Be ready for anything"—

"Ever hear of Al Ana, Aedan?" Harry said, his voice a raspy, low pitch that sliced through the quiet of the nearly empty store.

"Al Ana?" Aedan repeated, his voice edged with curiosity.

"Cheboygan's very own demon," Harry said, his eyes narrowing to slits as he watched him closely. "Legend says she's been here since before the town itself, lurking in Chook River, stealing the souls of the unwary, and driving folks insane."

"Stealing souls? Come on, Mr. Harry, that sounds like something straight out of a campfire tale."

"Maybe so," Harry acknowledged, leaning on his cane. "But there are things in this world, boy, darker and older than you can imagine. Things that lurk just beyond the corner of your eye."

Aedan shook his head but couldn't deny the tug of fascination. The thought of a hidden history, a secret entwined with Cheboygan, was... enticing. "So, this Al Ana," Aedan ventured, "is there more about her? Any books or stuff about these legends? What all do you know?"

Harry's lips twitched, a hint of a knowing smile creasing the corners of his mouth. "Books, he asks!" He chuckled dryly. "Boy, the stories I could tell aren't found in any library. But"—he paused, tapping his finger against his chin—"perhaps there might be something that could cure that curiosity of yours."

"Anything would help," Aedan admitted, his eagerness getting the better of him. "I mean, if there's truth to it, I'd like to know more. About Al Ana, about all of it."

"Truth is a slippery fish," Harry mumbled. "But alright, Aedan O'Connor. I'll see what I can do for you." He gave Aedan a long look, the kind that seemed to weigh on one's soul for its worth. "Be careful, lad. Some waters are too deep and dark to tread lightly in."

"I'll keep that in mind," Aedan said, though his heart raced with the thrill of uncovering what secrets lay beneath the surface of Cheboygan, beneath the rippling waters of Chook River.

Harry shifted uncomfortably, his eyes dropping to his knotted hands before he glanced back up at Aedan through those thick glasses. "Aye, there's a book," he admitted in a gravelly, quiet tone, as if the very shelves might be listening. "Tattered old thing, more scribbles than pages. Belonged to my granddad, it did."

"Could I see it?" Aedan asked, trying to keep the eagerness out of his voice, to sound casual even though his pulse hammered with anticipation.

"Listen, Aedan," Harry leaned in, his voice dropping to a clandestine hush. "This isn't child's play. That book...it's a gateway to things better left alone. Cheboygan's got its share of shadows, and some are darker than a moonless night on Chook River."

Aedan swallowed hard, but his determination didn't waver. "I need to know, Harry. If there's something strange going on in this town, I can't just ignore it."

"Stubborn like your father," Harry grumbled, then he sighed, his breath rattling in his chest. He reached into the inner pocket of his coat, producing a small, worn leather-bound tome, a scholarly book that looked as ancient as Harry himself. "Here it is. Ancient Local Mysteries is the title. But remember, I warned you. Don't go off chasing after demons that are better to stay hidden."

"I'll be careful," Aedan promised, taking the book reverently. Its cover was cracked and faded, the title illegible. But it felt like holding a piece of Cheboygan's heart—or maybe its secrets. "Thank you, Harry. I'll take good care of it."

"See that you do," he said, fixing Aedan with one last piercing stare. "And Aedan?

Sometimes a bit of ignorance is bliss. Don't lose yourself in the chase for the truth."

As Harry shuffled away, his warning echoed in Aedan's mind. But the weight of the book in his hands, the scent of aged paper and mystery—it was too intoxicating. Aedan was ready to dive into whatever depths awaited, ready to face whatever truths lay hidden within those tattered pages, leaving his mind buzzing with possibilities and a day that had suddenly become a lot more interesting. After his shift ended at closing, it was time for him to go home and explore this ancient book that had become a slight obsession.

2

Aedan's Curiosity

The moment Aedan closed his front door behind him, the book was in his hands again, its leather cover cool and slightly sticky from years of handling. Aedan retreated to the sanctuary of his room, flopping down on his bed as he flipped open the first page. The musty smell of old paper flooded his nose, and a thrill coursed through him.

"Let's see what you've got," Aedan breathed, barely audible above the faint creak of the binding yielding to his touch. His fingers traced over the delicate pages, feeling the indentations where the ink had been pressed into them decades, perhaps centuries, ago.

Aedan turned the pages with reverence, each offering cryptic drawings and spidery handwriting that interested him more. There were sketches of Chook River, depicted with an eerie accuracy that made the hairs on the back of his neck stand at attention. But it wasn't just the illustrations—it was also the stories they told and the legends they discussed.

And then, there she was—the demon Al Ana. Her name sprawled across the top of a chapter like a dark cloud presiding over a doomed land. The text beneath her name was a mix of history and myth, detailing her existence as if she were as real as the river itself. Words like "vengeance," "souls," and "water" jumped out at him, and he could almost hear the ripple of water accompanying them.

"'An ancient demon of vengeance who roams Chook River grounds stealing souls...'" Aedan read aloud, letting the reality of the words sink in. A chill ran through him, but it was met with an insatiable curiosity that pushed any fear he had into the background. Aedan needed to know more, to understand if this legend was responsible for the oddities happening around Cheboygan.

As he perused the book thoroughly and carefully, he heard faint voices humming all around him. Unsure where they were coming from, he disregarded them and continued reading.

Aedan's mind raced, connecting dots that seemed to have been laid out just for him. The sluggish movements of those customers at the store, their lifeless expressions—could Al Ana be more than just a tale? Was she influencing his town, right under his nose?

"Okay, Aedan, think," he coached himself, sitting up straighter. "How does this all fit together?" Theories began to form, wild and unproven, yet they felt grounded in something tangible. It was as if Aedan was part of the story now, a character in a mystery that had been unfolding long before he was born.

Determined, Aedan leaned closer to the dim lamp on his bedside table, intent on uncovering every secret held within the worn pages. The clock ticked away the minutes, but time didn't matter. He was on the precipice of something monumental and couldn't tear himself away. He became entranced in the book, reading every word twice, turning page after page. The disembodied whispers, *"Come here," "Water,"* and *"Careful,"* grew silent.

"Cheboygan, what are you hiding?" Aedan muttered into the quiet of his room, his eyes locked on the tattered book that seemed to pulse with ancient knowledge. Whatever answers it held, he was going to find them. No matter how deep he had to go, no matter what it took, he was ready to face the truth about Al Ana and the dark secrets of his hometown.

"Okay, so where to first?" Aedan asked himself, the book's spine creaking as he laid it delicately on his desk—a map of secrets ready to be navigated. His fingertips brushed against the pages, each piece of paper like a silent plea for discovery. He grabbed a pen and notepad from the drawer, his chosen tools for his impromptu investigation.

As Aedan flipped through the pages, meticulously reading every detail and making notes, a folded newspaper clipping caught his attention, unveiling a concerning revelation—Tommy Canfeld and Emma Taylor missing, last seen by the river.

"Tommy Canfeld and Emma Taylor," Aedan said aloud, as if speaking their names might conjure them up from the past. He scribbled down their names, followed by a list of places where they were last seen, according to the newspaper clipping, with Chook River at the top.

"Emma used to hang out at the old mill, right?" Aedan said. He recalled a detail from the book, adding it beneath her name. "And Tommy...he worked at the old lumber mill before, you know, before they both disappeared."

Aedan's heart thumped in eager anticipation, the same rush he'd get when a particularly tricky shipment came into O'Connor's Market, and he'd figure out how to stack it just right.

Only this time, the stakes were higher. This wasn't about apples not bruising; it was about unearthing truths that could change everything.

"Alright, Aedan, you got this," he encouraged himself. Visions of his heroics played out in his mind—he'd be the one to crack the case, the guy who brought answers to Cheboygan. And maybe, just maybe, Lindsey would see him as more than the clumsy kid who drops soup cans when she smiles.

Aedan let out a breath he didn't realize he'd been holding and glanced back at the book. Its cover was faded, edges frayed, but its contents? They were alive, pulsating with the potential of untold stories and hidden dangers. With a final nod to the room, he pushed away from his desk.

"Here goes nothing." Aedan's voice carried the weight of his newfound bravery.

He laid aside the tattered book, now a beacon of adventure, and stood up, a mix of nerves and excitement buzzing through him. It was time to step into the unknown, chase down legends, and face whatever awaited him in the shadowy corners of his town. Cheboygan's dark secrets wouldn't remain buried for much longer—not if Aedan had anything to say about it.

Aedan zipped up his jacket with a steady hand, the cool Michigan air seeping through the cracks of his old house. The list he'd scribbled down earlier was folded neatly in his back pocket; the tattered book's warnings echoed in his mind. But nothing could shake the feverish excitement that pulsed through his veins. Aedan snatched a worn-out notebook from the kitchen table, its pages filled with half-scribbles of grocery lists and homework assignments. But today, it would serve as the chronicle of his investigation.

"Pen," Aedan chirped to himself; he'd forgotten his in his bedroom. A simple ballpoint lay on the counter, cap chewed, courtesy of countless evenings he'd spent there mulling over history notes. It wasn't much, but it was all he needed. With a quick swipe, it joined the notebook in his pocket. His fingers lingered for a moment on the cover, feeling the indentations left by the pressure of many anxious thoughts.

"Okay, Aedan, you've got this," he said quietly, voice muffled, more to brace himself than out of any real need to hear the words. In the reflection of the small mirror by the door, he caught a glimpse of his eyes—determined, maybe a bit scared, but burning with a fire that even the sight of Chook River couldn't dampen.

As he stepped outside, the familiar creak of his front porch beneath his feet felt different, like a starting block just before a race. He pulled the door shut behind him, listening to the click of the latch falling into place. The town awaited, draped in its everyday quietness, stories and secrets churning, desperate to break free.

* * *

Aedan's sneakers met the pavement with a resolute thud as he made his way toward downtown Cheboygan. No turning back now. Each step carried the weight of the town's hidden past, the thoughts of Al Ana winding around him like tendrils of mist along the riverbanks. He could feel her presence, almost tangible, lurking at the edge of his consciousness—the demon of Cheboygan, an entity as inseparable from this land as the water was from the river.

"Tommy Canfeld. Emma Taylor." Their names bounced around Aedan's head, keys to unlocking some of the enigma that shrouded his peaceful town.

The deeper Aedan ventured into the heart of Cheboygan, the stronger his nerves grew. This wasn't just about solving some age-old mystery or proving his worth to peers who saw him as nothing more than the clumsy kid behind the grocery counter. No, this was bigger. This was about saving his town, protecting it from the dark influence that clung to it like an obsessed ex-lover.

"Cheboygan needs me," Aedan thought aloud. There was no audience to hear the declaration, no one to witness the fierceness in his stride. But that didn't matter. Aedan was the protagonist in a story yet to be written, armed with nothing but a notebook, a pen, a flashlight, and a heart full of courage.

And so, with the determination of someone having everything to prove, he pressed on, ready to face whatever truths lay hidden in the shadows of Cheboygan.

While wandering through the town in search of information about the disappearance of Emma and Tommy, Aedan's curiosity led him down a troubling path. The eerie silence of the deserted streets should have been a warning sign, but he pressed on, unaware of the unseen dangers lurking in the shadows. Suddenly, a fleeting movement caught his eye—a dark, formless figure that seemed to defy the laws of physics. His heart raced as the chilling presence drew nearer, its ominous aura sending shivers down his spine. At that moment, self-preservation kicked in, and he knew better than to tempt fate any further. Without hesitation, Aedan turned on his heels and raced back home, the haunting memory of the shadow person etched into his mind as a grim reminder to exercise caution when venturing into the unknown.

As Aedan sprinted through the dimly lit streets, his breaths quick and shallow, his perceptions hung heavy in the air. The echo of his hurried footsteps reverberated off the empty buildings, adding to the eerie atmosphere surrounding him. Every shadow seemed to whisper of hidden perils, every gust of wind carried a chilled warning.

His heart pounded as he continued his frantic sprint, and he glanced over his shoulder with each turn. The hairs on the back of his neck stood on end, an unseen force urging him to run faster, run farther. He couldn't shake the feeling that something sinister lurked behind him, stalking his every move. The once familiar streets now seemed twisted and menacing, the darkness concealing unknown threats around every corner. Aedan's mind raced, trying to understand the situation that had spiraled so quickly out of control. He needed to find safety, needed to escape whatever evil force pursued him relentlessly. As he pressed on, his lungs burned and his legs ached, but the fear that gripped him refused to let him slow down. The night had taken on a nightmarish quality, and Aedan could only hope that he would make it through until dawn's first light pierced the inky blackness.

Finally reaching the safety of his home, Aedan fumbled for his keys, hands shaking with lingering fear. As he stepped inside and locked the door behind him, he leaned against it, trying to steady himself. The encounter with the shadow person had left a mark on him, a scar in his mind that refused to fade.

With a trembling sigh, Aedan realized that the disappearance of Emma and Tommy was just the beginning of something far more sinister than he could have imagined. As he sank into an uneasy sleep that night, haunted by nightmares of dark figures and unseen dangers, he knew that his search for the truth would lead him down a path fraught with peril and darkness.

Time was slipping away, and the night grew ever longer. Aedan's restless body refused to surrender to slumber, leaving him tossing and turning in a desperate bid for rest. The clock ticked relentlessly, mocking his futile attempts to find solace in sleep. Midnight came and went, and still, he remained wide awake, grasping Harry's book like a lifeline. The pages turned, but the hours slipped through his fingers like grains of sand. Two a.m. arrived, a harsh reminder that the workday loomed ever closer. With a sense of urgency, Aedan tried to force himself to sleep, lest he face the consequences of exhaustion in the morning. But the battle against insomnia raged on, each minute a precious commodity that couldn't be wasted.

The fight intensified as the night wore on, the shadows growing longer and the silence more deafening. Aedan couldn't stop thinking; he was consumed by a whirlwind of thoughts that refused to settle. He tossed and turned, the sheets tangling around him like a twisted web, trapping him in a state of restless torment. Desperate, he tried every trick in the book—deep breathing exercises, counting sheep, even the age-old remedy of a warm glass of milk. But nothing seemed to work, and the minutes ticked away mercilessly. As the first hints of dawn crept through the curtains, Aedan felt a dread wash over him. The workday beckoned and he knew he must find a way to conquer this relentless foe. With a heavy heart and weary eyes, he readied himself for the battle ahead, determined to make it to work.

3

Twisted Truths

The early evening air was cooling down, and the sky stretched out with emptiness. "Tim, man, you got a sec?" Aedan's voice hitched slightly with urgency as he caught up to his friend outside the back door of the loading dock.

"What's up," Tim replied, turning around, eyebrow raised like he was Dwayne "The Rock" Johnson.

"Listen," Aedan started, running a hand over his eyes, as if trying to stay awake. "I've been thinking a lot about all those weird stories we heard growing up—the ones about people losing control of their lives. And, well, things have been off lately, haven't they? With the river and everything?"

"Off how?" Tim leaned against the brick wall, arms crossed but attentive.

"Man, I'm tired...it's more than just strange, Tim. I think there's truth to the legends.

More than we ever thought." Aedan's look was intense, pulling Tim into the gravity of his conviction. "I mean, think about it—why else would all these bizarre things be happening now?" "Like what, though? Give me something concrete, Aedan."

"When I was downtown on Main Street yesterday, I saw something. A ghost—no, more like an apparition, and when Lindsey and I were by the river near the high school we saw a banshee," Aedan said excitedly.

"A banshee...a ghost," Tim replied, concerned.

"Something is stirring, and I don't want to leave for college without getting to the bottom of it," Aedan replied. "The ghostly apparition I witnessed was as real as you and me. Something paranormal is going on, and we can't simply turn a blind eye. And you know when a banshee howls at you, she's warning you of potential doom. This is our chance to unravel a mystery that could change our understanding of the supernatural. Before we leave for college, we owe it to ourselves to investigate this phenomenon thoroughly. Who knows what secrets we might uncover? This is an opportunity we can't afford to miss. Trust me, once you see what I've seen, you'll be convinced too."

"Alright, so what do you suggest we do?" A flicker of interest sparked in Tim's mind, the allure of a mystery too tempting to ignore entirely.

"We investigate, buddy. Before we head off to college, and our lives change forever.

We've got to figure this out, for Cheboygan's sake...and maybe for peace of mind," Aedan said with optimism in his voice.

"Investigate how?" Tim pushed himself off the wall, the warrior within him rising to the challenge despite his reservations.

"Think about it, we've got the whole summer ahead of us. It's now or never, Tim. Are you in?" Aedan held his breath, knowing that Tim's agreement could be the deciding factor in embarking on this uncertain journey.

"Alright, Aedan. I'm in." Tim clapped a hand on Aedan's shoulder, that easygoing smile creeping onto his face. "But we're doing this carefully, agreed? No running headlong into trouble."

"Agreed!" Aedan exhaled in relief, a grin spreading across his face. His curiosity, once a quiet voice in the back of his mind, was now a roaring call to adventure. With Tim by his side, Aedan felt like they could take on even the shadows of Al Ana themselves.

"Okay, so where do we start?" Tim asked, his previous skepticism giving way to an earnest curiosity.

"First things first," Aedan replied, his mind racing with possibilities, "we hit the library. There's got to be something in the archives or some old books that can give us a lead on Al Ana and these weird happenings."

"Library, huh?" Tim rocked back on his heels, considering it. "Haven't been there since Mrs. Bannister made us do that history project junior year."

"Exactly," Aedan said, his eyes lighting up. "Remember how much stuff they had? All those records and newspapers from, like, a hundred years ago? If there are answers, that's where we'll find them." Aedan was already moving toward his beat-up car, eager to put their plan into action.

Tim followed. The trendsetter within him responded to the call of adventure. "Alright, man. Let's dig up skeletons." Tim's tone was light, but the way his jaw was set told Aedan he was all in.

"Thanks, Tim. I knew I could count on you," Aedan said, clambering into the driver's seat. He fumbled with the keys for a moment, his usual clumsiness at odds with the gravity of their mission.

The engine coughed to life, and they pulled out onto the quiet street, leaving behind the familiar sight of their employer. As the library's stately silhouette came into view, a mix of adrenaline and camaraderie settled between them. This was it—the beginning of their last great adventure before adulthood claimed them for its own.

* * *

The musty scent of old books and polished wood filled the air as Aedan and Tim entered the library, its quiet hush a stark contrast to the clamor of unease that had been following them around town. Aedan glanced at Tim, his easygoing demeanor now sharpened with focus, and for a moment, Aedan felt a surge of gratitude.

They both noticed library patrons behaving strangely, wandering around like lifeless forms of themselves, doing peculiar things. A few of the patrons picked up books and dropped them, then walked away as if nothing happened. It was a surreal and perplexing sight, reminiscent of a twisted nightmare. These weren't just isolated incidents either—they were happening everywhere Aedan and Tim looked. Regular, everyday people, suddenly acting utterly bizarre, their behaviors erratic and inexplicable.

"Okay, so where do we start?" Tim said out of earshot of any potential listeners so as not to startle the strange library zombies, scanning the rows upon rows of bookshelves towering around them.

"Local history section," Aedan muttered back, already steering them toward the familiar corner of the library. They navigated through the maze of shelves, their sneakers squeaking softly on the polished floor. The deeper they ventured into the library's heart, the more sensitive time became, with each shelf holding information about Cheboygan's past.

There it was, nestled between a hefty volume on the logging industry and a photo-laden book about the Great Lakes—a book with a spine so faded you'd almost think it wanted to hide.

Legends and Lore of Cheboygan, the gold lettering said, barely legible under years of accumulated dust. Aedan's fingers trembled slightly as he reached out and lifted the book from its place, a small cloud of sediment billowing up and dancing in the slanting sunlight filtering through the high windows.

"Whoa," Tim said as he peered over Aedan's shoulder, his voice low but tinged with excitement. "This looks ancient."

"Feels like it too," Aedan replied, blowing across the cover to clear the dust before opening it. The pages crackled in protest, resisting after years of neglect. But there, in the dim light, the secrets of their town lay sprawled across the ancient paper.

"Check this out." Aedan pointed to an illustration, dark ink depicting a shadowy figure looming over a stylized rendition of the town. Underneath, in Old English handwriting, the caption read: "Al Ana— The Shadow Over Cheboygan." On the next page, folded up, was a newspaper clipping that read "Local Resident Susan Smith Loses Her Mind Near Ojibwa Native Lands, Discovered By Native Elder Sakima."

"Creepy," Tim said, pulling out his phone. "Let's get pictures of everything."

They flipped carefully through the pages, the accounts growing stranger with each turn.

There were stories of inexplicable mists rolling in from Chook River, chilling tales of voices heard in the dead of night, and a list of names— people who'd vanished without a trace. One entry detailed a night when the entire town fell silent, stars blotted out by an unseen force.

Goosebumps riddled Aedan's skin as they took turns snapping photos of the pages, capturing every scrap of lore the book offered.

"Man, this is some serious stuff," Tim said, his usual confidence undercut by a hint of nervousness. "You think any of it's true?"

"Got to be some truth in legends, right?" Aedan replied, swallowing the lump in his throat. "Otherwise, why would people keep telling them?"

"Good point," Tim conceded with a nod, his charismatic nature unable to fully mask the concern creeping into his eyes.

"Let's keep looking." Aedan was eager to move on from the eerie illustrations that seemed to watch them as they pored over the dusty pages.

With every photograph and scribbled note, the weight of their quest grew heavier. But so did their resolve. If Al Ana was more than just a legend, Tim and Aedan were going to uncover the truth. Together.

They headed for a different section on local history, where Aedan had found another book. Running his fingers along the dusty spines, Aedan spotted a promising title: *Chook River: A History.* He pulled it from the shelf and brought it to a table, Tim crowding around expectantly.

Flipping through the pages, Aedan found it—a chapter titled "The Trials of 1843."His pulse quickened as he read aloud a passage describing the witch trials that gripped the town, claiming innocent lives.

"'One of the condemned was Heather Lowe, a young widow who had moved to Chook River a year earlier," Aedan read. As he spoke her name, the lights flickered ominously, warning of some type of malicious force nearby. He pushed on, filled with curiosity. "After being accused of witchcraft, Lowe was found guilty and hanged in the forest just north of town.'" Aedan looked up, meeting Tim's wide eyes. "This is it," Aedan said. "We must find where she was killed. The answer's in those woods."

Above the bookshelves behind them, smokey black shadows swirled, seemingly agitated.

Tim hesitated, glancing around fearfully at the writhing shadows. "You're right," he said firmly. "Let's go." Tim touched Aedan's arm gently. "It's getting late. We need to leave now."

Aedan sighed but agreed. As they quickly left, he knew with chilling certainty that they would be venturing into those woods at night.

Stepping out into the crisp Cheboygan air, Aedan zipped up his jacket before glancing over at Tim. "We gotta talk to someone who's been around, someone who knows the stories," Aedan said.

Tim nodded, agreeing with Aedan. "You're right. This whole situation is starting to feel way over our heads." He scanned the quiet streets as if searching for answers in the quaint storefronts and flickering streetlamps. "But who can we trust? These old legends have been buried for a reason. Whoever we talk to might not take too kindly to a couple of kids stirring up ancient secrets."

Aedan sighed heavily, his breath forming a misty cloud in the chilly air, which was strange because it was summer.

"Hey, we should check in with Mrs. Staples and see if she's got the scoop on what's been happening around here lately," Aedan said in a casual tone.

"Mrs. Staples, huh? The pie lady?" Tim chuckled, but there was approval in his eyes. "Yeah, she might know something."

"Exactly," Aedan agreed. " Her memory is sharp as a tack, despite her age."

"Lead the way then, Aedan O'Connor, Sherlock detective extraordi-naire," Tim teased, and he couldn't help but grin. His charisma always had a way of lightening the mood.

As they were walking a middle-aged woman in a business suit stopped abruptly on the sidewalk, stared vacantly at her briefcase for a moment, then tossed it into the street without a care. Across the street an elderly man shuffled aimlessly into a cafe, only to stumble back out a few seconds later, mumbling incoherently to himself. Even children weren't immune, some of them wandering off from their parents.

It was as if a strange spell had been cast over the city, robbing its inhabitants of their free will and turning them into mindless automatons. No one seemed aware of their bizarre behavior or they had no way to snap out of it. A cold feeling of anxiety washed over Aedan as he realized whatever bizarre phenomenon this was, it was rapidly spreading through the population like a contagion.

Aedan felt utterly helpless, unsure of what could be causing this nightmare scenario to unfold. All he knew was that he needed to get away from there as quickly as possible before they too fell under its eerie influence.

They hadn't gotten far when the familiar sight of Sheriff Bill's patrol car pulled up beside them. Bill Ford had that look about him, the one that said he'd seen things. Today, it seemed more pronounced.

"Evening, boys," Bill called out, rolling down his window. There was a seriousness in his voice that stopped them in their tracks.

"Sheriff," Aedan greeted, trying to sound casual. "Just headed to see Mrs. Staples."

"Be careful out there," he warned, his eyes sweeping from Tim to Aedan. "Especially around the River. Folks have been acting strange lately... weirder than usual."

"Strange how?" Tim asked, curiosity edging into his tone.

"More sightings, more rumors," Bill replied skeptically. "People avoiding the River, complaining about Al Ana. It's got them all spooked."

"Thanks for the heads up," Aedan said, feeling a shiver creep up his spine and run to his neck that gave him a cold shiver. "We'll keep an eye out."

"Good boys," Bill nodded, his expression softening just a bit. "Stay safe. And if you find anything..." He trailed off, leaving the rest unsaid.

"We'll let you know," Aedan promised, and Bill gave them a final nod before driving off.

"Guess we're not the only ones thinking there's more to these legends," Tim said, watching the patrol car disappear around the corner.

"Seems like it," Aedan agreed, his determination renewed. "Let's go get those stories from Mrs. Staples. Something tells me we're on the right track."

With a shared glance, they set off toward the small, cozy house at the end of the lane, where the scent of baking often ventilated through the neighborhood.

* * *

Aedan and Tim stepped onto Mrs. Staples' porch, the old wooden boards creaking under their weight. Without hesitation, Aedan knocked on the door, his knuckles echoing against the sturdy oak. The anticipation was like static in the air, making his fingertips tingle. Tim shifted from foot to foot beside him, his easygoing nature doing little to mask the eagerness in his eyes.

Mrs. Gloria Staples had always been a pillar of strength, her unblemished commitment to being a caregiver for the patients at the sanatorium earned her the respect of all who knew her. Born in Norwich, England, she had crossed the vast ocean in pursuit of a better life, her eyes shining with hope and determination.

Her years at the sanatorium had been both rewarding and challenging. She had seen the depths of despair in the eyes of the patients, their haunted memories echoing through the dimly lit corridors. Susan Smith had been one of her dearest patients, the woman's gentle nature a stark contrast to the darkness that lurked within her. And then there was Al Ana, the ancient demon that had plagued the sanatorium for centuries, its malevolent presence a constant source of fear and distress.

Through it all, Mrs. Staples remained attentive, her incorruptible spirit a beacon of light in the darkness. She listened to the stories of the lost souls within the sanatorium, offering comfort and solace where she could.

The door swung open, revealing Mrs. Gloria Staples, her silver hair catching the light like wisps of moonbeam. "Boys," she greeted, her voice carrying the warmth of a freshly baked pie. "To what do I owe this pleasure?" As she looked upon Aedan and his friends, a glimmer of humility shone in her eyes. She knew that the shadows of the past were reaching out once more, and she stood ready to face them with unfaltering determination.

"Mrs. Staples, we were hoping to talk to you about Al Ana and Susan Smith," Aedan blurted out, his words tumbling over one another in a worried rush. An awareness gripped him as her eyebrows rose, a flicker of surprise crossing her features before she stepped aside. Aedan's heart raced with apprehension, fearing the worst about the situation involving Susan Smith that he had read about at the Library.

Mrs. Staple's eyebrows rose, a flicker of surprise crossing her features before she stepped aside. "Well, come on in then. I can't say no to a couple of curious minds."

They entered her living room, a cozy space filled with floral patterns and the smell of cinnamon. She gestured them toward the plush couch and they sank into the cushions, feeling tiny amidst the array of handmade afghans and throw pillows.

"Al Ana, and Susan Smith you say?" Mrs. Staples mused as she settled into her armchair. "There are two names I haven't heard spill from young lips, ever."

"Everyone's been talking about the strange things happening around town," Tim chimed in, leaning forward. "And you're the best person to tell us about the town's past, the legends."

"Ah, yes, the echoes of the wind," she said, her tone taking on a somber note. "The mere thought of Al Ana, the demon queen, sends chills down one's spine. This ancient and evil entity, accompanied by her sinister army of intangibles, poses a grave threat that cannot be taken lightly. The notion of a vengeful demon roaming the grounds of Chook River, stealing souls, and inflicting irreparable damage upon the lives of innocent people, is deeply terrifying, it's the fact that Al Ana has the power to drive individuals into the depths of insanity, just like in the tragic case of Susan Smith, a harrowing reminder of the dark forces at play," Mrs. Staples explains.

"The mere existence of such a powerful and malicious entity is a cause for grave concern. One can only hope that the mystery surrounding Al Ana can be unraveled and her reign of terror brought to an end before more lives are irreparably damaged or lost to her insidious influence," Aedan chimed in.

"My great-grandfather was a brave man, or so I've been told. One of the few who looked into the abyss that is Al Ana and lived to speak of it."

Aedan leaned in, his breathing picking up. "What happened to him, Mrs. Staples?"

"Horror, pure horror," she began, her eyes distant as if she could see the past unrolling before her. "He was a woodsman, spent his days among the trees and streams. One evening, he was returning home when a mist descended like a shroud over Chook River."

"The mist?" Tim asked, nervously.

"Yes, the mist," Mrs. Staples confirmed. "It's said that Al Ana rides on such vapors, creeping into the soul. My great-grandfather saw figures moving through the fog and heard voices that clawed at his sanity. He ran, and ran until his lungs burned and his legs gave out."

"Did he see... did he see the demon?" Aedan pressed, his mouth dry.

"By an abandoned cabin in the woods, enough to haunt him for the rest of his days," Mrs. Staples replied. "Eyes, red as the blood moon, and a smile that promised endless torment. He spoke of it only once, and his voice trembled like autumn leaves in a gale."

Tim and Aedan exchanged a look, the gravity of her words settling on them like a heavy cloak. This was no longer just a legend; it was real fear etched into the lines of Mrs. Staples' face, a fear that had been passed down through generations.

"Thank you, Mrs. Staples," Aedan said, finding his voice. "This means a lot to us."

"Be wary, boys," she cautioned, her eyes were piercing. "Some truths are better left in the shadows. But if you're set on shining a light, be sure you're prepared for what might scurry out."

They nodded, a silent vow passing between them. Armed with the chilling details of her great-grandfather's encounter, they stepped back into the world, the weight of their quest heavier, but their purpose was clear.

"Let's find the truth," Tim said, his voice steady.

"Let's," Aedan agreed, fueling his steps. "Let's check out the abandoned cabin she was talking about," Aedan felt uneasy. "Sure," Tim's response carried an undercurrent of apprehension, mirroring Aedan's trepidation. The prospect of exploring the eerie, forsaken structure filled them both with fearfulness, yet a morbid curiosity propelled them forward, despite their misgivings.

4

Abandoned Cabin

The sun hung low in the sky, casting elongated shadows that reached out like fingers as Tim and Aedan approached the outskirts of Cheboygan. "Are you sure about this?" Tim asked, his eyes scanning the dense tree line that bordered the river.

"Mrs. Staples's story...it got to me," Aedan admitted, his hands shoved into his pockets as he trudged forward. "We've got to at least try to find something. Anything."

The eerie silence of the trail gave Aedan and Tim chills as they made their way toward the cabin. Suddenly, a loud crack pierced the stillness, causing their hearts to race with fear.

Aedan quickly looked to the ground, where he discovered the culprit—a mere broken stick that had snapped beneath his weight. Despite the innocuous source of the sound, a lingering sense of the calmness before the storm hung in the air, leaving them to wonder what other unseen dangers might lurk along the path ahead.

With each step they took, the abandoned cabin came into view, its dilapidated structure an eerie testament to the forgotten and forlorn. The windows, covered by vines, once clear passageways to the soul of the home, now stood vacant, like blind eyes that refused to see.

"Here we are," Aedan declared, though his voice barely rose above a babble out of fear.

The gravity of their quest seemed to sap the strength from his words.

They hesitated at the door, which hung off rusty hinges, its wood splintered. Taking a deep breath, Aedan bravely pushed it open with a creak that sang of disuse and decay.

"Let's split up. You take the back room," Tim suggested, ever the pragmatic one, even in the face of potential danger.

"Got it," Aedan replied, his heart pounding against his chest as if trying to escape.

The interior of the cabin was a tableau of abandonment. Cobwebs clung to the corners; the furniture lay overturned, a silent scream acknowledging the abandonment amidst the quietude. Aedan began his search, running his fingers along the rough wood of the walls, seeking any anomaly, any sign that might reveal the presence of where Al Ana might have been.

And then, there it was—a floorboard that didn't quite match the others, sitting just a tad higher, looking a bit newer. Aedan knelt, fumbling with clumsy fingers, feeling the rush of adrenaline that sharpened his senses.

"Tim, I found something!" Aedan called out, not taking his eyes away from the prize.

Tim was at Aedan's side in an instant, his charismatic ease replaced by a focused intensity. Together with bated breath, they pried the board loose, revealing a hidden compartment that cradled an old journal, its leather cover worn and pages yellowed with age.

"Whoa!" Tim shouted as they carefully extracted the book.

A chilling feeling of fear crept in as a spectral figure observed them from across the room, its unnoticed and terrifying presence silently witnessing Aedan and Tim's actions. The pages seemed to hold secrets long forgotten, and they couldn't help but worry about the unsettling revelations that might unfold. Foreboding lingered, a wordless warning that some truths are better left undisturbed.

There's a mystery about this place, a feeling of a presence that I can't quite shake off." He glanced out a window at the dense foliage in the distance, as if expecting something to emerge from the shadows at any moment. Neither of them could see the spectral figure that continued to observe them.

"Look at this," Aedan said, thumbing through the pages filled with scrawling handwriting, cryptic entries that spoke of shadows not caused by light, in a language foreign yet familiar.

"Check out these sketches," Tim pointed out, his finger tracing over the images that adorned the margins—dark figures with elongated limbs, symbols that made the hairs on the back of their necks stand on end.

Both Aedan and Tim couldn't shake the feeling they were being watched, observed by something unseen and supernatural. No matter how hard they tried to rationalize it, the atmosphere in the room had taken on an ominous feeling.

Every shadow seemed to conceal a lurking figure, and the slightest sound made them jump with trepidation. Aedan desperately wanted to believe his mind played tricks on him, but the lingering sensation of being under the scrutiny of an unseen entity was becoming increasingly difficult to ignore.

"Al Ana," Aedan breathed, the weight of the name heavy on his tongue. Still unnoticed, the ghostly figure silently lurked, defying gravity as it scaled the walls and ceiling, its hollow threatening look fixated upon them from above, watching their every move with malicious intent.

"Seems like we're onto something," Tim said, his eyes meeting Aedan's. There was fear present in them, yes, but also the spark of determination that had first drawn them together as friends.

A part of Aedan longed to confront the unknown, while another urged him to flee before whatever evil force was at work could manifest itself fully. "Let's document everything. We'll need all the evidence we can get if we're going to convince anyone else," Aedan suggested, already reaching for his smartphone to snap pictures of the pages.

"Good idea," Tim agreed, surfacing from under the wave of paralysis that held him in place.

As the last rays of sunlight vanished beyond the horizon, plunging the world into twilight, they sat amidst the ruins of the past, surrounded by a legend of a demon whose influence had seeped into the very bones of Cheboygan. But with each page they turned, each entry they decoded, they felt a step closer to unraveling the mystery of Al Ana.

"Whatever happens," Aedan said, meeting Tim's steady look, "don't chicken out now."

"Always," he affirmed, and in the silence of the cabin, their shared resolve was as tangible as the journal that lay open before them.

The cabin creaked with a language of its own, groaning under the weight of their discovery. "Did you hear that?" Tim's words cut through the thick air.

Aedan cocked his head, listening. There it was again—a rustling from outside, a shuffling that didn't belong to the wind. They exchanged a glance, silent communication perfected over years of friendship. With a nod, Aedan tiptoed to the window, his clumsy nature momentarily subdued by adrenaline. The glass was grimy, but through the grime, a shadow moved—fluid and purposeful. The ghostly figure slipped through the top of the window, defying all logic, and vanished into thin air, still unseen.

"Someone's out there," Aedan said, his voice riddled with concern.

"Can you see who it is?" Tim's question hung in the air, charged with a mix of excitement and apprehension.

"Too dark, too quick," Aedan replied. "But definitely not human...or at least, I think so." "Let's find out." Tim stood, already inching toward the door, his charismatic presence giving him strength. "Are you nuts? What if it's Al Ana?" Aedan knew how absurd it sounded the moment the words left his lips. But Tim just shot him that grin—the one that said he'd already made up his mind.

"Then we'll ask for an autograph. Come on, Aedan."

There was no arguing when Tim got like this. He had a way of making the danger seem like an adventure the two of them couldn't pass up. So Aedan followed him, his blood pressure pounding a staccato rhythm through his body as they slipped from the safety of the cabin into the embrace of the forest.

The sudden darkness carved shadows into the woods, turning trees into specters. They tread softly, their sneakers sinking into the forest floor without sound. Every snap of a twig underfoot made them wince, but Tim's reassuring presence kept Aedan moving forward. "Keep your eyes peeled," Aedan said, remembering the journal's strange sketches. "If those drawings are anything to go by..."

"Shh," Tim interrupted, holding up a hand. "Focus on following. We can freak out later."

Right. The mission. Uncover the truth, protect the town, and don't get caught by a potential demon—or worse, townsfolk who'd ask why they were sneaking around after dark. Simple enough.

They pressed on, the shadow person leading them deeper into a part of the woods that felt untouched by time. The air grew colder, and denser, as if they were walking into the lungs of the forest itself. But they were determined, driven by the need to know, to understand. Whatever secrets Cheboygan held, whatever power Al Ana wielded, they were going to face it head-on. Together.

The dark shadow figure halted at the edge of a clearing, and so did they—crouched behind a thicket, their breath fogging in unison. The dim light from the breakage of the dark clouds barely illuminated the space, but what it revealed sent shivers down their spine. A crowd of townsfolk faces obscured by shadows circled an ancient stone altar. Their hums and chants rose like a chilling breeze through the trees, weaving an eerie melody that set the hairs on their arms standing on end. "Can you believe this?" Aedan said to Tim.

"Shh, just watch," Tim replied, his voice barely audible.

Aedan squinted, trying to understand the ritual before them. Figures swayed, their movements synchronized and deliberate. At the center of the circle, an effigy smoldered, its flames casting long, dancing shadows that seemed to twist and contort with a life of their own.

"Al Ana..." The name slipped from Aedan's lips in a poisoned tone that confirmed the fears clutching at his gut. This wasn't just local folklore or tall tales spun by the old-timers. It was real, all too real, and it had ensnared the people they'd grown up with.

"Look at them, Aedan," Tim said, his voice a mix of awe and trepidation. "They're not themselves. It's like they're...possessed."

"Or controlled," Aedan added, the word tasting bitter. "We have to do something." "Like what? March in there and demand answers?" Tim's sarcasm held an undercurrent of fear.

"Of course not." Aedan shook his head, trying to formulate a plan.

"But we can't let this go on."

"Right. And we need help," Tim replied.

"This is bigger than any childish adventure we've dreamed up over the years," Aedan said excitedly.

Settling themselves, they retreated, each step away from the clearing making them feel both relieved and guilty. They needed a strategy, resources, and most importantly, allies who hadn't fallen under Al Ana's spell.

"Tomorrow," Aedan said as they emerged from the woods, the day suddenly less oppressive around them, "we'll start putting this puzzle together."

"Agreed," Tim said. "For now, let's get out of here before we end up part of that...whatever it is."

"Ritual." Aedan supplied the word he hesitated to say.

"Right. Ritual." Tim exhaled sharply. "Let's just keep moving."

As the cabin came back into view, their sanctuary against the night's revelations, Aedan knew one thing for certain: the battle for their town's soul had just begun to fully reveal itself, and they were right at the heart of it. However, panic lingered in their young minds, a shadow cast over their carefree spirits. The days were growing shorter, the nights cooler, and the inescapable march of time seemed to quicken with each passing moment. The weight of responsibility loomed ever closer, threatening to shatter the idyllic bubble they had so carefully constructed.

As they trudged along, the sound of their feet dragging on the pavement could have easily been mistaken for a herd of weary elephants. Despite the heaviness of their steps, their spirits remained high, buoyed by the knowledge that tomorrow would bring a fresh batch of shenanigans and misadventures.

As they parted ways, each boy silently vowed to himself to savor the remaining days of summer, to cherish the fleeting moments before the harsh reality of homework and bedtimes came crashing back into their lives. For in the ephemeral nature of childhood, they understood that these moments were precious beyond measure, and the weight of growing up would soon bear down upon them, ushering in a new chapter of their lives.

But for now, they were content to bask in the afterglow of another day well spent, dreaming of the endless possibilities that awaited them in the coming adventures.

5

Emma's Flyer

The next day, the mop dragged across the linoleum floor of O'Connor's Market with a rhythmic squelch, back and forth, like the steady ebb and flow of the ocean's tide. Aedan was lost in the motion, his mind replaying last night's eerie tableau by the cabin, when the bell above the store's entrance chimed. He glanced up, and there she was—Lindsey Merritt—in all her casual grace, like she had this aura of bright white light around her radiating generosity, balance, and harmony, walking with rhythm as if she were on a fashion show runway.

"Hey, Aedan," she greeted him with a smile that left Aedan daydreaming about marriage possibilities.

"Hi, Lindsey." He popped back into reality, the words tumbling out awkwardly as he propped the mop against an aisle end cap. Lindsey walked toward the milk. "Milk's...uh, it's on sale today."

"Great, thanks for letting me know," she said, continuing toward the dairy section. She could make something as mundane as buying milk look like a scene from a movie.

Aedan followed a few steps behind, pretending to straighten items on the shelves while stealing glances at her. She was focused on choosing the right gallon of milk—skim, one percent, two percent, vitamin D—oblivious to the storm of thoughts raging in Aedan's head. He needed to say something, anything that would sound remotely normal.

"Um, so, have you seen any good movies lately?" Aedan asked, mentally wincing at the banality of his question.

"Actually...I haven't had the chance. Been busy with...family stuff," Lindsey replied, turning to him with a slightly furrowed brow that suggested curiosity.

"Right, yeah, families can be...demanding," Aedan shot back. He leaned against the shelf and knocked over a display of cereal boxes. Scrambling to set them right, he continued, "But maybe we could go see one together? Sometime?"

"Are you asking me out on a date, Aedan?" Her eyes twinkled with amusement, and for a moment, he thought he caught a hint of hopefulness in her voice.

Aedan could see Tim shaking his head vigorously and chuckling to himself as he watched his buddy stumble over his words, trying to muster the courage to ask Lindsey out on a date.

"Uh, yeah...yes. That's exactly what I'm doing," Aedan managed to stammer, surprising himself with a sudden burst of courage. But as quickly as it came, it dissipated, leaving him fumbling with the boxes again.

"Dude, you're about as smooth as a cheese grater right now! At this rate, you'll have better luck asking out one of these blocks of cheddar I'm stocking," Tim said jokingly.

"Sounds fun," Lindsey said, surprising both of them, before letting out a laugh that was both kind and a little bit pitying. "Let's plan it out sometime soon, okay?"

"Yeah, sure...definitely. Soon." Aedan nodded, overcompensating with enthusiasm as he tried to regain some semblance of coolness.

Tim let out a hearty laugh, playfully tossing a chunk of cheese at Aedan, who fumbled to catch it while still attempting to woo Lindsey.

"Alright, I'll hold you to that, Aedan O'Connor." With her final choice of two percent milk, she headed to the register, and he couldn't help but watch her go, feeling a mixture of elation, embarrassment, and infatuation.

"Movie," Aedan mumbled to himself, trying to cement the idea into reality. It was just a simple outing, but with everything going on, it felt like another world—one where demons didn't lurk in shadows and rituals didn't bind townsfolk to an evil force. Shaking off the thought, he grabbed the mop and resumed his work, hoping he'd find the same determination when facing Al Ana as he did when inviting Lindsey to a movie.

Aedan attacked the floor with renewed vigor, the mop becoming an extension of his arm as he slayed invisible foes. In his mind's eye, he was a dashing hero vanquishing evil forces, clearing the path for his romantic endeavor. With each swipe, he envisioned fighting a dastardly demon or wicked warlock, until the tiles gleamed like polished armor. Of course, the real battle would be mustering the courage to follow through with his movie plans.

Lindsey's radiant smile and twinkling eyes had momentarily emboldened him, but now self-doubt crept in like a nefarious villain. What if she thought it was a date? What if she didn't? Aedan gripped the mop handle, settling his nerves. He was no coward—he'd faced down far more terrifying foes than a potential romantic misunderstanding. With a determined nod, he vowed to woo Lindsey with all the heroic charm he could muster. After all, compared to the forces of darkness he routinely confronted, asking a pretty girl to the movies should be a cakewalk. Aedan grinned, feeling invincible. Al Ana didn't stand a chance against his newfound bravery and freshly mopped floors.

* * *

Tim Spencer's arms moved rhythmically as he scrubbed the hood of his parents' 1998 Chevrolet Lumina sedan. It was a bright Saturday, and the sun beat down on his back, causing droplets of sweat to trickle down his forehead. Bubbles foamed up around the sponge, and the sound of water splashing against the car's surface filled the quiet neighborhood.

"Need some help with that, Timmy?" said a voice dripping with sarcasm, and without looking up, Tim knew it was Henry Gills, walking down the sidewalk, his shadow falling across the wet pavement.

"Hey, Henry," Tim said, trying to keep his tone neutral. "Just doing some chores." "Looks like you missed a spot," Henry jeered, and before Tim could react, a sharp pain stung his shoulder. A small rock clattered to the ground, evidence of Henry's idea of a joke.

"Really...was that necessary?" Tim asked, rubbing the sore spot, but he refused to give Henry the satisfaction of seeing him upset or angry.

"Lighten up, Tim. Just having some fun," Henry scoffed, continuing on his way with a swagger that seemed to say he owned the place. As the distance between them grew, Tim felt that familiar twinge in his gut—the one that reminded him he wasn't confrontational by nature. Splashing water over the car again, Tim tried to wash away the irritation along with the suds.

A few blocks away, Mary Thompson walked at a leisurely pace toward Lindsey's house.

Her eyes roamed over the quaint storefronts of Cheboygan, each holding memories of her childhood. As she passed an old antique store, something caught her attention. It was a flyer, torn and weathered by time, flapping weakly against the brick wall.

MISSING: EMMA TAYLOR read the bold letters at the top. Mary stopped, taking in the black-and-white photo of a woman with search-ing eyes that seemed to look right through her. Emma Taylor, the girl who vanished by the river a few years back. It was a story that had haunted the town, talked about in hushed tones and fearful glances.

Mary felt a shiver run down her spine as she took in the image, the edges of the paper frayed and curling. She remembered how the mystery of Emma's disappearance had gripped everyone, how it had turned into a local legend. And now, with recent events, the past seemed to be resurfacing, demanding attention.

Just then, the sheriff appeared, his expression grave. "I just wanted to provide you with some information, Mary, regarding the potential risks associated with Emma's disappearance," Sheriff Ford stated, advising her to remain vigilant, similar to the approach he'd recommended to Tim and Aedan.

"I'm warning you to be careful like I warned Aedan and Tim," the sheriff said, being cautious.

"We can't rule out foul play at this stage," Sheriff Ford continued his expression grave. "Until we have more information, it's crucial that you remain alert and take precautions. Don't go anywhere alone, and keep your doors and windows locked at all times. If you notice anything out of the ordinary, no matter how insignificant it may seem, report it to me immediately."

The sheriff paused, letting the weight of his words sink in. "I know this is a difficult and unpleasant situation, but we need to consider all possibilities.

"What about Aedan and Tim?" Mary inquired, wanting answers.

"I spotted Aedan and Tim cruising around town, looking like they're on some kinda investigation. I believe they're looking for the demon Al Ana," the sheriff said casually.

"Oh, I see," Mary responded.

The weight of his words hung heavy in the air, leaving Mary annoyed. It was clear that she was getting into something far more sinister than she could have imagined, and the risks were mounting with every step she took.

"Emma..." Mary said to herself, her thoughts drifting to Aedan and Tim's newfound mission. She snapped a quick picture of the flyer with her phone, thinking it might be useful. With a last glance at Emma's face, she turned away, feeling the weight of unsolved mysteries as she continued her walk to Lindsey's house.

She arrived at Lindsey's and showed her the flyer with Emma's picture from her phone, her eyes filled with worry. "I'm deeply concerned about the situation unfolding," said Mary.

"About what?" Lindsey replied with curiosity, standing outside her front door. Mary's words carried an aura of mystique that left Lindsey thoroughly spellbound.

"Let me show you," Mary uttered, her voice laced with intrigue. She unveiled her cell phone, revealing the picture of Emma's missing person flyer, and Lindsey found herself drawn into a realm of bewilderment.

"Did you know that lover boy and his best friend are investigating this rumor about a demon in town by the river or something?'" Mary exclaimed, her eagerness appreciable, igniting awe within Lindsey.

"No, I didn't. And lover boy, huh?" Lindsey responded, her humorous tone a stark contrast to the supernatural revelation, yet failing to diminish the profound accomplishment of wonder that consumed her.

Mary's footsteps echoed with reverence as she accompanied Lindsey toward the aged antique store, the place where the missing person flyer of Emma had captured her attention. The air seemed to hold its breath, as if the very walls of this timeless establishment harbored secrets waiting to be unveiled. Each step felt like a pilgrimage, a journey into the unknown, where the tales of the past mingled with the hopes of the present.

"Come on, it was right here!" Mary said, frustration lacing her voice as she pointed to the space on the brick wall where the flyer had once been. Lindsey's eyes searched the ground, looking for any scrap that might have been the missing piece of paper.

"Maybe someone took it down?" Lindsey suggested, her tone gentle, trying to ease Mary's irritation.

"Where did that flyer about Emma Taylor go?" Mary again pulled out her phone, looking at the picture she snapped earlier. "You remember her story, right? Disappeared without a trace…"

"Yes I remember, and I believe you," Lindsey replied.

Mary nodded, her brows knitting together in concern. "Yeah, it's so creepy. Every time I pass by that river, I get the chills."

They started walking back, their steps matching in rhythm as they headed away from the antique store. Their conversation shifted awkwardly, like a radio trying to find the right frequency.

Mary's voice trembled as she recounted overhearing Sheriff Bill Ford mention them, and how the two boys were determined to uncover the truth.

"Hey," Lindsey said, her voice taking on a lighter note, "how's Aedan doing with all this investigation stuff? Does he seem really into it?"

Mary chuckled. "Aedan? Oh, he's determined, for sure. Thinks he's some kind of detective now. But between you and me"—Mary leaned closer, dropping her voice to a whisper—"I think he's just glad to have an excuse to hang around you more."

"Mary!" Lindsey's cheeks flushed a pretty shade of pink as she swatted at Mary's arm playfully. "Don't be silly, of course he does," Lindsey replied playfully.

"Am I wrong, though?" Mary teased, nudging her with her elbow.

Before she could reply, they rounded the corner near the old oak tree that marked the halfway point to their neighborhood. That's when Mary saw it—a figure, pale and spiritual, standing just beyond the bark. Her heart skipped a beat, and her breath caught in her throat.

"Lindsey…" Mary's voice said eagerly. Mary grabbed Lindsey's arm, pointing shakily. "Do you see her? That's…that looks like…"

Lindsey followed Mary's eyes, and she felt her body tense beside her best friend's.

There, beneath the twisted branches, stood a woman—translucent, with a transcendental glow. Her features were unmistakable, with the same searching eyes from the flyer staring back at them.

"Emma..." Lindsey breathed out, her words a ghostly echo of her thoughts.

Panic seized them, a primal fear that urged their legs to move before their minds fully comprehended what they were seeing. They turned on their heels, their footsteps pounding against the pavement as they ran, leaving the apparition of Emma Taylor behind. Their hearts raced and their breaths came in short gasps as they dashed through the streets, desperate to escape the confusing image that would undoubtedly linger in their thoughts.

"Keep going!" Mary gasped, not daring to look back, knowing Lindsey was right beside her, fueled by the same terror. Cheboygan's shadows seemed to reach for them, screaming secrets they weren't sure they wanted to uncover. But one thing was certain: they couldn't *unsee* what they'd just witnessed, and they couldn't ignore the chilling mystery that had settled over their town.

Their hearts pounded in sync as they sprinted through the dimly lit streets, fear propelling them forward. The shadows seemed to shift and twist as if concealing untold horrors just beyond their line of sight. Each alleyway they passed felt like a gaping maw, ready to swallow them whole if they faltered even for a moment. Despite their burning lungs and aching muscles, they dared not slow down.

The image of what they had witnessed was seared into their minds, a haunting specter that would forever taint their perception of reality. The town they had once thought they knew so well had revealed itself to be a labyrinth of secrets, and they found themselves lost in its depths, unsure of whom or what to trust. As they reached the perceived safety of Mary's house, they collapsed onto the porch, gasping for air.

The adrenaline that had fueled their flight began to dissipate, replaced by a creeping fright that settled deep within their bones. They exchanged a wordless glance, their eyes reflecting the same question: What had they stumbled upon, and what would be the price of their newfound knowledge?

As the night wore on, sleep eluded Lindsey and Mary. Restless, they tossed and turned in bed, haunted by the events of that evening. The darkness outside seemed to press against their windows, softly talking half-formed truths and eerie promises.

The girls felt a chill run down their spines, goosebumps prickling their skin despite the warmth of their blankets. Every creak and groan of their houses made them jump, their imaginations running wild. What had seemed like harmless fun earlier was now taking on a sinister undertone, and their minds conjured up shadowy figures lurking just out of sight.

Lindsey clutched her stuffed bear tighter, its worn fur offering little comfort against the growing emotions of alarm. Mary stared wide-eyed at the ceiling, straining her ears for any sound out of the ordinary. The ticking of the clock on the nightstand seemed deafening in the stillness. Neither dared to close their eyes, fearing what terrors might await them in the realm of dreams. The night stretched on endlessly, each minute feeling like an eternity as they waited with bated breath for the first rays of dawn to break through the gloom. Then finally they both fell asleep.

6

Roadside Park

The next day, Aedan leaned forward on a grassy hill at a roadside park, his eyes wide as Lindsey described her and Mary's ghostly encounter. "Her dress was a nice warm summer sunflower dress. And her face— it was exactly like the missing flyer!" she said as she shrugged her shoulders at the memory.

"You think it was Emma Taylor's ghost?" Aedan asked. His mind raced, thoughts of vengeful spirits and restless souls flashing through his imagination.

"It had to be her. The apparition by the river, the same spot where Emma disappeared," Mary added, her usual composure shaken. "I didn't believe in ghosts before, but now..."

Aedan glanced at Tim, who seemed just as captivated as he was.

"What did she do, the ghost?" Tim leaned forward intently and interrupted Mary.

Lindsey wrapped her arms around herself, fighting back a shiver. "She just stood there by the water, staring. Like she was waiting for something or trying to tell us something, then she vanished."

"What was she trying to tell you?" Aedan asked as his pulse quickened.

There was more to Emma's disappearance than missing flyers and local folklore. Whatever happened here a few years ago, her spirit was still trapped, unable to move on. And he aimed to find out why.

"I'm not too sure…I think she was trying to give us…say something about the river," Mary said cautiously as she started shaking with fear, remembering Emma's image.

Aedan stood up abruptly, a surge of determination flowing through him. "Remember that article at the library we found about Heather Lowe, we should go to the forest by the river and look around to see if we can find some clues about her."

The others rose to join him with some hesitation, curiosity and apprehension playing Aedan led the group with urgency, his mind racing with possibilities. The forest loomed before them, its twisted branches and gnarled trunks casting eerie shadows that seemed to reach out and grasp at them.

Despite the uneasy atmosphere, Aedan pressed on, undeterred. "There's something in there, something we need to find," he declared, his voice low and resolute. "I can feel it, like a breeze in the wind, calling us deeper into the woods."

The others exchanged wary glances, silently questioning his decision, but there was no turning back now. They had come too far, and the allure of the unknown was too strong to resist, even for their newly found doubts.

With a collective deep breath, they followed Aedan into the forest's embrace, their hearts pounding with an equal mixture of fear and exhilaration. The path ahead was shrouded in mystery, but Aedan's determination was precise, like Thomas Edison's when he invented the light bulb. Whatever lay waiting for them in the depths of the forest, he was convinced they must uncover it, no matter what the cost was. The stakes were high, and the risks were great, but the promise of discovery burned brighter than any doubt or fear.

"Woah, what was that?" The hairs on Aedan's neck prickled as he felt an unseen presence nearby. From the corner of his eye, he thought he saw a flicker of movement, a blurry figure keeping pace from behind them.

He glanced at his friends, who were now looking in the same direction—they had seen it too. Tim scanned the surroundings warily while Lindsey and Mary huddled close together as they walked.

Aedan couldn't resist cracking a joke to lighten the tense mood. "Looks like we've got some unwanted company," he quipped nonchalantly. "Either that, or the library's decided to send its overdue book poltergeist after us."

Tim rolled his eyes, but the corner of his mouth twitched with a suppressed smile. "Very funny, man. You know how I feel about paranormal stuff," Mary said giggling nervously.

"Well, if it is a ghost, at least it has good taste in haunts," Aedan added.

"The library's way cooler than some dusty old mansion," Lindsey said, swatting playfully at Aedan's arm. "Don't even joke about that! You know I scare easily." She glanced around apprehensively, sticking close to her friends.

Chuckling, Aedan looped his arm through hers reassuringly. "Relax, it's probably just Mrs. Perkins from next door, out for her daily power walk and glaring disapprovingly at us youths again," he said, trying to ease the tension.

Despite their laughter, the group couldn't shake the nerve-racking feeling of being watched as they hurried the rest of the way to the forest's safe, naturalistic sanctuary. Or so they thought.

The four friends froze in their tracks, hearts pounding, as they whipped around to confront the unseen presence. But to their utter dismay, there was nothing there—the sinister entity had vanished without a trace, leaving them consumed by an immense sensation of terror and vulnerability.

The atmosphere carried an alarming weight, as Aedan's words lingered with a hint of angst. "It's like we are being investigated," he remarked.

Tim responded, amplifying the pensive mood, "I think we are," as if weighing the implications of such a possibility. At that moment, uncertainty hung in the air, inviting a thoughtful pause to consider the potential ramifications that lay ahead.

The four friends stood in front of Chook River. Crickets chirped and fireflies blinked in the encroaching shadows. "You sure about this?" Tim asked, peering into the gloom.

Aedan nodded, jaw set. "We have to find where they hanged Heather. I just know the answer's out there."

Tim clasped his shoulder. "Then let's do this."

Switching on their cell phone flashlights, they trekked the woods. The canopy of leaves blocked out the fading light, immersing them in eerie darkness. Disembodied voices echoed around them, barely audible. Using an old map, they located the approximate site of the hanging tree. Aedan's light glinted off something ahead. Approaching cautiously, they discovered a frayed length of rope dangling from a thick branch.

"This is it," Aedan breathed. As he grasped the rope, the disembodied voices began to intensify, swirling around them saying *"Hi"* in static tones. The hanging remnant swayed slightly as if tugged by invisible hands. They spun around as a bush rustled violently behind them. Lindsey let out a loud deafening scream.

More disembodied voices cried out, unintelligible words echoing *"We see you"* mournfully.

"What could they possibly mean?" Aedan uttered, his voice laced with worry. The uncertainty gnawed at their very core, leaving their minds racing with disturbing possibilities that seemed to grow darker by the second.

"I can't help but worry about the ominous implications behind those hushed, unintelligible words," Tim replied, his gaze darting around in all directions, desperately trying to pinpoint the source of the eerie voices that seemed to envelop them from every angle.

The friends' hearts hammered as they clung to each other. "Let's get out of here!" Lindsey yelled over the swelling, loud, confused, and inharmonious sound.

They all fled blindly, ghostly wails giving chase. Whatever lurked in these woods did not wish to be discovered. But Aedan knew they had found a clue, one that would unravel the dark mystery enshrouding Chook River.

They all ran as fast as their legs could carry them, the eerie wails pursuing them like a malicious force. The dense foliage whipped at their faces, and branches scratched their arms, but they dared not slow down. Their breaths came in ragged gasps, mingling with the cacophony of otherworldly sounds that seemed to surround them from all sides. Aedan risked a glance over his shoulder, his heart pounding with a mixture of terror and intrigue as they ran toward Main Street.

The woods appeared to shift and distort behind them as if the very trees were alive and reaching out with long, twisted limbs. He stumbled, nearly falling, but Tim's firm grip on his arm kept him upright. Finally, after what felt like an eternity, they burst onto the corner of the street and into the safety of the open public. Doubling over, they gulped in lungfuls of air, their bodies trembling from the harrowing ordeal. Aedan's mind raced, piecing together the fragments of what they had witnessed. He knew, deep down, that they had stumbled upon something sinister, something that defied explanation. And yet, the burning desire to uncover the truth about Chook River burned brighter than ever before.

* * *

Later that day, Aedan worked his usual shift at O'Connor's Market. As he scanned and bagged items methodically, his thoughts kept drifting back to the chilling experience in the woods. What were those voices trying to tell them?

The chime above the entrance jangled as a customer walked in. Aedan glanced up to see Sakima ambling casually down the aisle. Aedan recalled him from a newspaper clipping he read regarding Susan Smith.

Sakima was the medicine man of the Ojibwa Native American Tribe. He had always possessed a deep connection to the spiritual realm. From a young age, he displayed a keen discernment, attentiveness, and honesty, traits that endeared him to his people. As he grew older, Sakima took on the role of a healer, using natural remedies and ancient rituals to aid those who were in need.

Though reserved, Sakima had a wealth of knowledge about local history and legends. As Sakima placed his items on the counter, Aedan made a split-second decision. "Hey Sakima, can I ask you something?"

Sakima raised an eyebrow. "Go ahead, young Aedan."

Aedan lowered his voice. "What do you know about Susan Smith? A news reporter said she was possessed on your lands."

Sakima's expression darkened. "Susan was an innocent soul, corrupted by forces beyond her control."

He recounted the tale in hushed tones. A few years back, Susan had been hosting a séance with friends by the river when an evil presence possessed her. A priest had tried to exorcise the demon, but it drove Susan insane instead. She now lived, wheelchair bound, in the Northern Woods sanatorium. "The demon's name is Al Ana," Sakima said. "An ancient evil that feeds on souls."

Aedan shivered, glimpsing the deeper darkness plaguing his town. After paying for his groceries, Sakima clasped his shoulder. "Be wary, young one. Some secrets are better left buried. You might be able to seek more information from an old gypsy fortune teller named Elara Wildheart."

Elara Wildheart was born into a long line of Romani people, inheriting the gift of foresight that had been passed down through generations. From a young age, Elara's vivid visions of future events set her apart from her peers. Her family nurtured her abilities, teaching her the ancient art of divination and the delicate dance of reading fortunes in the shimmering patterns of crystal balls and tarot cards.

Growing up on the open road, Elara traveled far and wide, offering her insight to those in need. People were drawn to her animated presence and captivating views, finding solace in her accurate predictions and comforting words. Yet, the weight of knowing what lay ahead took its toll on Elara, her youthful exuberance tempered by the somber knowledge of life's twists and turns.

Despite the burden she carried, Elara remained adventurous, always seeking new experiences and connections. Her encounters with different cultures and beliefs enriched her understanding of the world, shaping her into a wise and empathetic soul.

With those ominous words, Sakima was gone, leaving Aedan to ponder this new piece of the puzzle. What was Al Ana's connection to everything happening now? And how could he hope to stop such an ancient evil?

Aedan could not get Sakima's warning out of his head. He had to know more about what happened to Susan Smith. He enthusiastically bounced out from behind the cashier's counter, his steps filled with energy as he made his way over to the aisle where Tim was diligently stocking the shelves with bags of crispy chips.

"Hey, Tim, want to take a ride with me after work?" Aedan asked as

Tim worked. Tim raised an eyebrow. "Where to?"

"The sanatorium on the edge of town. I want to see if we can talk to Susan and find out what happened to her."

Though skeptical, Tim agreed to go along. He knew once Aedan got an idea in his head, there was no talking him out of it.

* * *

Aedan and Tim arrived at the imposing wrought iron gates of the sanatorium. Patients in robes and hospital gowns wandered through overgrown gardens. A chill ran down their spines as they peered through the bars of the gate, unsettled by the eerie silence that seemed to hang over the sanatorium grounds.

The unkempt gardens only added to the neglect and decay, as if the facility had been left to crumble and be reclaimed by nature. Aedan swallowed hard, his grip tightening on the straps of his backpack. "Are you sure we should be here?" Tim said, his voice trembling slightly. "This place gives me the creeps."

Aedan tried to appear nonchalant, but his covert glances betrayed his anxiety. "Don't be such a baby," Aedan scoffed, though his bravado rang hollow. "We came all this way, didn't we? We can't turn back now." He silently prayed they wouldn't come to regret their decision to explore the Northern Woods Sanatorium.

Tim spotted a guard patrolling, holding a baton. "We'll have to sneak in," he said. They found a tree next to the wall and climbed onto a sturdy branch extending over the grounds.

Dropping down, they crept along the shadowed perimeter, ducking behind bushes when orderlies passed. In a far corner, next to a crumbling wall, sat a woman in a wheelchair. Her straggly hair covered her face as she rocked back and forth, mumbling to herself. "That looks like her," Aedan said, matching the hair of the woman rocking to a picture of her he brought from the library. "Susan Smith."

They approached cautiously. "Susan?" Aedan called softly. She gave no response. "Is your name Susan?" Again, no response. As they drew nearer, Aedan saw her lips moving rapidly, and they caught glimpses of wild, darting eyes between strands of her hair. Susan was lost in her own world, oblivious to the boys' presence. What unspeakable torment had she endured at the hands of the demon Al Ana or the institution in which she was being forced to live?

"We should go before someone spots us," Tim urged nervously. Reluctantly, Aedan agreed it was too risky to linger. As they snuck back to the wall, Aedan glanced back at the rocking, demented figure of Susan Smith. They might never learn her full story, but Aedan was more determined than ever to defeat Al Ana and free his town from its curse.

Aedan hesitated, feeling desperate—he had to at least try to reach Susan one last time. "I'll catch up with you," he told Tim. Before his friend could protest, Aedan approached the wheelchair.

"Susan?" he said gently. She continued rocking and rambling, oblivious to anything around her. He crouched down, trying to meet her darting eyes. "My name's Aedan. I want to help you." At the sound of his voice, her stream of murmuring halted briefly. Aedan caught his breath. Was she listening? "Can you tell me what happened with the demon Al Ana? What happened to you?"

Her lips moved soundlessly as she resumed rocking. Aedan persisted. "Please, if you know anything that could stop Al Ana, you have to help me. The town's in danger."

No response. Aedan sighed, knowing it was hopeless. Whatever Al Ana had done to her, Susan was lost to the world. He stood, sadness weighing on him. "I'm so sorry," he gasped. As he turned to leave, a disfigured hand shot out, seizing his wrist. Her arm at the elbow was covered in bruises from the use of several IVs. Susan's clouded eyes bore into him with sudden, startling clarity. In a cracked, hissing voice, she uttered a single word:

"Beware…"

Aedan staggered back, shocked. He recalled hearing that same voice from the disembodied voices saying *"Hi"* in the forest earlier. Before he could react further, Tim was grabbing his arm, pulling him away. "We've got to move, now!"

They scrambled over the wall just as a flashlight beam cut through the darkness. It was the sheriff. Aedan's heart pounded as they slipped away into the night, Susan's chilling warning echoing in his mind.

Aedan and Tim hurried through the darkness, putting distance between themselves and the sanatorium. "That was too close," Tim said. "If the sheriff had caught us…"

"I know, but I had to try talking to Susan," Aedan replied. "Even if she's lost her mind, she might know something about Al Ana."

Tim nodded. "So what now? Back home?"

Aedan hesitated. "Not yet. I want to check out Susan's old house. Maybe we can find some clues there."

"Her house?" Tim raised an eyebrow. "You think that's a good idea this late at night?" "We'll just take a quick look around. I can't shake this feeling that the house is important."

Tim sighed. "Okay, fine. But we'd better be quick."

They changed direction, heading toward the abandoned Smith house on the edge of town. As they approached, Aedan felt uncomfortable. The house loomed against the night sky, sagging and silent.

Tim shivered. "Gives me the creeps."

Aedan readied himself. "Let's just get this over with." They crept up the weed-choked walkway and tried the front door. Unlocked. The hinges creaked ominously as they entered the dark foyer. Dust coated every surface.

"Where do we even start?" Tim said.

"Upstairs. That's where the exorcism happened." They moved carefully through the downstairs and ascended the staircase. Aedan's heart pounded as they reached the upstairs landing. Tim's breathing grew shallow beside him. They moved down the shadowy hallway, floorboards groaning underfoot. Aedan tried the first door—locked.

The second swung open with a protesting creak, revealing a disheveled bedroom. "This must be it," Aedan said, running his fingers along the faded wallpaper.

Tim swallowed hard. "You think something's here? After all these years?" A faint scrabbling noise made them both freeze. It seemed to emanate from the far corner. Aedan's mouth went dry as he slowly turned his cell phone flashlight beam toward the source of the sound.

At first, he saw nothing. Then a shape began to materialize in the inky blackness—a hunched, spindly form, like a grotesque human silhouette. Aedan's scream caught in his throat as two pinprick eyes snapped open, glowing with an unholy light.

"Oh, shi…" Tim's voice was barely audible. "We need to get out of here. Now."

The entity stirred, rising from its crouched position with agonizing slowness. Aedan felt rooted to the spot, his limbs turned to lead. He wanted to run, to flee this cursed place, but some unseen force held him transfixed in the creature's baleful wickedness.

At the top of the stairs, a hallway stretched into darkness. As they ran, the floorboards groaned under their feet. Suddenly, the temperature dropped sharply. Their breath misted in the frigid air. Aedan's heart hammered. "You feel that?" Tim nodded, eyes wide.

Then—a scratching sound. Something darted at the edge of Aedan's vision, a small, hunched figure that vanished around a corner. "What was that?" Tim gasped.

More skittering shadows flickered past, barely viewable. The scratching grew louder, more insistent, coming from all around them now. Aedan's mouth went dry. "I think it's a poltergeist. We should go, now!" They ran for the stairs. Behind them, a door slammed open and closed violently. The scratching on the walls rose to a frenzied, striking combination of a chaotic mixture. The walls shook with the force of some unseen rage.

They fled downstairs, nearly tumbling in their retreat. As Aedan risked a backward glance, his blood turned into ice. A writhing black mass poured from the second floor, boiling down the walls. Hundreds of shadows, swarming toward them. Aedan and Tim burst outside into the cold night air. They sprinted down the walkway as the door slammed shut behind them, muffling the shrieks and scratching. Panting, they slowed to a halt under a streetlamp. Aedan's mind reeled.

"What the hell was that?" Tim gasped.

Aedan shook his head. "I think we just met the poltergeist." He shivered. Susan's warning echoed once more through his mind:

Beware...

Aedan and Tim shivered as they walked briskly back to their houses, eager to put some distance between themselves and Susan's haunted residence. The image of that writhing mass of shadows swarming down the walls was seared into their minds. Aedan bid Tim good night before slipping inside, bolting the door behind him. The warmth and familiarity of home was comforting, but Aedan still felt rattled by the experience.

He tried to distract himself by turning on the TV, and flipping channels until he found a ghost-hunting show. *Maybe I can pick up some tips,* he thought. As the investigators on-screen discussed EVP recordings, a chill breeze brushed the back of Aedan's neck. He glanced over his shoulder just as the window creaked open by itself, letting in the night air and whatever other invisible mass that followed.

That's weird, he thought. *Did I just see that?* He crossed the room to pull the window shut. As he grasped the frame, an eerie undertone drifted through the gap:

"Beware the river..." Aedan froze. The hairs on his arms stood on end. That was no ordinary breeze carrying those words through the window. The low disembodied voice came again, more insistent. *"The river...BEWARE..."*

Aedan's heart pounded with fear, his stretched-out arms shaking as he slammed the window shut and turned the lock. He took a step back, wobbling. The bedroom light flickered restlessly. Shadows skated across the walls. The picture on the TV warped and scrambled. For a second, Aedan was certain the room was closing around him, and he couldn't breathe.

"Go away," he mumbled through gritted teeth. "You don't scare me," he said, still scared and shaking. For another tantalizing moment, the presence came closer and closer, as if testing his will. Then, gradually, the flickering flame congealed, and the room blew steady.

Aedan sucked in his breath and hesitated. But then the warning rang in his head. He couldn't walk away from this now. There were mysteries yet to be solved, with or without the will of this spirit.

The next morning, Aedan knew that he needed help understanding the strange things happening in town. He had an idea of where to go, but it wasn't a place from his childhood. He would have to venture some distance outside of town, to the home of an elderly man named Harry, a local gossip who always seemed to know more about the town's legends and folklore.

7

Harry's Haunted Life

The next morning Aedan drove over to a dilapidated Victorian house where Old Man Harry lived. As he walked up an overgrown path, he noted the KEEP OUT signs and wind chimes made of animal bones that adorned the gate. Taking a deep breath, Aedan rang the doorbell.

After several long moments, he heard shuffling footsteps approach from within. The door creaked open, revealing a disheveled older man with wild gray hair, walking with a wooden cane and wearing a flannel shirt. "Harry?" Aedan said. "It's me, Aedan. From the store. I was hoping I could ask you some questions about some local legends. I think something...unnatural is going on in this town."

Harry's eyes narrowed. "So, the book I gave you did the job—you're the newest meddler, nosing into things best left alone, huh?" He stared hard at Aedan, then sighed. "Well, you might as well come in. Watch the books and mind the raccoon in the corner."

Aedan followed Harry inside, carefully stepping over teetering piles of books and artifacts that looked more like a pile of junk. He sat in a moth-eaten armchair, glancing warily at the raccoon perched on a nearby shelf.

"Now," Harry said, sitting on his outdated 1970s sofa splashed with bright colors, covered in bold patterns, and shaped like something from a sci-fi movie. "Tell me what sort of trouble you've gotten yourself into."

Aedan began recounting his experiences, watching Harry's expression grow more excited with each detail. He described the strange events he and his friends had witnessed around town— the moving shadows, eerie sounds, and the sensation of unseen eyes watching them.

Harry listened intently, nodding when Aedan mentioned the name "Al Ana." Then he visibly stiffened. "Where did you hear that name, boy?" he asked sharply.

"I saw it written on some old documents at the library," Aedan explained, not revealing his true source. "It seemed connected to bad things happening in the town's past. What can you tell me about Al Ana?"

Harry leaned back with a weary sigh, steepling his fingers. "Well...Al Ana is an ancient evil that has plagued humans for centuries. Some say she is a demon, others say a vengeful spirit, but all agree she isn't to be messed with...period, point blank."

He rose from the sofa and retrieved a large, leather-bound book from a splintered plywood bookshelf. "Ah, yes, here it is. It is said Al Ana is a powerful demon who is after the souls of the living, humans or animals." Flipping through the book's fragile pages, Harry showed Aedan images depicting a dark-haired woman named Heather Lowe being hanged. At the same time, villagers looked on, and behind the onlookers was a dark figure Aedan had seen before, resembling the demon.

Underneath the images of the woman was an old map, circled on a spot that showed the image of strange markings near an old lumber mill in the woods. Aedan took notes on the location as Harry pointed at the image.

A chill ran down Aedan's spine as he studied the map, his eyes fixated on the ominous markings near the old mill. What secrets did those woods hold? What horrors lay waiting in the shadows? He couldn't shake the curiosity that crept over him. His scribbling seemed to echo in the tense silence, each stroke of his pen a haunting reminder of the unknown he was about to confront.

Harry's subtle gestures only heightened the eerie atmosphere, as if he too felt the grave danger lurking ahead. Aedan's mind raced with awful possibilities. Was he venturing into a realm better left undisturbed? A part of Aedan yearned to turn back, to bury this discouraging mystery. Yet, the lure of uncovering the truth burned brighter than any fear.

"I have to ask you a question, lad. Do you know who Tommy Canfeld was?" Harry asked, his voice laced with deceitful implications.

"Yeah, I read about his and Emma's disappearance at the library a few days ago," Aedan replied, his tone unnervingly hyper, betraying an underlying curiosity.

Aedan's heart raced as the implications of Harry's question sank in. Tommy and Emma's disappearance had been shrouded in mystery, with no concrete answers ever emerging. A nagging feeling crept up his spine, hinting at sinister undercurrents beneath Harry's seemingly innocent query. "What do you know about it?" Aedan probed cautiously, his eyes narrowing as he studied Harry's expression for any telltale signs of deception. The air grew thick with tension, each word carrying the weight of unspoken secrets and buried truths.

"You know, Aedan, I know of the location where they went missing," Harry said, his eyes squinting like he was harboring some dark secret. The ominous tone in his voice filled Aedan with caution, leaving him deeply worried about what he might be implying, or the trouble he could be plotting.

"How can you be certain of that information?" Aedan cautioned, his voice laced with apprehension.

" Listen, over the generations, Al Ana has been responsible for many unexplained tragedies and disappearances—she steals away souls and wreaks havoc on the living," Harry continued grimly. Aedan stared wide-eyed at the disturbing images, a chill running down his spine. What had he gotten himself into?

He glanced nervously around the cluttered study, as if worried the demon might materialize right then and there.

"I know you're trying to help the town, but don't take this lightly," Harry cautioned. "There are forces here beyond your understanding." The old man's eyes bore into him, deadly serious.

Aedan shifted, the responsibility suddenly feeling heavy. "I'll be careful," he promised. "Really. This isn't just some adventure to me."

Harry studied him for a moment before nodding. "See that you remember that. Al Ana has destroyed far stronger men than you, boy."

Aedan swallowed, imagining the demon's shadow falling over him. But he stood tall. "I won't let her win. Whatever she's done, it ends."

Harry smiled slightly. "You've got courage, boy. Use it wisely." He clapped Aedan on the shoulder. "Now, come on. Come with me to the river and I'll show you where they went missing."

He rose from his seat and began to make his way out of the room, a worrisome gesture that sent a wave of anxiety throughout Aedan. "No, I'm good for now...I believe you," Aedan replied, his voice laced with worry as a nagging feeling crept in, hinting at an ulterior motive behind Harry's seemingly innocuous offer. The air grew thick with tension, and Aedan couldn't shake the worrying feeling that something wasn't quite right.

Aedan stepped out of Harry's cluttered study behind him, his mind swirling with questions. The old man's dire warnings echoed in his ears, sending a chill down his spine. But he couldn't turn back now. Not when his curiosity had gotten the best of him.

Supported by Harry's sudden change of emotions, Aedan turned toward the door. "There are answers out there, waiting for me to find them," Aedan said, trying to stay focused. With a final fake wave to Harry, he stepped outside, ready to unravel the mystery of Al Ana.

He paused on the porch, gazing out at the dense forest surrounding Harry's isolated cabin. Somewhere in those shadowy woods lurked the malignant spirit of Al Ana.

With a deep breath, Aedan descended the creaking steps of the front porch. His boots crunched on the gravel path as he made his way to his dusty, old, beat-up car. Despite the looming threat, excitement vibrated through him. He was getting closer to the truth; he could feel it.

As Aedan climbed inside his car, he caught a glimpse of Harry staring at him incessantly, then he glanced at his own determined expression in the rearview mirror. "No turning back now," he told himself firmly. He had a job to do. A town to save. And he wouldn't rest until Al Ana was stopped for good.

The engine sputtered to life. Gripping the wheel tight, Aedan pulled out onto the lonely dirt road lined with rows and rows of pine trees. The answers were out there, waiting. And one way or another, he was going to find them. Aedan's mind raced as he drove away from Harry's cabin, replaying their conversation. The dire warnings about Al Ana echoed in his thoughts. He knew confronting the demon could put him in grave danger, but the alternative was unthinkable. If he didn't act, the evil spirit would continue terrorizing Cheboygan, stealing souls, as it had for centuries.

The responsibility felt heavy on his shoulders. He was just an eighteen-year-old with a crush on a girl, working at the family store. How could he defeat such an ancient and evil force? Self-doubt crept in as the trees flew past in a blur. What if he wasn't up to the task? What if his clumsiness got him killed before he could save the town? Aedan took a deep breath, steadying his nerves. He couldn't let fear stop him, not when so much was at stake.

* * *

Aedan pulled his beat-up car to the side of the winding forest road. He killed the engine and sat in silence, mentally preparing for the next phase of his investigation. Despite his determination, doubts still lingered within him. What if he wasn't clever enough to outwit the demon? What if his clumsiness got him into trouble again? Shaking his head, he pushed the negative thoughts away. He had come too far to turn back now.

With his courage in tow, Aedan stepped out of the car. The forest around him was eerily still and quiet. He knew these woods held secrets...and dangers. Al Ana could be lurking anywhere.

Alone, Aedan bravely walked along the overgrown trail, slowly; his attention was alert, in search of the markings he saw on the map Harry showed him. Though nervous, he felt empowered by his purpose. Protecting Lindsey and the town gave him courage. He would face whatever came next. As the path twisted deeper into the shadowy woods, Aedan mentally prepared himself. The answers were close now, he could feel it. Step by step, he was getting closer to the truth. And when the time came to confront the demon, he would be ready.

The farther Aedan ventured into the forest, the heavier the air seemed to get. The pine trees cast long, twisted shadows that played tricks on his eyes. He thought he saw movements out of the corners of his vision, but when he turned, there was nothing. As Aedan examined the map, he recognized the circled area he had previously marked. After searching the vicinity for several minutes, he spotted what appeared to be the tree in question. However, upon closer inspection, there were no distinguishing markings, leaving Aedan disappointed and the feeling of being misled.

Aedan's heart pounded as he recalled Harry's warnings about the demon's powers.

According to legend, Al Ana could drive someone mad just by being near them.

Crack! A branch snapped loudly behind Aedan. He whirled, eyes wide. "Who's there?" he called out, voice wavering slightly. Silence answered. After a tense moment, he continued. The ruins soon appeared, just as Harry's map had shown.

A cold wind whipped up, howling through the trees as he crossed the threshold. The hairs on Aedan's neck stood. He was being watched; he could feel it. "Al Ana," he said loudly. "I know you're here. Come out!" A raspy cackle echoed around him. Aedan's breath caught in his throat.

The cackle faded, replaced by an eerie silence that seemed to press in on him from all sides. Suddenly, a shadowy figure emerged from behind a broken concrete parking block in the old mill's parking lot, its form shifting and distorting as it glided toward him. Aedan prepared himself, his heart pounding in his ears. "Al Ana," he growled, raising his hand. "Your reign of terror...will..." Aedan didn't get to finish what he was saying.

"Look," the figure said in a disembodied voice, sending a shiver down Aedan's spine.

One false step, one moment of hesitation, and it could all be over. As the mysterious shape loomed closer, Aedan braced himself for the inevitable clash, determined to face whatever horrors lay ahead with optimistic courage.

Suddenly, the figure manifested itself, morphing into an old theater, and then reverting to its original form, which frightened Aedan but reassured him that at least it wasn't the demon. Out of nowhere, the figure vanished into the air, leaving Aedan bewildered. He cautiously approached the brush, peering around in vain for any trace of the mysterious entity. Unable to figure out the awkward occurrence, Aedan's mind raced with concern, urgently prompting him to reach out to his friend Tim. Aedan pulled his cell phone out and called his buddy.

"Tim, I'll be over to pick you up immediately. We need to go to the Calumet Theatre right away—there's no time to waste. Something serious is happening," Aedan said.

"Alright, I'll be ready. Where are we going?" Tim's response was simple and to the point.

"I will explain later," Aedan cryptically replied.

As Aedan and Tim sped down the winding road toward the Calumet Theatre, the conversation hung heavy between them, broken only by the occasional breeze outside. The looming presence of the mysterious figure still weighed on Aedan's mind, the memory of its eerie transformation replaying in his thoughts.

"Listen up, Tim! You won't believe what I just witnessed. I was at Harry's place, grilling him about this demon, right? After that, I followed his map to the forest near the old mill, and there it was, by this decrepit parking block—an apparition, man, I'm telling you! At first, it was just a black cloud of smoke, but then it morphed into the Calumet Theatre. I'm not sure if it was evil or not, but we need to figure this out, now. There is some seriously weird stuff happening, and we can't afford to waste any time. We've got to investigate further and get to the bottom of this before it's too late," Aedan said in a startled state of mind.

8

The Calumet Theatre

The Calumet Theatre stood before Aedan and Tim like a grand dame of old, her walls steeped in mystery and suspicions of the supernatural. They couldn't help but feel its history seep into their bones as they approached the grand entrance, their footsteps reverberating through the hushed corridors that seemed alive with secrets.

"Man, can you believe this place?" Aedan said to Tim, his voice quiet and soft, as if he were afraid to disturb the spirits that might be lingering just beyond sight. "Madame Modjeska, here. Can you imagine?"

Tim gave a low whistle, his eyes sweeping over the ornate trimmings and velvety drapes that filled the interior with an air of faded elegance. "Dude, haunted theaters are the stuff of legends. And Madame Helena Modjeska—she's practically royalty."

"Royalty that doesn't want to leave," Aedan added, recalling the tale that had become almost as famous as the theater itself. "In 1958, Adysse Lane, an actress of some renown at the time, stood on this very stage.

"During her performance, Adysse experienced a momentary lapse in memory. She blanked out, lost in her lines, and coincidentally glanced up toward the balcony. To her astonishment, she claimed to have witnessed the presence of Madame Helena, who silently mouthed the forgotten lines to her. With the ethereal assistance of Madame Helena, Adysse successfully concluded the play," Aedan explained with enthusiasm.

"Supposedly, since then people hear things," Aedan continued, his voice echoing off the walls, lending a chilling resonance to the story. "Music drifting through the air when no instruments are playing. Or they'll feel this sudden drop in temperature, like winter just walked in and brushed past them," Aedan said with feistiness.

"Creepy," Tim acknowledged, though his tone held the thrill of their upcoming adventure. His protective instincts were always at the ready; it was one of the reasons Aedan trusted him with his harebrained schemes.

"Here we are," Aedan said, pausing at the threshold of the near-empty ticket booth. The hallway was dimly lit, casting long shadows that seemed to dance just out of the corner of his eye. "Do you get the feeling we're not exactly alone?"

"Always," Tim replied, unfazed by the eerie atmosphere. That was Tim for you—solid as the earth itself, no matter how deep they delved into the unknown.

They made their way closer to the booth, their presence a mere forewarning against the quiet hum of the Calumet Theatre's restless soul. They were here to seek answers, and something told them they lay hidden within these walls, waiting for the right moment to emerge from the shadows.

Stepping into the muted glow of the ticket booth's single flickering light, Aedan couldn't help but feel a tingle of tension. There he was— Mr. Jenkins, the man whose very appearance seemed to scream tales of the paranormal. He was as much a fixture of the Calumet Theatre as the aging velvet seats and the spectral rumors that breathed life into its walls.

"Look at him," Aedan said to Tim, his attention fixed on the ticket seller. Mr. Jenkins towered above the counter, his lanky form draped in an usher uniform that seemed to hang from his frame like garments on a forgotten scarecrow. The fabric, once a deep maroon, now washed out to a somber hue, told stories of countless days working. And that bow tie—it was a relic, an untamed thing that defied the passage of time with its stubborn presence.

Tim leaned in closer, his curiosity piqued by the sight. "He looks... hollow," he observed, a note of concern threading through his voice. Indeed, there was something about Mr. Jenkins that suggested he was more spectral than flesh. His skin held the pallor of a man who hadn't felt sunlight in years, almost translucent under the theater's dim lights.

Aedan watched intently as one customer after another approached the booth, each exchange with Mr. Jenkins more soulless than the last. Every motion he made was sluggish, as if he waded through a reality different from their own. His hands moved with a strange lethargy, tickets passing from his grasp like leaves falling from a weary tree.

"Doesn't seem like there's much going on behind those eyes," Aedan said, squinting to make out the finer details of Mr. Jenkins's expression—or lack thereof. It was as if the man had retreated far within himself, leaving only a shell to interact with the world. A shell that could smile, yes, but even that rare occurrence had the warmth of a winter's chill, the corners of his mouth twitching upward in a semblance of human emotion that failed to reach the depths of his haunted eyes.

"Something's not right," Aedan concluded, the words barely a breath between them. The haunted look in Mr. Jenkins's eyes was a silent scream, a testament to sights unseen and secrets buried deep within the heart of the Calumet. Whatever it was that caused this man to wear such an empty mask, they had the unshakable feeling that it was intrinsically tied to the ghostly legends of Al Ana that clung to this place like cobwebs.

"Let's keep watching," Tim replied, his voice steady yet edged with a growing intrigue. Together, they stood watch over Mr. Jenkins, their presence unnoticed as they tried to decipher the enigma of the man before them and the lingering mystery hidden in the shadows of the theater.

Tim and Aedan edged back into the shadows, a recess in the wall providing just enough cover to keep them out of sight. It was a snug fit, with old promotional posters peeling off the walls around them, but it gave them an unobstructed view of the ticket booth where Mr. Jenkins continued his spectral-like duties.

"Perfect spot," Aedan quietly muttered, glancing at Tim's broad frame packed in beside him. Tim nodded, his eyes never leaving the peculiar spectacle before them.

From their vantage point, they could see every detail of Mr. Jenkins's movements. There was something unnervingly precise about the way he tore each ticket—one smooth motion, no more, no less—and he handed them over with the same lifeless efficiency. The repetition was hypnotic, almost as if he were a marionette, with invisible strings guiding his every action.

"Watch his hands," Aedan said, focusing on the monotonous task. The hands moved with an eerie autonomy, unaffected by the ebb and flow of human emotion that should've accompanied such interaction. The dim light from the chandelier above cast long, sinister shadows across his fingers, accentuating their skeletal appearance.

"Like clockwork," Tim replied, his voice low and hushed.

It was true; there was no hesitation, no fumble, no sign of life. Each customer received the same vacant stare, the same rigid posture, and the same mechanical service. His eyes, those sunken pools of despair, looked past the patrons, fixated on some unseen point in the distance.

"Doesn't even seem to see them, does he?" Aedan couldn't help but feel a pang of sadness for Mr. Jenkins—whatever had sapped the life from his face must have been truly harrowing. Or perhaps it wasn't just the past haunting him, but something much closer, something within these very walls that kept him bound to this creepy routine.

As another patron approached, Aedan leaned forward slightly, his curiosity inching toward a conclusion that felt as cold and unforgiving as the air that sometimes swept inexplicably through the theater. Whatever the truth, one thing was clear: Mr. Jenkins was more than just a ticket seller; he was a mystery wrapped in the enigma of the Calumet, a puzzle begging to be solved. And Aedan was determined to unravel it.

"Tim," Aedan said, talking under his breath, a silent flutter against the backdrop of eerie stillness that encased them. "You ever think... maybe it's not just him? Maybe there's something else here, meddling with the way things should be?"

Aedan could feel the weight of the question hanging in the air between them, dense with implications that stretched beyond the realm of logic and into the supernatural—a concept he'd always kept at arm's length until now.

Tim's eyes, those vigilant sentinels, never ceased their watchful roaming, even as he gave a subtle nod. His profile was etched with concern, a testament to the gravity of their shared suspicion. It was enough to confirm that Aedan's instincts weren't leading him astray; there was an unseen force at play, something that cloaked the Calumet Theatre in an intangible veil of mystery.

"Keep your eyes peeled, Aedan," Tim said back, his voice carrying the command of someone who had faced the unknown before and stood firm. "There's gotta be more to this. We're missing pieces of the puzzle."

Aedan shifted his focus, following Tim's example, seeking out the telltale signs of the peculiar. The atmosphere was thick with secrets, as if the very walls of the old theater were poised to divulge tales of forgotten spectral spirits—if only they knew how to listen.

"Let's find them, then," Aedan breathed with clarity, the thrill of the chase reigniting the fire within him. "The truth is here somewhere, hiding in the shadows. And we're going to drag it into the light."

The creak of the double doors heralded their arrival. One by one, ushers filed into the grand foyer, their silhouettes casting elongated shadows on the walls as they passed beneath the flickering lights. They moved with an eerie synchronicity that sent a chill crawling up their spines—a procession of marionettes drawn by unseen strings.

"Watch," Aedan said to Tim, nudging him slightly. With rapt attention, they observed from their hidden alcove as the ushers approached the theatergoers, their gestures devoid of the warmth you'd expect in such a place of entertainment. There was a cold efficiency to the way they directed people, hands extending stiffly to point out the aisle, faces as blank as freshly wiped slates.

"See that?" Tim's voice was low, his eyes locked on the peculiar sight before them. "Jenkins isn't the only one, Aedan. It's like they're all...programmed."

Aedan nodded, unable to tear his eyes away from the ushers as they shuffled past. Their movements lacked the fluid grace of humanity; it was as if someone had drained them of their essence, leaving behind these hollow vessels to perform the duties of the living.

"Something's got them all," Aedan mused, a frown tugging at his forehead. "It's like they're not even here, not really. Just shells." The eerie lack of emotion displayed by the customers was also a concerning sight. Their lifeless motions, devoid of any genuine enthusiasm or engagement, resembled mere robotic routines—purchasing a ticket, handing it over, and finding their seat, all without a hint of emotional investment. This hollow, apathetic behavior raised red flags, suggesting an underlying issue.

"Exactly." Tim's agreement was clipped, almost terse. His body tensed beside Aedan's— a silent signal of his readiness to act.

Their eyes met, and without a word, they understood each other perfectly. The strange behavior wasn't confined to the man in the ticket booth. No, it was an infection that had spread through the entire staff of the Calumet Theatre, infecting them with this unnatural stillness.

Whatever haunted the corridors of this old place had its fingers entwined in every aspect of its operation.

"Something's very wrong here," Aedan breathed. The sentence hung in the air between them, heavy with the weight of unspoken fears. And yet, beneath it all, there stirred the undeniable excitement of the unknown—the adventure that beckoned them to delve deeper into the theater's secrets.

They slinked back into the shadows, trailing an usher who glided down the aisle with a stiff stroll. His movements were precise, devoid of any human warmth as he escorted a middle-aged couple to their seats. Aedan kept his head low, blending in with the ornate wallpaper that adorned the walls of the Calumet. Tim's eyes darted about, his keen instincts on high alert.

"Careful," Aedan said to him, "we can't risk being seen." Tim nodded subtly, his thousand-yard stare never leaving the eerie procession before them.

The couple seemed oblivious to the strangeness of their guide, almost like they didn't care, chattering away about the performance they were about to see.

"Got your phone?" Tim mouthed, so quietly that Aedan barely caught it.

"Always," Aedan replied, fumbling with the device in his pocket. He powered it on, ensuring the sound was off, and lifted it just enough to frame the shot. His hands were steady, despite the adrenaline coursing through his veins.

Aedan pressed record, capturing the usher's empty mannerisms as he turned to walk back toward the lobby. His face was a mask, betraying nothing of what might lie beneath. The light from the opulent chandeliers above cast deep shadows over his features, accentuating the hollows of his cheeks and giving him an almost spectral appearance. "Did you get it?" Tim asked, his voice low and urgent.

"Every second," Aedan confirmed, tucking the phone away with grim satisfaction. "This...this isn't right, Tim. They're like puppets with their strings cut."

"Let's hope that footage helps them figure out who—or what—is pulling the strings," Tim said, his tone grave.

"Let's go see what this movie is about," Aedan said cautiously.

Aedan and Tim stepped into theater number 13, their eyes wide with awe, as if entering a sacred realm. The dimly lit space enveloped them in hushed reverence, and the air seemed charged with anticipation. Mr. Jenkins, oblivious to their presence, mechanically accepted the tickets that Aedan and Tim pulled out of a nearby trash can. In that moment, Aedan and Tim were transported, their emotions heightened, ready to embark on a journey of cinematic wonder that would leave them forever changed.

The movie began with a captivating black screen; as the minutes ticked by, the screen remained an ominous black void that didn't change. All eyes in the theater were fixated on the darkness, and an interest began to settle over the audience. The prolonged blackness felt suffocating to Aedan and Tim, like being trapped in a lightless void, but the rest of the crowd was fascinated. An uneasy feeling began to creep in as the darkness persisted.

The prolonged stillness and lack of any visual stimuli started to feel upsetting, as if something sinister lurked just beyond their perception. A few audience members shifted restlessly in their seats, obviously not under the spell, while others remained transfixed, perhaps questioning whether this was an intentional message from their leader. The oppressive blackness seemed to stretch on endlessly, toying with them and leaving them disoriented.

Low-level chatter rippled through the theater, betraying the growing unrest that gripped many of them. It was as if the darkness itself was an almost tangible force, slowly suffocating the anticipation and curiosity that had initially captivated them. As the minutes dragged on, fear overshadowed their fascination, leaving them to wonder whether they had unwittingly stumbled into a psychological experiment or a twisted form of entertainment. The unrelenting void felt like a haunting presence, challenging their perception of reality and leaving them questioning what lay in store once the veil of darkness finally lifted.

Aedan couldn't shake the feeling that they were standing on the edge of something vast and unknowable. But whatever lay ahead, they were in it together, determined to peel back the layers of mystery shrouding the Calumet Theatre. In the shadowed recesses of the theater's grand hallway, Tim's hand shot out, gripping Aedan's arm. His brown eyes, usually so warm, were edged with an urgency that cut through the dimness like a beacon. "Look," he hissed, nodding toward a sliver of darkness where a door stood slightly ajar. A brass sign, tarnished by age, hung askew beside it: STAFF ONLY.

"Restricted area," Aedan stammered back, feeling the itch of curiosity tug at his insides.

This was it—the uncharted territory that could hold answers to the theater's startling enigma. With a shared glance that conveyed volumes, they skirted the edges of the main foyer, their steps muffled by the plush carpet. The air grew heavier as they approached the door, laden with the must and silence of secrets long kept.

Tim pushed the door wider, revealing a room swallowed by shadows, except for the faint light spilling in from the hallway. The scent of musk and aging fabric hit them, a tangible reminder of the past that this hidden chamber cradled. "Whoa," Tim breathed, his voice echoing

Aedan's awe.

Old props loomed like forgotten totems against the walls—twisted tree branches from a long-ago production of *Macbeth*, a chipped chariot from some ancient Greek tragedy, and racks upon racks of costumes draped in spectral shrouds of musky sheets.

They tiptoed farther inside, their hearts thudding in tandem against their ribs. With each step, the atmosphere thickened, charged with the electric hum of discovery and the fact that they felt like they were trespassing through time.

"Check this out," Aedan said, reaching for a velvet cloak that had seen better days, its color dulled but its regal air undiminished. It felt heavy in his hands, weighted with the echoes of applause and the drama of scenes played out beneath the spotlight.

Tim ran his fingers over a faded jester's hat, its bells silent, and then looked up at Aedan, his expression mirroring the thrill of their clandestine exploration.

"Imagine the stories these costumes could tell," Tim mumbled, and Aedan nodded, feeling the pull of history and the chill of the unknown ripple across his skin.

As they explored deeper into the room, Aedan couldn't shake the feeling that every prop, every frayed hemline, held a fragment of the theater's soul—a soul that now seemed to be crying out for someone to listen, to understand the silence that had fallen over the Calumet.

The air was raunchy with the musk of old leather and the faint taste of metal. With careful steps, they moved through the labyrinth of ancient stagecraft, their hands skimming over relics that seemed to tell secrets into the stale air. Aedan couldn't help but feel like a detective in one of those noir films, piecing together clues from the shadows of history.

"Anything?" Tim's voice cut through the silence, barely above a mumble.

"Nothing yet," Aedan replied, his fingers tracing the outline of an ornate mask, half expecting it to come alive with stories of its former glory.

They were knee-deep in research, rummaging through piles of props that felt like they hadn't been touched since the theater's golden age. The more they searched, the more they connected everything—a thread woven not just through the theater's present strangeness, but back into its past.

"Look at this," Aedan called out softly as Tim's eyes landed on a stack of yellowed playbills, the names and dates long faded. They crumbled at the edges, yet the act of holding them felt like touching history itself.

"Old scripts," Tim noted, his voice tinged with awe as he handled the sheaf of papers, their lines filled with dialogue never again spoken.

And then, tucked behind a moth-bitten curtain, Aedan's eyes caught something: a photograph. Not just any photograph, but one where the faces of the people captured looked hauntingly familiar. "Tim, get over here," Aedan said, urgency lacing his words.

Tim was by his side in seconds, peering over his shoulder at the sepia-toned image: a group of theater employees—ushers, actors, stagehands—all standing rigidly, their expressions devoid of life, as though frozen by the camera's flash.

"Look at their eyes," Aedan said, unable to hide the shiver that ran down his spine, making his legs shake. It was like looking into a mirror reflecting the very same emptiness they had seen in Mr. Jenkins and the others.

"Exactly like the staff today," Tim breathed, his expression mirroring Aedan's realization.

There was no mistaking it; the eerie atmosphere that permeated the Calumet Theatre wasn't confined to the present. Whatever held sway over this place had roots reaching far deeper than they could have imagined. They exchanged a glance, the weight of their discovery pressing down upon them. It was as if the very walls urged them to delve even further, to unravel the mystery that clung to the theater like a shadow.

"History repeating itself..." Tim said, his voice low and pensive. He leaned closer, his breath stirring the dust from the surface of the picture.

"Or maybe never stopped happening," Aedan countered, his mind racing with possibilities. "What if whatever affected them back then is still at work? Like a curse or some spirit?"

"Could be Madame Modjeska working with Al Ana," Tim proposed. The skepticism that usually laced his tone was absent now, replaced by a genuine concern. "But why would she target the staff?"

"Maybe they're not targeted but rather...recruited?" The thought sent a jolt through Aedan, making him shiver like he'd gotten cold chills, as he glanced up at Tim, gauging his reaction. "Think about it, all these people bound to the theater, even after death?"

"Recruited for what, though, Aedan?" Tim's question hung between them, an unspoken challenge to piece together a puzzle whose edges were blurred by time and haunting sounds.

"Whatever it is, we need more than just theories." Determination laced his words as Aedan pocketed the photograph for safekeeping. "We need proof, something solid that can make sense of all this."

"Agreed. We'll have to comb through every inch of this place, past and present." Tim's view hardened with determination; his usual bravado tempered by the gravity of their discovery.

"Let's keep moving, then," Aedan said, stepping away from the photograph. "Every answer we find only leads to more questions, and I've got a feeling we're close to something big."

"Right behind you, man." Tim's presence was reassuring.

"Keep your eyes peeled for anything out of the ordinary," Aedan told Tim, his voice sounding alarmed. The thrill of the hunt surged within Aedan, an adrenaline-fueled craving for truth that he knew Tim shared.

"Always do," Tim replied, a spectral smile flickering across his face before being swallowed by the intensity of their task.

Together, they stepped deeper into the labyrinth of the Calumet Theatre's secrets, each creaking floorboard and hushed echo a testament to the enigma that lay before them.

The air grew thicker, carrying the weight of untold stories trapped within these crumbling walls. Every shadow seemed to shift and contort, playing tricks on their eyes. Aedan's grip tightened around the flashlight, its feeble beam cutting through the inky blackness like a knife.

He fought the urge to quicken his pace, knowing that haste could lead to careless mistakes. Tim's steady presence behind him was a comforting reminder that he wasn't alone in this difficult quest.

A sudden creak from above made them both freeze in their tracks. Aedan's heart pounded in his ears as he strained to listen for any other sounds. The silence was deafening, amplifying the weight of the unknown that surrounded them. He exchanged a wary glance with Tim, silently communicating their shared doubts. With a deep breath, Aedan pressed on, each step more cautious than the last. The thrill of the hunt had given way to thoughts of retreat, but he knew they couldn't turn back now. The truth they sought lay somewhere within this labyrinth, and they had to unravel its mysteries, regardless of the consequences.

Suddenly, a low, guttural growl reverberated through the darkness, freezing them in their tracks. They exchanged nervous glances, their hearts pounding in unison as they realized they were not alone. Something ancient and malevolent lurked within these walls, waiting to unleash its wrath upon unsuspecting intruders.

With trembling hands, Aedan reached for Tim's arm, silently urging him to retreat with him. But before they could make their escape, a pair of glowing eyes emerged from the shadows, locking on to theirs with a ferocious intensity.

At that moment, they knew they had trespassed where no living soul should venture. Al Ana had appeared at the Calumet Theatre, and her fury was about to be unleashed upon them.

The hushed echo of their frantic footsteps mingled with the menacing growls behind them as they fled from the labyrinth of secrets, forever haunted by the enigma that lay within those cursed walls.

As Aedan and Tim sprinted through the twisting passageways of the Calumet, their breath ragged and panicked, the evil presence pursued them relentlessly. Al Ana's growls echoed ominously, reverberating off the walls, a chilling warning of impending doom.

Their only hope lay in finding an exit before it was too late. Adrenaline fueled their flight as they turned corner after corner, the oppressive darkness seeming to constrict around them like a suffocating embrace. With each step, the weight of the stress pressed down upon their shoulders, urging them to surrender to the inevitable fate that awaited them. But just when it seemed all was lost, a faint glimmer of moonlight pierced through a crack in the cinder block wall ahead that illuminated a door. Aedan's heart leaped with newfound hope as he pushed himself harder, his determination assured even in the face of certain peril.

As they burst into the open air outside the Calumet, gasping for breath and hearts racing, they dared not look back. The echoes of the demon's furious roars faded into the night behind them, a reminder of the narrow escape they'd just made.

In silent agreement, Aedan and Tim knew that their curiosity had led them dangerously close to the edge of darkness. As they walked away from the looming shadow of the theater, relief washed over them mingled with the haunting knowledge that some secrets are better left undisturbed.

The memory of that fateful night would linger in their minds forevermore, a cautionary tale of forbidden knowledge and the price one pays for delving too deep into realms best left untouched. And so, as they disappeared into the veil of night, the legend of the Calumet Theatre and its ancient demon remained shrouded in mystery, waiting patiently for another foolhardy soul to awaken its wrath once more.

9

Gypsy Detroit

The next day the steady drone of a lawnmower pulled Aedan's attention away from the cracked sidewalk as he walked down Inverness Trail Road. Mr. Reynolds was methodically shearing his lawn to an even height. Spotting Aedan, he let go of the mower's handle just long enough to offer a wave, which Aedan returned with a quick upward flick of his wrist.

Unlike Mrs. Staples, whose intelligence was due to her wisdom that comes with age, Reynolds was a very smart man, a borderline genius. His intellect was truly awe-inspiring, transcending the bounds of ordinary comprehension. With a mind that seemed to defy the limits of human potential, Reynolds possessed a brilliance that left one in a state of reverent wonder. His cognitive prowess was nothing short of extraordinary, a marvel that evoked a profound feeling of amazement and humility in the face of such remarkable mental acuity.

Mr. Reynolds was one of those fixtures in town you could set your watch by—midforties, tall, and spindly like the antique grandfather clock that stood stationary in his study. His hair, once a deep chestnut, had surrendered to streaks of dignified gray, which he maintained with the precision of someone who respected the past and its impact on the present.

Aedan always admired Mr. Reynolds for more than his sartorial choices. The guy was a walking encyclopedia; if there was something to know about any little corner of the world, he knew it, and he'd tell it to you with a sharp wit that made history feel less like a subject and more like a story.

"Hey, Aedan!" he called over the motor's rumble. "What brings you by?"

"Hey, Mr. Reynolds," Aedan shouted back, feeling the familiar tug of curiosity as he considered asking Reynolds about the old stories of the town. "Just passing through. You know how it is."

"Indeed, I do," Mr. Reynolds replied with a knowing smile before turning back to his task, guiding the mower to finish up the last strip of grass as if it were a chariot of lore cutting through fields of ignorance, uncovering narratives hidden in the very earth beneath their feet.

Reynolds meticulously put the mower away; each movement was deliberate and reverent. As he turned and walked back toward the roses, Aedan observed his steps were filled with childlike wonder, as if he were witnessing the beauty of nature for the very first time.

Aedan paced the length of Mr. Reynolds's well-tended lawn, each step deliberate, the gravel crunching underfoot like a timer counting down to the inevitable bombardment of questions. Aedan's heartbeat pulsated in his ears—a staccato rhythm urging him to break the silence that hovered between them.

"Mr. Reynolds," Aedan began, raking a hand through his thick, curly hair as he came to a halt at the edge of Reynolds's garden, where he was now pruning roses with almost surgical precision. "There's something...odd going on, and I think it's related to Cheboygan's past."

Reynolds straightened up, wiping the sweat away from his forehead with the back of his hand, interest piquing in those keen brown eyes.

"Odd, you say? Historical oddities are my specialty, Aedan." He set down his shears, giving Aedan his full attention now. "What seems to be the trouble?"

"Unexplained occurrences seem to be taking place across various locations in the town.

At the Calumet Theatre, both moviegoers and ushers exhibited lifeless and robotic behavior, deviating from their usual demeanor. Similarly, customers at the family store displayed the same eerie, lifeless mannerisms," Aedan said with concern.

"My visit to Susan Smith at the sanatorium yielded no meaningful response, as she appeared oblivious to my words, uttering only a cryptic warning: 'Beware.' Peculiar incidents were also observed at the library, where patrons picked up books only to drop them and walk away," Aedan continued. Adding to the mystery, Aedan mentioned the disappearances of Emma Thompson and Tommy Canfeld, as well as sightings of apparitions that materialized and vanished within minutes. Furthermore, he reported a persistent feeling of being watched, heightening his emotions. "My friend Mary saw a missing person flyer that inexplicably vanished," Aedan said.

"And I spoke to Old Man Harry the other day..." Aedan acknowledged. However, before he could elaborate further, Mr. Reynolds abruptly interrupted, his tone grave and unsettling.

"Harry, you say? Tread cautiously, Aedan, for that man harbors a sinister aura that should not be taken lightly."

The warning hung heavy in the air, leaving Aedan confused. "What's wrong with Harry?" Aedan asked curiously.

"I can't help but feel weird when you mention speaking with Old Man Harry," Mr. Reynolds admitted, his voice laced with concern.

"Harry may seem like a harmless, eccentric old fellow, but there are rumors that he dabbles in the dark arts," Mr. Reynolds continued, his expression grim. "Tales of strange occurrences and unexplained phenomena have long swirled around him, not to mention he is the uncle of Tommy Canfeld, and those who've crossed his path have often found themselves entangled in misfortune."

Aedan's eyes widened, captivated by the ominous revelation. "But how can that be?

Related to Tommy. He's just a kindly old man who lives alone in that dilapidated cottage on the outskirts of town. I was there."

Mr. Reynolds leaned closer, his voice dropping to a hushed tone. "Appearances can be deceiving, my boy.

"Harry's true nature remains shrouded in mystery, but the rumors suggest he was suspected in the disappearance of both Emma and Tommy. I implore you, for your well-being, to steer clear of that man and his alleged dark dealings."

A chill ran down Aedan's spine as he contemplated the weight of Mr. Reynolds's words. The once harmless figure of Old Man Harry now took on a sinister feeling, leaving Aedan torn between curiosity and caution.

"These unexplained occurrences you've described are indeed unsettling, Aedan. It appears that something strange and potentially sinister is affecting various locations and individuals across the town. The lifeless, robotic behavior observed at the Calumet Theatre and family store, coupled with Susan Smith's cryptic warning at the sanatorium, suggests a disturbing pattern that demands further investigation," Mr. Reynolds explained.

"The disappearances of Emma Thompson and Tommy Canfeld, as well as the sightings of apparitions that materialize and vanish, add an eerie supernatural element to the mystery, young Aedan," Mr. Reynolds continued. "The persistent feeling of being watched and the mysterious flyer that disappeared only heightened the anxiety and uncertainty surrounding those events. While the causes behind these occurrences remain unclear, it is evident that you are investigating unusual and potentially dangerous circumstances. I suggest that you collaborate with local authorities and enlist the help of experts who may have experience in dealing with such unexplained phenomena."

"Local authorities...got it," Aedan replied.

"I have another question," he said with curiosity.

"Go ahead," Mr. Reynolds replied with a friendly tone.

"It's about Elara Wildheart," Aedan said. The name felt foreign on his tongue, like they were words from another time. "I heard she was a fortune teller around these parts, long ago."

"Ah, Elara Wildheart, a gypsy," Mr. Reynolds mused, stroking his chin thoughtfully. "A fascinating character indeed. Some considered her a visionary, others, a charlatan. She was well-versed in local legends, especially concerning supernatural entities."

"Entities like Al Ana?" Aedan prodded, watching as Mr. Reynolds's expression shifted to one of recognition.

"Al Ana," he echoed, his voice dropping to concern laced with gravity. "You're delving into deep waters there, Aedan. Al Ana is more than just a mere ghost in tales told to frighten children. It's said she is an ancient demon, connected intrinsically to the natural elements of this region, particularly the waterways."

"Like the river?" Aedan asked, recalling the eerie sensations that had washed over him whenever he was near its banks.

"Exactly," Mr. Reynolds confirmed with a nod. "Legend has it that Al Ana draws strength from the river's currents. But every creature has its Achilles' heel, even demons."

"And what's hers?" The urgency in Aedan's voice betrayed his fear, mingled with a growing purposefulness.

"I do believe it's holy water," Mr. Reynolds revealed, and the simplicity of it almost made Aedan laugh—if the situation wasn't so dire. "But not just any holy water, mind you. It must be sanctified in a place of old faith, steeped in the genuine belief of the townsfolk."

"Like an old church?" Aedan ventured, thinking of one ancient structure dotting their town like a relic of a forgotten time.

"Perhaps," Mr. Reynolds replied cryptically. "But remember, knowledge is your most potent weapon."

"Then that's what we'll do," Aedan declared with a newfound determination.

The hesitation in Mr. Reynolds's voice was noticeably laced with a questionable amount of confidence. It had Aedan concerned. "We'll do," he uttered, his words tinged with confusion and uncertainty.

Aedan couldn't help but feel a twinge of guilt for involving him in this precarious situation. "Yeah, we'll Mr. Reynolds, I could use your help," Aedan suggested, trying to mask the growing apprehension within himself.

"Okay, fine, I'll go this time, but I can't guarantee I'll do any more for this investigation you've got going on. After all, I don't do well in dangerous situations," Mr. Reynolds said, his tone protective and laced with trepidation.

The weight of responsibility for Mr. Reynolds's safety weighed heavily on Aedan's shoulders, and he silently prayed that his curiosity wouldn't lead them down a path from which there was no return.

Together, they would unearth the secrets that bound this demon to their town—and find a way to protect it. Clutching the old, frayed map Mr. Reynolds had unearthed from his extensive collection, their steps quickened as they approached the telltale mark that indicated Elara Wildheart's dwelling.

* * *

The woods around Aedan and Mr. Reynolds were dense and untamed, a labyrinth of shadows that seemed to shift with each windy breeze. Aedan could almost feel the weight of unseen eyes tracking their progress, and a shiver crawled up his spine despite the humidity that clung to the air like a diamond on a woman's finger.

"Are you sure this is the right way?" Aedan asked, his voice barely louder than the rustling leaves above them.

"Quite certain," Mr. Reynolds replied, pushing aside a low-hanging branch with more confidence than Aedan felt.

"I just hope she's expecting company," Aedan said confidently, trying to shake the eerie sensation that the forest itself was alive, watching, waiting.

The map led them deeper into the heart of the woods, where the sunlight struggled to pierce the thick canopy. And then, there it was— the Elara Wildheart residence. It wasn't so much hidden as part of the woodland tapestry, nestled between full-grown trees with roots that clawed at the earth like the fingers of the dead. Overgrown vines clambered over its walls, and the windows peeked out from behind curtains of moss, suggesting eyes that hadn't blinked in decades.

Elara Wildheart's home was every bit as forgotten and spooky as the rumors suggested. Its wooden planks were weathered by time, etched with grooves that spoke of years gone by and secrets held tight. An aura of otherworldliness cloaked the structure; it was as if the cabin itself was an extension of Elara, sharing in her enigmatic existence.

"Creepy doesn't begin to cover it," Aedan said, taking a cautious step toward the door, which seemed to sag on its hinges as if sighing in resignation.

Mr. Reynolds nodded, adjusting his bow tie with a nervous twitch. "Elara has always been...eccentric. But don't let appearances deceive you; her mind is sharp, and her knowledge vast."

Aedan couldn't help but wonder what lay beyond that creaking doorway, what ancient tales echoed within the walls of her cabin. With each step closer, his heartbeat thudded louder in his chest, a rhythm that seemed to sync with the pulse of the forest around them. This was it, the threshold between the known and the unknown.

Taking a deep breath, Aedan raised his hand to knock on the door that might as well have been a portal to another world. It creaked open before his knuckles could knock against its aged wood, and the scent of incense and old paper fanned out from inside. Elara Wildheart, with her jet-black hair and red bandanna, wearing jewels, stood framed in the doorway, her piercing brown eyes locking on to Aedan's as if she'd been expecting them.

"Come in." She waved them in, dirt on her fingers, her voice a bit raspy and seeming to sway with the creaking trees. Mr. Reynolds and Aedan exchanged a glance, his scholarly curiosity momentarily overriding any trepidation. They stepped over the threshold into a realm that felt detached from time, where the flicker of candles cast a supernatural glow.

"Ah, my young demon hunter...what brings you two here?" Elara asked with a warm smile. "How did you know I was looking for the demon?

"Well...honestly, I'm fascinated!" Aedan exclaimed, his eyes sparkling with excitement despite a hint of shyness.

"I know everything, I see the future, young one...Al Ana," she began without prompting, as though the name itself conjured an icy draft, "is ancient and cunning. Water blessed by faith...holy water, it is her bane." Her fingers danced through the air, sketching invisible star-shaped pictorial symbols.

"Is there anything I can do to protect myself from Al Ana?" he asked.

"Hold on a second, I think...no, I have it..." Elara said, turning around and walking toward her bookshelf in the living room. "Yes, here it is." She grabbed an ancient Bible with a slightly aged front cover. "How old is that Bible and where did you get it?" Aedan asked, intrigued by the aged look.

"During my travels, years ago, I found myself in the Hubbard-Richard neighborhood of Detroit, at an old Catholic church located at 1000 St. Anne Street. The Basilica of Sainte Anne de Detroit was established on July 26, 1701, by French settlers in the region once known as New France. It holds the distinction of being the second-oldest Roman Catholic parish in continuous operation in the United States...Here," Elara said as she handed Aedan the Bible.

Elara walked across the room to a dusty cabinet, retrieving a small bag with a string around it. Mr. Reynolds shook his head in disbelief.

"This contains protective herbs: rosemary, salt, and dragon's blood. While dragon's blood, the resin from a tropical palm tree, holds significance in certain spiritual practices, it's crucial to approach its usage with caution and discernment, Aedan. Rosemary is *so* strong and requires very little activation—keep it on you at all times." Elara placed the pouch around Aedan's neck. "You must also recite these holy words if you encounter Al Ana's presence." She handed Aedan a slip of paper with strange words written on it.

They read: *Seek and you shall find. I adjure you by the Father, Son, and Holy Spirit that you grow no larger but that you dry up...Cross Matthew, cross Mark, cross Luke, cross John.*

"Memorize those words, speak them aloud, holding the sacred Holy Bible I just gave you," Elara said intensely. "It will help dispel the demon's dark energy."

Aedan looked down at the strange herbs in his hands, knowing his life depended on using them correctly.

"Be very careful, boy," Elara warned gravely. "You tread a dangerous path. Do not let curiosity cloud your judgment."

Aedan nodded, looking up at the old woman. "I'll be cautious. Thank you for the guidance." He meant it—this was not a game. With Elara's help, he felt prepared to confront the lurking evil of Al Ana.

He tucked the herbs and the holy words into his pocket, the pouch still hanging around his neck. He could feel the weight of responsibility settling on his shoulders.

Elara got up from her chair and walked to a different cabinet in the living room, grabbed a clear bottle, and walked back over to Aedan and Mr. Reynolds.

She handed Aedan the clear bottle of holy water, explaining that she obtained it from a sacred water supply deep within the church. "If you require more, Aedan, you can venture there and locate the same source. This water is imbued with divine properties, rendering the water holy and suitable for various rituals or purposes," explained Elara.

"The sacred water is said to be guarded by ancient angelic spirits who have protected its purity for centuries. With the right knowledge and intentions, the sacred water can aid in cleansing, purification, and various mystical practices, lending power to those who wield it responsibly," Elara said with intense emotion.

"Water carries purity, clarity...it disrupts her essence, her web of lies." Elara's gaze flitted between them, sharp and assessing. "Sprinkle it upon her deceits and watch them wither."

Mr. Reynolds, ever the academic, adjusted his bow tie again—a nervous tick betraying his intrigue. "And this holy water, how does one properly wield it against such a creature?"

"Faith, courage," she said decisively, "and conviction. Without belief, the water is but droplets in the wind against her. You must be doubtless with your belief and strike all evil with it."

Aedan shivered, not from the chill in the room but from the weight of her words. It was one thing to face a demon, quite another to believe wholly in what you doubted. "Her strengths?" Mr. Reynolds pressed, leaning forward eagerly.

"Deception. Despair. She preys on the cracks within one's soul, widening them until one is consumed by darkness." Elara's countenance grew somber, her eyes reflecting a well of sorrow. "She takes forms most pleasing, makes fake promises, fabricates allurements..."

"And the souls?" Mr. Reynolds asked with conviction. The question loomed heavy, a shadow stretching across the cabin's confines.

"Ah," she sighed, turning her look upon a solitary flame that danced atop a blackened candle. "Al Ana hungers for the essence of life—human souls. They are her currency, her sustenance, her trophies, her food. With each one taken, she weaves herself deeper into the fabric of our world."

"Like a parasite," Mr. Reynolds muttered under his breath, his historian's mind undoubtedly drawing parallels with past plagues.

"Exactly," Elara confirmed with a nod. "But not just any souls. She craves those teetering on the edge—lost, searching, and vulnerable. She ensnares them with illusions of what they most desire, then drags them beyond the veil."

"Then we must be on the defense," Aedan stated. A newfound confidence settled over him, an armor forged from the eerie truths Elara had unveiled.

Elara's lips quirked in a shadow of a smile, cryptic and knowing. "Indeed, young Aedan.

The battle for souls is a battle of wills. Protect yourself, for Al Ana, will seek to unravel your fortitude."

Upon acquiring the desired information from Elara, Mr. Reynolds decided to terminate his involvement and return to his residence. "At this juncture, my role in this investigative endeavor has reached its conclusion," Mr. Reynolds stated.

"Well, I extend my gratitude for your help, Mr. Reynolds," Aedan responded formally.

With a firm handshake, they parted ways, each embarking on their path. Aedan's footsteps crunched against the fallen leaves as he ventured toward the mysterious woods lurking behind Elara's house. Meanwhile, Mr. Reynolds, ever the pragmatist, turned on his heel and marched homeward, no doubt already pondering what would happen next in Aedan's journey.

* * *

Holy water, faith, the Holy Bible, herbs, holy words, and a steadfast heart were now Aedan's weapons in the looming confrontation with an insidious demon.

Aedan trudged bravely through the underbrush, the weight of destiny heavy on his shoulders. The old Native American trail before him wound its way through the heart of the woods like a sleeping serpent, and Aedan had chosen to walk it alone.

"Protect them," Aedan said to the rustling leaves, his vow dispersing in the wind. Protect Cheboygan from Al Ana's dark grasp. It was a mantle Aedan never sought, but now it clung to him, as tangible as the mist clinging to the branches overhead.

The river was close; Aedan could hear its rumble, a natural lullaby that had soothed generations. But for him, it was a siren call to a grim reckoning. Each step felt purposeful, drawn by an unseen force that tugged at the core of his being.

"Who knew a history buff's sidekick gig came with ghost wrangling?" he babbled, trying to inject some humor into the worry coiling in his gut. No laugh came, only the echo of his footsteps and the distant hoot of an owl. Then he saw it—a wisp of fog that danced across the river's surface, defying the breeze. It swirled and stretched, shaping itself into a form that made his heart skip a beat. A spectral entity, edges blurred but undeniably human, hovering above the water.

"Al Ana," Aedan breathed, not a question but a recognition. His heart raced, adrenaline surging as he reached into his pocket, fingers brushing the vial of holy water Elara had given him. The apparition shifted, eyes piercing the veil between worlds, locking on to his.

"Aedan," it hissed, a voice like the scrape of dead leaves on stone.

"Stay back," Aedan commanded, more bravado than certainty fueling his words. The figure cocked its head, considering him, an intruder in this realm of shadows.

"Defender," it shouted, a mocking lilt in its tone. "Do you truly understand what you protect? The souls here are ripe...deliciously uncertain."

"Enough!" Aedan's hand shook as he drew out the vial, brandishing it like a talisman. "You won't find any willing victims here."

It laughed, a sound that fractured the night, and then faded, leaving behind a silence so profound Aedan could hear his heartbeat echoing in his ears. "Stay strong, Aedan," he told himself, the words a buoy in the darkness. "This is your fight now."

With a deep breath, Aedan turned from the river, running away, the spectral encounter etched into his memory. There was work to be done, and preparations to make. Al Ana wouldn't rest, and neither would he. Not until Cheboygan was safe from her clutches.

Aedan's mind raced with thoughts of how to protect the town and its residents from the evil spirit's wrath. Every shadow seemed to conceal a lurking threat, every river a potential portal for Al Ana's return.

Night had fallen by the time Aedan reached the outskirts of town, the moon casting a pale glow over the deserted streets. He knew he needed allies in this battle, individuals who understood the supernatural threat that loomed over them all. Determination hardened his demeanor as he made his way to his house.

10

OConnor's Market

The clang of cans and the rustle of packages were a steady rhythm to Aedan's restocking efforts the next morning at O'Connor's Market. The mundane nature of arranging soup tins in precise rows was almost meditative, a small reprieve from the supernatural Al Ana chaos that had consumed him.

Aedan's hands moved methodically, but his mind raced with questions and fears. What new horrors awaited him next? Were the strange occurrences confined to his small town, or was this just the beginning of something more sinister spreading across the region...the country...the world?

Aedan shuddered at the thought, nearly tripping over his feet. The gentle tinkling of the bell above the store's entrance snapped him back to reality. He glanced over, half expecting some eldritch abomination to come slithering through the doorway. Instead, it was just Old Man Jenkins from the Calumet Theatre, likely seeking refuge from the madness outside, like so many others. Aedan forced a weak smile, trying to project a calmness he didn't feel.

How much longer could they carry on like this, tiptoeing around the darkness creeping in from all sides? Aedan's mind conjured night-marish visions of shadowy tentacles bursting through the windows, shattering the fragile peace. He blinked hard, pushing the thoughts away. One thing was certain—this eerie quiet couldn't last forever.

Fear washed over Aedan as he mopped the floor, lost in his thoughts about running into the demon herself the night before. Suddenly, his eyes fell upon the menacing figure of Henry Gills, the school bully, approaching him from the end of the aisle. With each step, Henry's demeanor exuded a foreboding aura of intimidation, sending Aedan into irritation mode. "What now, Henry?" Aedan said, mustering up the courage, his voice laced with apprehension and annoyance.

"Whatcha doing, wuss?" Henry taunted, his words dripping with malice, leaving Aedan to wonder what fresh torment awaited him at the hands of this relentless bully.

Aedan's heart pounded in his chest as Henry closed the distance between them, his menacing presence looming ever larger. Aedan racked his brain, trying to think of a way to defuse the situation, but Henry's reputation for cruelty preceded him.

Aedan stood tall and courageous; his voice was impervious as he implored Henry to leave him alone. Yet, in a breathtaking display of disregard, Henry seemed to glide past him, or so Aedan believed. In a moment that left Aedan utterly awestruck, Henry's stride carried him past, but not before his foot lashed out again, a seemingly favorite move of his, upending the mop bucket with a resounding clatter, unleashing a torrent of soapy water that cascaded across the floor in a mesmerizing, rippling expanse.

Aedan watched in stunned disbelief as the murky water rapidly spread, his heart sinking with each passing second. The once pristine floor now resembled a miniature lake, reflecting the harsh fluorescent lights above in a kaleidoscope of shimmering patterns. He couldn't tear his eyes away from the spectacle, transfixed by the sheer audacity of

Henry's actions and the mesmerizing dance of light and liquid. As the water reached the limits of its expanse, it seemed to pause momentarily, as if taunting Aedan with its defiance of gravity and order. Then, in a final act of rebellion, small rivulets began snaking their way outward, creeping ever closer to Aedan's feet, threatening to engulf him in the chaos.

The awestruck trance was abruptly shattered by Henry's mocking laughter, echoing through the hallway like a cruel symphony. Aedan's hands clenched into fists, his jaw tightening as a surge of emotions washed over him—anger, humiliation, and a newfound determination to stand his ground against this relentless tormentor. At that moment, the mundane task of mopping transformed into a battleground, and Aedan knew he could no longer remain a passive bystander.

"Damn." Aedan didn't get the chance to finish his statement before he snapped.

In a fit of rage, he tried to break the mop over his knee, but he struggled, and it didn't break. He tried his damnedest to snap that thing in half, but it just wouldn't budge. The mop had other plans, and it decided to give Aedan's shin a good ol' whack, leaving him yelping a cry of "OUCH!" that could have woken the dead.

Witnessing the confrontation unfold, Aedan's father, Eddie, couldn't help but feel compassion for his son. As a father, his heart ached to see his child navigate such a challenging situation. In that moment, Eddie's paternal instincts were heightened, and he longed to provide comfort and support, offering a reassuring presence amidst the turmoil. With empathy and understanding, he silently stood by, ready to embrace Aedan and guide him through this difficult experience when it was over.

Henry, the resident comedian, couldn't help but let out another hearty and boisterous laugh at the sight of Aedan's mop-taming misadventures. And just when Aedan thought the situation couldn't get any more embarrassing, Tim strolled in, took one look at the scene, and decided to play the role of the mop-breaking hero for his buddy. With a swift motion, he snapped the mop in two, leaving Henry to shake his head in disbelief. Henry, getting the picture, walked away and left the store.

"Aw, shucks," Aedan grumbled, his frustration as believable as a wet sock stuck to the bottom of his shoe.

Tim, ever the loyal sidekick, chimed in with a cheeky grin, "Hey, no sweat, Einstein.

You're the one with the big brain around here. I'm just the muscle." His attempt at lightening the mood was as subtle as a sledgehammer to the funny bone, eliciting a reluctant snort of laughter from his exasperated friend.

Eddie recognized the frailness of the two youths, the delicate nature of their emotions, and the profound impact such conflicts could have on their developing hearts and minds. A profound desire to nurture and protect welled up within him, transcending the boundaries of blood relations.

"Son, I understand how difficult that situation must have been for you," Eddie said with a gentle tone, placing a comforting hand on Aedan's shoulder. "You were incredibly brave to stand up for yourself, overcoming any fears you might have had in the past. I'm proud of the courage and strength you showed." Eddie's words were filled with warmth and compassion, offering reassurance and support to his son during his challenging situation. "It's okay to feel overwhelmed or uncertain. Just know that I'm here for you, every step of the way."

"Hey, Aedan." Tim's voice cut through his friend's embarrassment, his large frame shadowing him. Aedan straightened up, brushing a lock of curly hair from his eyes. "You up for some gaming tonight? Might be good to get your mind off things."

"Sure," Aedan replied, the corners of his mouth lifting slightly. "I could use a distraction."

"Great, swing by around eight?" Tim clapped a hand on Aedan's shoulder, his usual easy grin spreading across his face.

"Sure," Aedan said, nodding.

* * *

Later, in the familiar confines of Tim's room, the two friends sprawled on bean bags, with controllers in their hands, their focus locked on the screen where pixels danced and collided in an epic battle of digital warriors. Aedan and Tim laughed and trash-talked, the tension of the past days easing momentarily as they lost themselves in the virtual combat of a first-person shooter.

As headshots started raining down like confetti at a parade for the visually impaired, the trash-talking reached levels of creativity that would make Shakespeare blush. "Nice aim there, noob!" Aedan quipped, doing a little jig to avoid the pixelated hail.

Not one to be outdone, Tim flashed a grin that could've cured blindness and fired back, "Yeah, well, I'll bench press you!"

"Yo, Tim! Are you tryin' to play hide-and-seek with that barrel? Hate to break it to ya, buddy, but you're about as stealthy as a neon sign in a blackout!" Aedan chuckled as Tim's character crept along, oblivious to his surroundings. Then, BAM! With the reflexes of a ninja cat, Aedan landed a killer shot, leaving Tim's character in a virtual puddle of pixels. "Woohoo! The tea kettle is bubbling, baby!" Aedan exclaimed with infectious enthusiasm. "Dude, you might wanna consider taking up knitting or something. This gaming thing ain't working out for ya!"

The room erupted in a chorus of wheezes and snorts, their friendly roasts a stark contrast to the digital carnage unfolding on-screen. For a beautiful moment, they were just two pals indulging in that time-honored tradition of gaming and verbally eviscerating each other, leaving the real world's cares at the door.

But the serenity was short-lived. As Aedan's character executed a flawless combo, the room's atmosphere shifted. Chilling emotions crept in as they sat on beanbag chairs in front of Tim's bed, their eyes wide open in disbelief as the window mysteriously unlocked and opened by itself. An eerie silence hung in the air, amplifying the frightening nature of the inexplicable event. Thoughts raced through their minds, both wondering if this was a mere coincidence. A cold draft swept in, chilling despite the warmth of the evening. Tim and Aedan exchanged a glance, their amusement fading into confusion.

"Did you leave a window open?" Aedan asked, looking away from the game.

"Everything was closed before you got here," Tim stated, standing to check.

That's when it happened—the air seemed to thicken, charged with an unseen energy as he walked over to close the window. The lights flickered, casting eerie shadows against the walls. The rhythmic knocking sounded from above their heads—*knock, knock, knock*—seemingly mocking the Holy Trinity. In the gloom, they saw it: a shadow figure skirting the edge of their vision, dark form nebulous and shifting.

"Poltergeist," Tim breathed, his usual bravado wilting before the paranormal display. "Al Ana's doing," Aedan suggested, his hand inching toward his pocket where the herbs and Elara's holy water vial rested. "Should we—"

"Wait." Aedan held up a hand, dazed, eyes locked on the shadow in front of them. It swirled like smoke, coalescing into a more defined human shape. A face appeared within the darkness, contorted in a silent scream. "Al...Ana's watching us," Aedan said, shaking.

"Can it—can it do anything to hurt us?" Tim's voice trembled, the sight rattling his nerves.

"Elara said they're limited without a physical form, but..." Aedan words trailed off as the figure lunged forward, its visage morphing into a grotesque snarl before dissipating inches from the TV screen. "AHH..." Aedan screamed with a high-pitched tone as he jumped a mile in the air.

"Okay, that's enough!" Tim declared, scrambling away from the window, his protective instincts kicking in. "We're not dealing with this anymore."

"Yup," Aedan said as he stood beside him, heart racing. This was no longer just about Cheboygan. It was personal. Al Ana was drawing a line in the sand, and they were directly in her path. "Let's get out of here," Aedan said, and without another word, they bolted from the room, leaving the shadow figure behind.

With their breaths coming in short, sharp gasps, Tim and Aedan edged toward the living room. The air was charged with an unseen energy that prickled their skin and set every hair on end. "Did you see that?" Tim said fearfully, but in the thick silence, it sounded to him like he was shouting.

"See what?" Aedan asked, though he wasn't sure he wanted the answer.

"Th-the chair," Tim stuttered. His hand trembled as he pointed to the corner of the room where a computer chair sat. As if on cue, the chair began to twirl slowly, its movement deliberate and unnatural.

"Okay, that's not right," Aedan said, his heart thumping against his ribs like a caged bird desperate for escape. "Chairs don't just spin by themselves."

"Unless they're being pushed by something," Tim replied, his eyes wide with fear.

"Or someone," Aedan added, thinking of Al Ana and the sinister form they'd seen in the bedroom. The spinning grew more frantic, the chair's legs scraping against the wooden floor, a screech that seemed to echo throughout the house. And then, amidst the harsh, discordant mixture of sounds, a ghoulish voice—low and guttural—filled the room.

"Leave..."

The single word hung in the air, a command wrapped in malice that sent shivers down their spines. It resonated with a familiarity that chilled them to the bone. It was Al Ana's voice, the demon's demand seeping into the walls, infusing them with terror.

"Did you hear that?" Tim was pale, his knuckles white as he gripped the back of the sofa. "Hard not to," Aedan muttered, struggling to keep his composure.

Before they could ponder their next move, a series of violent slams erupted from the kitchen. Back and forth, over and over, the sound of the refrigerator door flinging open and slamming shut filled the air with a maddening rhythm.

"Is it trying to communicate or just scare us?" Aedan wondered aloud, each crash punctuating his words.

"Either way, I'm officially freaked out," Tim admitted. He moved cautiously toward the kitchen, his curiosity overcoming his fear.

"Be careful," Aedan warned, following closely behind with his bottle of holy water out in front of him, ready to strike. They reached the doorway, and the sight that greeted them was pure chaos. The fridge door flung open once again, the interior light flickering wildly before the door slammed shut with such force that bottles and containers inside rattled violently. "I got holy water," Aedan shouted, his mind racing through the litany of protections Elara had taught him.

"Right now, I'd settle for a regular bottle of water," Tim joked weakly, a feeble attempt to diffuse the tension.

"Let's grab what we can and get out of here," Aedan said, resolving to put an end to the nightmare. With each step to retrieve their shoes, the conviction grew stronger within them.

"Whatever it takes," Aedan said bravely. "You're not getting us, Al Ana."

They bolted out of Tim's house, their hearts pounding in their chests like drumbeats in a wild symphony. The crisp night air did little to cool the heat of their fear as they stumbled across the lawn, shadows from the moonlight reaching out like dark fingers.

"Man, Aedan, what the hell was that?" Tim's voice trembled as he glanced over his shoulder, half expecting a poltergeist to follow them into the street.

"Let's just get to my place," Aedan urged, not wanting to linger on the terror that had surrounded Tim's house. They picked up their pace, the familiar path to Aedan's house offering a semblance of safety in the madness that seemed to be swallowing their town whole.

As Aedan and Tim approached the edge of the woods near Aedan's house, a mist rose from the ground, coiling around tree trunks and roots like serpents. There, by the woods' edge, stood an apparition, its form wavering between solid and liquid—a spectral silhouette that spooked them.

"Tommy?" Aedan said, the name catching in his throat. The figure nodded, and as it raised a hand toward the river, its body rippled and transformed into a watery image. Droplets hung in the air, shimmering under the moonlight, arranging themselves into a symbol—a cresting wave encircling a crescent moon.

"Water...the moon...What are you trying to tell us, Tommy?" Aedan mumbled, the pieces of the puzzle eluding his grasp.

"Could be something about the river at night?" Tim suggested, his eyes wide with awe and apprehension.

"Maybe," Aedan said, the clue embedding itself in his mind. "We'll figure it out, Tommy. I promise." The watery visage of Tommy gave a faint nod before dissolving into the night air, leaving them alone once more.

They continued to Aedan's house; the image of the water symbol was seared into their memory. Inside, the comfort of the home did little to ease the tension that clung to them like a second skin. Aedan led Tim to his room where he'd stashed the picture he found—the only tangible link to Emma and Tommy's disappearance.

"Look at this," Aedan said, handing him the faded photograph. It showed both Emma and Tommy, their youthful faces smiling back at them from a time before the darkness had taken them. "Man, they looked so...normal," Tim remarked, a hint of sadness in his voice.

Without warning, a picture on Aedan's wall began to move. It tilted to the side slowly, as if unseen hands were adjusting its position. Aedan's breath hitched, and Tim's head snapped up, the photo slipping from his fingers as they both stared at the wall in disbelief. "Did you see that?" Aedan asked, even though he knew the answer.

"Yeah," Tim replied, his voice a frightening warning. "It's like they're still here with them...or maybe it's Al Ana, taunting them."

"Or maybe," Aedan countered as his nerves hardened, "it's a sign that we're on the right track. That we're getting closer to the truth." Together, they straightened the picture and bolted from the house, thankful that Aedan's family wasn't home, their determination mirrored in each other's eyes.

Aedan and Tim darted through the deserted streets of Cheboygan, shadows stretching long and eerie in the fading light. Across the street, Aedan spotted Henry walking alone on the sidewalk. The sight filled Aedan with deep fear. As Henry strolled, a dark figure emerged from the shadows, taking the form of a woman—resembling his mother.

Aedan and Tim watched in trepidation as this spectral figure hovered a foot above the ground. Alarmingly, when Henry reached out to grasp what appeared to be his mother's hand, he collapsed to the ground, convulsing violently as if in the throes of a seizure.

"I can't believe what's happening to Henry!" Aedan said to Tim. Both petrified, they watched helplessly as the bully's soul was consumed by Al Ana's nightmarish mouth, which was stretched to an unnatural size.

Tim's eyes widened in horror as he watched the scene unfold. "This can't be real," he whispered, his voice trembling. The air around them grew thick with an oppressive energy, making it difficult to breathe. Aedan felt his heart pounding in his chest, his hands shaking uncontrollably as he struggled to process what he was witnessing. The bully's muffled screams echoed in their ears, a chilling reminder of the supernatural terror before them. As Al Ana's monstrous form continued to grow, Tim and Aedan bolted out of there, their minds racing with questions about what this meant for their safety and their fates.

The disturbing scene left them deeply troubled, their minds consumed by grave concerns for Henry's well-being and fear of the provoking presence they had just witnessed.

"First stop, the old church," Aedan said, panting from the running, and he led Tim down an overgrown path that snaked toward the outskirts of town.

"Are you sure it's open?" Tim's voice was laced with doubt, his eyes scanning the encroaching darkness warily, looking behind him to make sure Al Ana wasn't following them. "It has to be...Elara said the spirits keep it alive," Aedan insisted, more to inflate his courage. They moved swiftly, driven by an urgency that seemed to pulse from the very earth beneath their feet.

* * *

The majestic New England-style 1820s church stood before Aedan and Tim, its pointed Gothic arches and the exquisite Gothic-Palladian windows gracing its facade truly an architectural marvel, Aedan thought. The white clapboard exterior emanated a hauntingly beautiful aura against the twilight sky, a sight that filled their hearts with awe and appreciation for the craftsmanship of bygone eras. Its steeple pointed accusingly at the heavens, while the surrounding gravestones stood like silent sentinels. The church's history was etched into each weathered plank and pane of stained glass that adorned the outside walls.

"Check this out," Aedan gasped, motioning toward the plaque by the entrance. "In 1874, the parishioners of Ste. Anne's Church worshipped here." Aedan traced the engraved letters reverently. "Imagine the prayers, the hope...now we're here, borrowing a bit of that faith."

"Feels weird being here without a congregation," Tim said, pushing open the heavy wooden door with a creak that disturbed the silence like a damsel in distress.

"Let's just find what we need," Aedan replied, stepping into the cool interior. The church was empty, yet it felt alive, as if the echoes of past sermons and songs vibrated through the air. Their footsteps were muffled by the aged floorboards as they moved down the aisle, past rows of polished pews that gleamed softly in the dim light filtering through the windows.

"Over there, the holy water fountain." Aedan nodded toward the stone basin near the altar, his heart thudding with anticipation as his blood pressure rose. They filled a couple of small bottles, the liquid clear and cold to the touch—a stark contrast to the warmth of his racing pulse. The priest emerged from around the corner, having listened compassionately to the voices of the boys within the church altar.

"Bless us, Father...we need to know if you've seen anything... unusual," Aedan pressed, his voice sounding slightly distressed.

The priest, an aging man with deep-set eyes that seemed to carry the weight of his flock's confessions, clasped his hands tightly. "Children, this is not the place for ghost stories," he admonished softly, though the creases in his brow betrayed his concern.

"It's not just stories," Tim interjected, a tremor of urgency in his tone. "It's Al Ana. We think she's..."

Before he could finish, the overhead lights flickered erratically, casting strange shadows across the priest's face. A shiver scuttled down

Aedan's spine, and the air seemed suddenly charged with electricity, heavy with unspoken warnings.

"God help them," the priest said, and swiftly etched a sign of the cross over his chest. "She stirs."

Aedan and Tim exited the church, leaving behind the sanctity of its walls for the uncertain journey ahead. Terror crept in as they began walking down the dimly lit street toward their homes. The eerie silence and deserted surroundings made every step feel heavier, their hearts pounding with apprehension.

With each step closer to their houses, the weight of their mission bore down upon them, but they were resolute. "Going home...right," Aedan said, his voice tinged with understanding.

"Yeah, I guess," Tim's responded, carrying a weight of uncertainty and, perhaps, hesitation. "Better yet, call Mary and Lindsey and have them meet us at the Waltz's 24 instead of us calling it a night...Let's pull an all-nighter," he said.

"Okay," Aedan agreed, easily convinced. His hands trembled slightly dialing Lindsey's number, mind racing with a thousand worries, each more threatening than the last. What if something had happened to them? What if they were in danger?

He tried to push those thoughts aside, but the knot of anxiety in his stomach only tightened as the phone rang. When Lindsey finally answered, her voice sounded scared, and Aedan's heart sank. "Lindsey, are you okay? Tim wants us all to meet at the Waltz's 24 tonight." He paused, bracing himself for her response, fearing the worst.

Lindsey's words came out in a rush, her tone laced with panic. "Aedan, I'll get Mary, we will be there."

Aedan felt a wave of relief wash over him, but it was short-lived as Lindsey continued speaking. "Listen, Aedan, something really strange is going on. I was out running errands earlier, and I could have sworn someone was following me. At first, I thought I was just being paranoid, but then I noticed the same car trailing me no matter where I went."

His heart pounded in his chest as he listened intently, his mind racing with possibilities. "Did you get a good look at the car or the person?" he asked, his voice low and cautious.

"No, they were too far away, and the windows were tinted," Lindsey replied, her voice quivering slightly. "But I can't shake the feeling that it's connected to what we've been investigating."

Aedan nodded, even though Lindsey couldn't see him. "Okay, don't go anywhere alone until we figure this out. We'll swing by and pick you up, and then we'll get Mary and go to the Waltz's 24s. Stay safe, and keep your eyes peeled for anything suspicious."

With urgency, Aedan ended the call as he got to the front door of his house. He rushed inside, running next to his dad, who was sitting on the couch reading the paper, and grabbed his keys lying on an end table. Deep in thought about an article he was reading, Eddie didn't budge to see what his son was up to.

"Going out?" he said, lost in the depths of literary enlightenment, blissfully oblivious to the mischievous antics unfolding right under his nose.

"Yeah, Tim and I are going to pick up Lindsey and Mary and go to the coffee house," Aedan replied with a forced smile of smugness and self-satisfaction.

"How late do you plan on being?" Eddie replied as he turned a page of the paper. "Is it okay if we pull an all-nighter?" Aedan asked cautiously.

"I trust you, son. Don't do anything stupid," Eddie said charismatically.

"I won't, Dad." Aedan ran out the front door, sprinting toward his car, with Tim following right behind.

11

Waltz's 24s Gas and Coffee Shop

The bell above the Waltz's 24s Gas and Coffee Shop door jingled as Aedan pushed it open for his friends, and their eyes scanned the interior until they landed on a booth for them all to sit at by the window. Aedan and Tim huddled over the small table as Lindsey and Mary walked up to the counter to order coffee. When they returned to the booth, the boys had a scattering of papers and notes sprawled all over the tabletop. Aedan's heart pumped a rapid beat, echoing the excitement already dancing in all their expressions.

"Guys, you won't believe what I've found out," Aedan announced, sliding into the seat next to Lindsey, who was just sitting down, her sharp brown eyes sparkling with anticipation.

"Spill it, Aedan," Tim urged, leaning in, his body tensing as if ready to spring into action in an MMA octagon.

"Alright, alright," Aedan chuckled, raking a hand through his curly brown hair. "So, it turns out Old Man Harry is related to Tommy and might be responsible for Emma and Tommy's disappearance. He even tried to get me to go to the river with him."

Lindsey leaned forward, arms crossed on the table. "Related? That

120

sounds...ominous.

Did you go to the river with him?"

"No...and yeah, related, he's Tommy's uncle. Mr. Reynolds told me yesterday," Aedan exclaimed urgently.

"Man, that's messed up," Tim responded casually, grasping the gravity of the matter.

Mary took a sip of her coffee, her face laced with concern as she uttered a single word: "Cringe." The apprehension in her voice was distinct, hinting at an underlying timidity that seemed to permeate the air around her.

"So, what does Harry being related to Tommy have to do with anything?" Tim said, trying to shed light on Harry's potential motives and involvement in the tragic incident.

"Harry knew of the presence of the demon near the river. Exploiting this information, he deliberately lured Tommy and Emma to that location, leading to their unfortunate demise," Aedan explained.

"And more than ominous, Lindsey. The demon's been pulling strings for centuries, and I ran into her in the woods behind Elara the Gypsy's house. There's this old journal at the library—dates back to 1850. It mentions Al Ana by name," Aedan said. "And get this, some of the townspeople back then feared her and also vanished."

"Vanished?" Tim's voice had an edge to it now, a mix of skepticism and the kind of curiosity that made him an invaluable part of their group. "You think it's all connected to what's happening now?"

"Has to be...there's a cycle," Aedan said, his determination swelling within him like a wave about to break.

"What's the cycle?" Tim chimed in, his voice laced with concern, seeking understanding of this ominous revelation.

"Al Ana feeds on our souls, she manifests into our gullibilities and consumes them, driving the healthy insane, or even worse, they die. So be careful," Aedan shot back.

"And I think we're smack in the middle of it. We need to figure out how to break it before..." He didn't finish the sentence, but he didn't have to.

"Before Al Ana comes for us," Mary finished for him, her words a quiet echo of the fear they all felt, yet laced with the strength that defined her.

"Exactly." Aedan nodded, blue eyes locking on to his friends'. "We're going to stop her this time. We have to."

The coffee shop's ambient chatter faded into the background as Aedan sifted through the tattered pages of his notebook, each scribbling a breadcrumb on their trail to uncover the truth behind Al Ana's mystery. Lindsey, Mary, and Tim leaned in, their faces mirrors of focus and concern.

Aedan flipped through the pages, the weight of their investigation growing heavier with each cryptic note and half-formed theory. He couldn't shake the nagging feeling that they were missing something crucial, some vital piece of the puzzle that would bring everything into focus. The others remained silent, their expressions a mix of determination and apprehension. Aedan feared they might be in over their heads, but the thought of giving up now, after coming so far, was unthinkable.

With a heavy sigh, Aedan closed the notebook, his mind racing with thoughts of their next move. One wrong step could spell disaster, not just for them but for anyone caught in Al Ana's crosshairs.

"Harry knew about the disappearance and cycle, he had to. And he didn't mention it," Aedan muttered to his friends as he traced a line of thought only half-formed. "He mentioned it once, didn't he? Before we even found these old journals."

"Kinda," Tim said, scratching his chin. "But he was all cryptic about it, like always." "Too cryptic," Aedan said, his words carrying an unusual weight. His bright blue eyes, usually sparkling with the thrill of the hunt, now clouded over with suspicion. "It's like he's been feeding us just enough to keep us interested, but not enough to get to the bottom of things."

Lindsey tilted her head, a strand of hair falling across her face. "You think Harry's holding back on purpose?"

"Maybe." The word hung between them, heavy and unwelcome.

Aedan's mind whirled, replaying every encounter with the old man they had trusted implicitly. Harry's tales, once a beacon of guidance, now felt like a maze designed to lead them astray. It gnawed at him how Harry would often change the subject whenever they got too close to something concrete, or how his anecdotes seemed to skirt around the edges of their most burning questions.

"A few days ago, when I was at Harry's house, he showed me a map that had a page with a circle on it!" Aedan said, tapping the notebook. "With the markings near the old mill? The next day, I went there, and nothing. It was like he sent me on a wild goose chase."

"Could've been an honest mistake," Tim offered, ever the voice of reason.

"Could've been," Aedan conceded, but the doubt had taken root, spreading its tendrils through his thoughts. "Or maybe Harry's got his reasons for keeping the full story under wraps. Reasons he doesn't want us to know....kinda like his nephew Tommy."

"Like what?" Mary's eyebrows knit together in concern.

"I don't know," Aedan admitted, feeling a twist in his gut. "Maybe he wants to get rid of us too." The possibility of betrayal, especially from someone they had considered an ally, left a bitter taste on his tongue. "But I'm going to find out. If there's one thing I've learned, it's that secrets have a way of coming to light. And if Harry's hiding something..."

"Then we need to know what and why," Lindsey finished, her voice reflecting Aedan's own.

"Exactly. We can't afford blind spots, not with Al Ana lurking in the shadows." Aedan closed his notebook with a snap, the sound echoing his newfound determination.

"Alright, then," Tim said after a moment, clapping his hands together. "We dig deeper. We trust the facts, not the stories. And we keep our eyes open for any more...inconsistencies."

"Agreed," Aedan said, his voice firm. "Starting now, we're on our own."

The four friends exchanged a look that sealed their silent pact, the air around them charged with the gravity of what lay ahead. They were stepping into the unknown, but they were doing it together.

"Is that Harry over there?" Mary said, pointing to a man in the corner reading a newspaper.

"There's no mistaking it—that's definitely Harry over there in the corner, engrossed in his newspaper," Lindsey said confidently.

"You can recognize his distinctive features and mannerisms from a mile away. I'm telling you, it's undoubtedly him," Tim replied eagerly as he put his coffee cup down on the table.

Aedan's hand gripped the edge of the table, his face turning a shade of red as he stood up abruptly, chair scraping back against the floor with a grating sound. He strode determinedly across the room, the scent of freshly ground coffee beans overpowering, yet unable to mask the bitter scent of treachery. His friends watched from across the store.

"Harry," Aedan said, voice steady but laced with a sharp edge as he approached the old man, who sat alone at a corner table, his face half-hidden behind a local newspaper. "We need to talk."

Harry lowered the paper slowly, peering over his spectacles with an expression that feigned annoyance. "Aedan, my boy, what do you want?"

Aedan bent over, hands flat on the table, his thin frame casting a long shadow over Harry in the dim light of the café. His blue eyes bore into the older man's with distinct intensity. "I feel like you've been lying to me, Harry. Hiding things. Important things and lying to me about the markings on that map."

"Betrayal is a strong accusation, lad." Harry's voice remained calm, but his fingers twitched, betraying a hint of nervousness.

"Strong but fitting." Aedan's words were like ice. "What are you not telling me? Why lead me down this path if you're just going to withhold the truth?"

"Listen to me, Aedan—" Harry began, but Aedan cut him off.

"No, you listen!" His volume rose, drawing glances from nearby patrons. "I trusted you.

We all did. And now I find out you're keeping secrets? What kind of game are you playing?"

"Game? This is no game, boy! And I didn't lie to you about no markings, you were the one who jotted down the location, not me" Harry's voice finally broke, rising to meet Aedan's fury. "There are forces at work here beyond your understanding!"

"Then help me understand!" Aedan slammed a fist onto the table, cups clinking and liquid sloshing over the rims. "What happened to Tommy Canfeld?

"Tommy?" Harry's demeanor hardened. "You think I've spent all these years, dedicated my life to protecting my land, just to play the fool now? There are layers, Aedan, layers you can't even fathom!"

"Try me." Aedan's challenge was fierce, his stance unyielding.

"Fine! Do you want the raw truth? It's dangerous, Aedan. Knowledge like this—it's a burden. One I thought to spare you from." Harry's voice wavered, a crack in his stern facade revealing a flicker of doubt.

"Too late for that," Aedan shot back. "Are we clear?"

"Crystal," Harry said, but his eyes held a stormy sea of regret. "If it's the full picture you want, then brace yourself. Because once I tell you, there's no going back."

"Good." Aedan straightened, the weight of their exchange settling around him like a cloak. "Because I'm not backing down, not when so much is at stake."

"Very well." Harry sighed, folding his newspaper with finality. "But remember, Aedan O'Connor, you asked for this."

"Tommy's behavior was bothersome, as he would persistently annoy me with his fanciful and unrealistic perception of his relationship with Emma," Harry's voice was laced with frustration over the situation.

"Wow, you are responsible, then, aren't you?" Aedan exclaimed, his voice brimming with fervor.

"That's neither here nor there, boy!" Harry roared back, his words dripping with unbridled passion, a fiery anger igniting within him.

Lindsey's brown eyes widened, shock etching her delicate features as she absorbed the gravity of Aedan's and Harry's heated exchange. She reeled back slightly in her chair as if the air around her had turned to ice.

Lindsey, Mary, and Tim got up from the table they were sitting at and walked over to Aedan's side. Beside Lindsey, Tim tensed, his protective instincts kicking in, but there was nothing he could shield Aedan from—not when the threat was woven into words and revelations.

"Harry," Mary said, disbelief lacing her voice, "how could you keep this from us?"

Tim's jaw clenched, his usual composure giving way to a simmering anger. "We trusted you, man," he said, the hurt clear in his tone. His shoulders rose and fell with each heavy breath, his brown eyes reflecting betrayal that mirrored Lindsey's and Mary's.

Tensions escalated rapidly as Harry found himself surrounded by the four imposing teens, their presence overwhelming him. Unable to bear the confrontation any longer, Harry abruptly rose from the table and stormed out of Waltz's 24s, leaving the group of friends behind.

"It's clear now," Aedan said, his voice solid cutting through the tension like a knife. "We've been leaning on broken crutches all along."

"Trust," Lindsey said softly, almost to herself but loud enough for the others to hear. "It's everything. Without it—"

"Without it, we're blind," Tim finished for her, nodding grimly.

"Blind and stumbling," Mary agreed, her fingers drumming on the wooden table. "But not anymore. We can't afford to be led astray, not with Al Ana lurking in the shadows."

"Then we trust in ourselves," Lindsey said, her athletic posture straightening as she spoke. "Our instincts haven't failed us yet."

"Exactly." Tim's voice was resolute. "We've got each other's backs. Always have, always will."

"Then it's settled," Aedan declared, his look meeting each of theirs in turn. "We'll carve our path, use what we've learned, and piece together the rest. Harry's secrets won't define our moves any longer."

"Agreed," Lindsey said, her spirit undiminished by the revelation. "We're more than capable. We've proven that much."

"Damn right," Mary added, the corner of her mouth lifting in a defiant half-smile.

Aedan leaned forward, his elbows on the scarred surface of the café table, eyes alight with a fierce glow. "We chart our course from here. No looking back. We've come too far to let Harry—or anyone—hold us back."

"Right," Lindsey said, her voice steady as she pulled a tattered map from her backpack. It sprawled open between them, dotted with notes and symbols only they could decipher.

"We start by retracing her steps, every site of disturbance we've recorded," Aedan suggested.

"Back to basics." Tim nodded, his arms folded across his chest as if bracing against the weight of their task. "We've faced down strange noises in the night, shadows that move against the wind."

"Exactly," Aedan agreed, his finger tracing a line from the river up through the old forest, then circling an area near the town's outskirts.

Aedan's hand shot out, snatching up the map from the table, creases etching deeper into the worn paper as he folded it with practiced haste. "Time's wasting," he said, his voice laced with urgency.

Lindsey scooped her notes into a leather-bound journal, her fingers deftly wrapping the attached string around its cover multiple times before tucking the end into itself. She looked up, nodding to Aedan and Tim, her backpack already slung over one shoulder.

"Let's go," she urged, her tone crisp and decisive.

Tim, who had been checking his phone for any last-minute clues or messages, slipped the device into his pocket and rose, towering over the small table that had been their makeshift command center. His eyes flickered with determination as he shouldered his bag, filled with the essentials they needed on their unpredictable journey ahead.

The clatter of chairs pushed back quickly, the shuffle of determined footsteps, and the final swish of Waltz's 24s door signaled their departure to anyone who might have been watching. But their focus was singular—on the path that lay ahead, the secrets veiled in shadow, the demon that lurked in the silent spaces of their town.

The four friends looked around Waltz's 24s as they noticed some of the coffee patrons appearing to be disoriented and having difficulty consuming their beverages, the liquid spilling down their faces alarmingly.

"How did we not see this?" A pensive silence lingered as Mary's question hung in the air. Her tone carried a hint of self-reproach tinged with a longing for clarity.

"We were too busy with Harry," Aedan responded with a measured cadence of words acknowledging the weight of their preoccupation, a gentle reminder of the distractions that had clouded their vision. An eerie silence fell over Waltz's 24s as the friends watched in stunned disbelief.

Patrons who mere moments ago were engaged in lively conversations now sat motionless, their expressions vacant and their movements unnervingly stilted. A woman across the room lifted her cup to her lips, but the liquid cascaded down her chin, staining her blouse in a grotesque parody of drinking. The friends exchanged wide-eyed glances, their hearts pounding in their chests.

"Remember, eyes sharp," Aedan commanded softly.

"Be alert," Lindsey said back, her stride matching Aedan's, while Tim and Mary moved like quiet sentinels at the rear, vigilant and unyielding as they approached the front door. They stepped out into the brisk air, the sky overhead a canvas of grays and blues swirling together as if reflecting the turmoil brewing within them. Aedan took point, leading them down the sidewalk, his curly brown hair tousled by the wind, his blue eyes piercing through the uncertainty that lay ahead.

"Cheboygan needs us," Aedan stated, his voice filled with a tone that resonated through the cool air. The four friends moved as one entity, a force melded by purpose and friendship, ready to unravel the woven threads of darkness and deceit.

"We're taking the shortcut, I don't want to go through town," Lindsey declared with confident conviction, her voice resonating with a fierce determination.

"You sure?" Aedan's eyes met hers, etched with concern.

"Yeah," Lindsey responded immediately.

"I agree." Mary's affirmation echoed with a fervent passion.

After crossing over Main Street, Mary and Lindsey separated from Aedan and Tim, choosing to go a different route home instead of going the downtown way.

As Aedan and Tim walked home down Main Street, a concerning sight caught Aedan's eye. He spotted what appeared to be Lindsey across the street, down an alleyway between two buildings. "Is that Lindsey? I thought she didn't want to go through town," Aedan asked, his voice laced with concern yet tinged with excitement.

"It looks like her," Tim replied anxiously, his tone suggesting caution.

As the two friends walked closer Tim noticed a frightening glow emanating from beneath what should have been Lindsey's feet, casting an eerie hue upon the ground. "STOP...IT ISN'T LINDSEY," Tim yelled to urgently warn Aedan.

Tim's heart raced as the realization dawned upon him. The figure before them was not their friend Lindsey, but something far more sinister. He gripped Aedan's arm, his voice trembling with seriousness. "We need to get out of here, now. Whatever that thing is, it's not human, and we can't trust it." The glow intensified, casting long, distorted shadows across the ground, as if the very earth beneath its feet was shifting and twisting.

Tim could feel the hairs on the back of his neck standing on end, every instinct screaming at him to flee. He knew they had stumbled into something far beyond their comprehension, a force that could potentially consume them if they lingered any longer. With a firm tug, Tim urged Aedan to turn and run, their footsteps echoing in the eerie silence. They couldn't risk looking back for fear of what they might witness. The only thing that mattered now was putting as much distance as possible between themselves and that supernatural presence before it was too late.

As Aedan and Tim fled the scene, they split up, each heading to their respective homes.

Meanwhile, Lindsey, began her walk home. The night was quiet, the only sound being the crunch of gravel under her feet.

Lindsey's heart raced as she walked down her house's street, her eyes fixated on a familiar figure ahead. A chill ran down her spine as she recognized the unmistakable silhouette of her late grandmother. "Grandma?" Lindsey called out, her voice tinged with a mix of excitement and trepidation.

The sight was unsettling, leaving her mind swirling with questions. Could it truly be her beloved grandmother's spirit, or was her mind playing tricks on her? The uncertainty weighed heavily, and Lindsey couldn't shake the nagging worry that something wasn't quite right.

As Lindsey drew closer, a perturbing sight gripped her with panic— the spectral, glowing image of her late grandmother appeared to emanate from behind her own body. A chill ran down her spine, and panic took over. She spun and ran away, seeking refuge within the confines of her house, her heart pounding with fear and confusion over the eerie apparition that had manifested before her eyes.

Lindsey ran inside her house, and the familiar warmth of her home enwrapped her, offering a fleeting feeling of solace amidst the chaos of emotions raging within.

With shaky hands, Lindsey dialed her mother's number, the phone ringing endlessly before finally connecting. As she recounted the bc wildering encounter with tears streaming down her face, her mother's soothing voice provided a glimmer of comfort amidst uncertainty.

Lindsey sat down at the kitchen table, her hands still trembling; she couldn't shake the feeling of strain that gripped her. "Mom, I don't understand. It felt so real, yet so...haunting," she said quietly, her voice barely above a breath."

"Sometimes, spirits try to communicate with us in ways we may not fully understand," her mother offered softly. "Perhaps there is something else trying to convey a message to you."

Lindsey's face furrowed as she pondered her mother's words. "I think I know who it was?" she said, her mind racing with thoughts of the demon after her.

Just then, a soft knock at the front door interrupted her thoughts. Lindsey's heart skipped a beat as she threw a wary glance toward the front door before rising from the table to answer it cautiously.

Standing on the doorstep was an elderly woman with blacked-out eyes and a harsh smile. "Lindsey, dear," she began, her voice carrying an unsoothing lilt and an accent of evil. "I couldn't help but feel a disturbance in the spirit realm. Your grandmother is trying to reach out to you, but her message is clouded by confusion and fear."

Lindsey's breath caught in her throat as she listened intently to the woman's words. "How do you know? Who are you?" she asked, her voice tinged with a mix of anticipation and apprehension.

The woman placed her disfigured hand on Lindsey's shoulder. "You must be open to receiving the message with an open heart and mind," she advised. "Only then will the truth be revealed."

Lindsey realized this woman must be connected to the demon; finding courage, she willed herself to confront the unknown forces that had intruded upon her reality. Just then, her mother's car pulled into the driveway. She quickly got out, racing toward the door where her daughter stood face-to-face with the mysterious visitor. In a blink, the ominous figure turned and took a few steps before vanishing into the night, leaving a trail of unanswered questions in her wake. Lindsey's and her mother's hearts pounded with trepidation as they wondered what dark forces were at play.

Together, they tried to piece together Lindsey's fragmented recollections of her day, attempting to unravel the mysterious visitation that had shaken Lindsey to her core.

As morning crept up, the world outside grew still, and Lindsey sat by her bedroom window, gazing out into the darkness with a mix of apprehension and curiosity. The echoes of that creepy encounter still reverberated within her soul, but were now tinged with a hint of defiance. She knew that she would not rest until she got even with the haunting presence that had crossed the threshold between life and death.

12

Abandoned Lumber Mill

The following afternoon, Aedan, Tim, Lindsey, and Mary found them-selves driving up and down Main Street, not with a particular destina-tion in mind but rather engaging in the typical leisurely wandering of teenagers. With the freedom of no parental supervision and a full tank of gas, they cruised aimlessly, singing along as they blasted the song "Beds Are Burning" by Midnight Oil from the car stereo, and playfully critiqued the questionable exercise choice of the only normal-looking person outside, briskly walking by himself down the sidewalk.

Aedan, ever the attentive observer, provided a running witty commen-tary that had the girls embarrassed. "No way...aside from the sweatband on his forehead he looks normal! Maybe he's lost!" he exclaimed. "Yo, buddy, are you exercising, or are you lost?" Aedan yelled out to the guy.

The guy peacefully looked up as Aedan slowed the car down next to him.

"Where's everyone at?" Lindsey asked the guy, reaching her head up in between the front seats.

"Things get the darkest before dawn," Tim said, cutting Lindsey off as he recited a line from the "Joe Dirt" movie.

The guy rolled his eyes like he was becoming annoyed. "Ha, ha, very funny, no," he replied to Tim, not actually finding the comment funny.

"Hey, where's everyone at?" Mary asked, backing Lindsey up.

"Don't you know?" the guy said, replying to Mary and leaning toward the passenger window.

"Know what?" Mary shot back instantly.

"No one comes outside anymore. Everybody stays inside outta fear," the guy replied.

A heavy silence fell over the group as the weight of the guy's words sank in. Fear had become a constant companion, casting a lingering darkness over their once vibrant community. Lindsey couldn't help but feel a twinge of sadness at the thought of people huddled inside, too afraid to venture out and experience the simple joys of life.

"Hey, man, how come you're not afraid?" Aedan shouted, a mischievous grin proudly displayed on his face as he revved the car's engine playfully.

The guy shot them an unamused glare, prompting Tim to chime in. "Stay safe man...you're all alone out here."

The stranger's eyes narrowed as he assessed the situation, clearly wary of the two young men in the car. He took a step back, his hand instinctively moving toward his pocket. Aedan's grin faltered slightly, realizing their attempt at intimidation might have backfired. "Look, you don't want any trouble," the man said firmly, his voice steady despite the tension in his posture. His eyes suddenly changed into solid black.

"I suggest you kids move along before she finds you."

Tim glanced nervously at Aedan, suddenly aware of the potential consequences of their actions. The isolated location, which had seemed perfect for their prank, now felt ominous and threatening. The stranger's calm demeanor in the face of their provocation made them both uneasy.

Aedan drove away, parking his car farther down the street in an empty parking lot of a hardware store. "There's Mrs. Blackwood's house... Should we see if she knows anything about what's been happening around here?" Aedan asked as he pointed over at Mrs. Blackwood's residence across the street.

"She knows something, she has to," Tim said.

Mrs. Agatha Blackwood, a retired baker, was once at the heart of her beloved small town.

Known for her attentive nature, big-hearted generosity, and charismatic presence, she was always able to lift the spirits of all those she came across.

However, her life took a dark turn when her late husband vanished without a trace, which sent shockwaves throughout the community. It was rumored Mrs. Blackwood knew more than she let on about the mysterious disappearance. Some believed she held the key to the truth, while others speculated she had made a deal with the town's demon, Al Ana, in exchange for her bakery's success. The burden of this knowledge weighed heavily on her, shaping her into a guarded and solitary figure in her later years.

"The window's open, she must be home," Lindsey said, observing the open shutters.

"I think it's a good idea," Mary said, supporting the suggestion. "But don't bring up her husband!"

"Got it," Aedan said as they all got out of the car and jogged across the street.

Aedan knocked on the door and Mrs. Blackwood answered. "Please come in," she said warmly, welcoming all four friends into her cozy home with a bright smile and a twinkle in her eye.

Her gray hair, set in a classic perm, framed a face etched with wisdom and time. It gave her a regal air, as though she were the guardian of the town's secrets.

The inviting aroma of freshly baked treats filled the air, beckoning them inside for what promised to be another clue to their curiosity. The scent was better than pleasant—clinging to the air and filling the space between the weathered walls, it carried the gravity of untold stories. It was almost like they were walking into a bakery.

"Mrs. Blackwood?" Aedan began tentatively, feeling somewhat like he was intruding upon her quiet life.

"Please, call me Agatha," she insisted, her voice soft but firm.

"Thank you," Aedan stated, tugging at the edge of a quilt that added a splash of hominess against the backdrop of the room's frozen-in-time decor. Knick knacks—ceramic cats with chipped ears, glass American robins that caught the afternoon light—watched them from their perches on the shelves. On the walls, family portraits in faded sepia tones held secrets of bygone days.

"You're here about the old tales, I suppose. The ones that have Cheboygan tossing and turning in its sleep."

"Exactly," Lindsey piped up, her researcher's curiosity evident. "We've been looking into the disappearances..."

"Of Tommy and Emma," Agatha finished, adjusting the glasses that rested on the bridge of her nose. Her scholarly appearance lent her an aura of authority, as if she was about to impart the most significant lesson of their lives.

"Agatha," Aedan began, "you mentioned knowing Tommy and Emma?"

"Child," Agatha replied, her regard deep and knowing, "there are layers to this town darker than the waters of Chook River on a moonless night. But tread carefully, for some secrets are like Pandora's box: once they're opened, they can never be shut again."

Her words made their skin run cold, even as Aedan felt the pull of the mystery beckon all the friends closer. In Agatha's guarded expression, Aedan saw the hint of secrecy—the suggestion that she knew more than she let on. It was a look that told them she had pieces of the puzzle they sought, yet also a warning that some truths might be better left buried.

"Is it true that you knew them?" Tim asked, his tone respectful yet eager for any morsel of information.

Agatha nodded slowly. Her vintage cardigan brushed softly against her long skirt, the fabrics rubbing together in hushed tones. The timeless quality of her garments wrapped around her like a shawl of mystery, unresolved for centuries.

"Ah, yes," she started, her focus returning to them, her glasses glinting with the reflections of lost years. "They were bright youngsters, full of life and laughter. But there was always something...off about their fascination with the river...maybe it was related to Old Man Harry. He was Tommy's uncle, you know."

"Yeah, I figured that out a few days ago. I think he had something to do with their disappearance too," Aedan replied as he recalled how Harry creepily tried to talk him into going down to the river with him.

"Off how?" Tim prompted, leaning in, his protective nature momentarily giving way to his intrigue.

"Rumors of a dark presence that seemed to envelop the town," Agatha said. "Dark presence? Like a curse?" Lindsey asked, her skepticism tinged with the nervousness of one who has seen the shadows move in ways they shouldn't.

"Perhaps," Agatha conceded with a slight nod. "There are those who believe in such things, and those who have been touched by them never remain quite the same."

"Did Tommy and Emma believe in the demon?" Aedan found himself asking, drawn into the tapestry of mystery she had woven with her words.

"Believe?" Agatha's chuckle was a dry leaf skittering across a tombstone. "My dears, they were consumed by it."

Agatha Blackwood's words resonated with profound inspiration. She looked out the window for a brief moment, as if gathering her thoughts from the garden beyond.

Her fingers traced the rim of her teacup, a small clinking sound punctuating the silence that had settled over her living room. "There is a place," she began, her voice as delicate as the china in her hands, "where the hints grow louder and the shadows stretch longer than anywhere else in Cheboygan." Her eyes met Aedan's, sharp despite their age. "The old mill by Chook River."

Tim straightened, his curiosity piqued. Lindsey's pen hovered above her notepad, ready to capture every detail.

"Tommy and Emma...they were seen there, before they..." Agatha's voice trailed off into a sigh, a cloud of sadness passing over her features.

"Before they disappeared," Aedan finished for her, the weight of their investigation bearing down on him.

"Exactly." Agatha set her cup down with finality. "But heed my warning, children. That room is said to be cursed. Evil clings to the mill walls like damp. The air within it is thick with despair."

"Can you tell us where in the mill to start looking?" Tim pressed gently.

With a sigh that seemed to carry the weight of decades, Agatha stood and walked to a window overlooking her unkempt garden, her back to them as she spoke.

"Start where all things lost yearn to be found, where echoes of the past still swirl amidst the silence. At the old lumber mill by Chook River, where memories reside, an ancient place where secrets sleep and time cannot hide," Mrs. Blackwood said, turning to face them with an expression that was both kind and somber. "In shadows deep, a cursed embrace, where evil dwells, in hidden space. Within forsaken walls, it hides, in darkness where the sorrow lies.

Beware the room no light can touch, where sounds echo, haunting far too much. A place of secrets, long submerged, in ancient halls where spirits surged. But remember, in the darkest gloom there lies a tale of woe and doom. For some places hold a curse, where an evil demon dwelt, now in reverse..."

Aedan leaned forward, elbows on his knees, his curiosity practically vibrating in the air around him. Tim sat back, arms crossed, his eyes sweeping the room with the careful scrutiny of a guard. The vintage lamp cast a warm glow across the crochet placemat, spilling over onto the carpet as if to soften the edges of reality. Lindsey and Mary were straight-up stunned by Agatha Blackwood's poem. They leaned back, exchanging looks of pure amazement, completely blown away by the poetic brilliance they had just heard.

"Hidden space?" Aedan repeated his pulse quickening. That was it—the next piece of the puzzle, laid bare by a woman who seemed as much a part of Cheboygan's history as the legends themselves.

"Go, if you must," Agatha said, a note of reluctance in her voice. "But do not underestimate the shadows that cling to that place. They are...persistent."

"Thank you, Agatha," Aedan managed, his mind racing with the implications of her words. "We'll be careful."

"See that you are," she responded, her eyes meeting each of theirs in turn—a silent benediction from one who had seen too much.

"Where exactly in the mill?" Lindsey asked, leaning forward, her reporter instincts kicking in.

"Through the main entrance, past the rusted machinery. There's a staircase descending into darkness. At its base, a door, concealed behind the remnants of an old wood stack. It's been untouched for years." Agatha's directions were precise, her memory unerring.

"Thank you, Mrs. Blackwood," Tim said with respectful gratitude. "We'll be careful." "Please do." Agatha's sight lingered on the family portraits adorning her walls, as if drawing strength from them.

They rose from the couch, the plastic crinkling beneath them as if bidding farewell. Aedan felt the urgency pushing them toward the door, toward the truth that lay shrouded in secrecy.

With a final nod, they took their leave, stepping back out into the daylight with hearts heavy and minds ablaze with the tales of Agatha Blackwood and the mystery of the mill that awaited them.

"Flashlights. We'll need them for sure," Tim muttered as they stepped into the waning light of day.

"Get cell phones ready," Aedan reassured him, patting the pockets of his jacket. "Let's not waste any time."

Lindsey nodded, her face set in determination. Together, they made their way through the quiet streets of Cheboygan. The town seemed oblivious to the dark currents running beneath its surface, but not to them.

"Here we go," Mary announced as they reached Aedan's car, parked at the hardware store lot, popping open the trunk to reveal a tangled mess of emergency supplies.

"Check the herbs," Lindsey reminded Aedan, as practical as ever.

"Good to go," Aedan confirmed after a quick test, handing one bag to each of his friends.

The abandoned mill was a short walk down the street toward the edge of the wood line next to the river, and they walked in silence, each of them lost in thought. What would they find in the hidden room? Clues? Answers? Or just more questions?

Soon, the old mill loomed ahead, its silhouette a dark stain against the dimming sky. Their cell phone flashlights cut through the twilight as they approached, beams dancing over decrepit walls and broken windows.

"Let's stick together," Aedan said, leading the way with anticipation. The adventure was thrilling, the mystery intoxicating, but the fear...the fear was real. It clawed at the edges of his mind, mentioning warnings he refused to heed.

The world around them seemed to hold its breath as they neared the desolate mill, a hulking giant silhouetted against the night sky. There was a stillness in the air that felt almost tangible, disturbed only by their footsteps crunching on the gravel path. Aedan couldn't shake the feeling of being watched, though he chalked it up to nerves and adrenaline.

"Here's the entrance," Mary pointed out, her voice sounding panicky. She pushed open the door, its hinges protesting with a screech that seemed to echo into eternity.

"Into the unknown through the main entrance, past the rusted machinery. There's a staircase descending into darkness. At its base, a door concealed behind the remnants of an old wood stack," Lindsey said, her words a battle cry against the creeping shadows.

They entered the abandoned mill, the darkness enveloping them like a shroud. Ahead of them, the staircase beckoned, a descent into the heart of Cheboygan's darkest secret.

"Feels like we're walking into a ghost story," Mary quietly said, her voice barely audible over the echo of their steps.

"Or writing one," Lindsey added, trying to sound more confident than Mary felt.

"Let's keep our wits about us," Tim said, his protective nature cutting through the ominous atmosphere.

Their flashlights cut swathes through the darkness, revealing the sad decay of what once must have been a thriving heart of industry. Now, it stood as a mausoleum to forgotten times, the dust bunnies dancing in the beams like spirits disturbed by their presence.

"Here, the door should be around this corner," Aedan said, leading the way down a corridor that seemed to stretch endlessly into the gloom.

"Got it," Tim called out from behind a pile of wood debris, gesturing toward an aged door, its surface marred by time and neglect. Cobwebs and rust clung to it like shrouds, and it hung precariously on hinges that looked ready to surrender to movement at any moment.

"Ugh, look at them all," Lindsey gasped, pointing her flashlight downward. The ground teemed with spiders skittering across the cracked tiles, their eight-legged ballet an eerie sight.

As Aedan swept his light along the walls, he spotted worms writhing in the crevices and bats that darted from the ceiling, their flapping wings stirring the stagnant air. "Careful," Aedan warned, stepping gingerly among the crawling chaos. It was then that one particularly bold bat swooped too close, its shadow flitting over Lindsey's face.

A scream ripped from her throat, high-pitched and laced with terror, echoing off the walls and sending shivers through their bodies. "Sorry, sorry," she panted, clutching her chest. "It just...it surprised me."

"Let's just find what we came for and get out of here," Tim said, his voice steady but his brown eyes betraying a flicker of anxiety. They gathered their nerves and pushed open the door to the hidden room. It groaned in protest, the sound a chilling herald of the secrets that lay beyond.

The room felt like a tomb, every step they took raising clouds of dirt that danced in the narrow beams of their flashlights. The air was thick with the smell of mold and disuse, and their throats tightened against it. Aedan led the way, his light sweeping over dilapidated chairs and a table that looked as though a single touch would collapse it into kindling.

"Watch where you step," he muttered, eyeing the rotten floorboards. "This place is a deathtrap."

"Imagine what secrets it's hiding," Lindsey said, her earlier scream forgotten in the face of her raw curiosity. She moved to a bookcase sagging under the weight of decayed books, their titles long since eroded by time and neglect.

Aedan trailed his fingers over a moth-eaten sofa, imagining the conversations it might have absorbed, the confessions it had heard. Were Tommy and Emma ever here? Did they sit on this very couch, oblivious to their impending fates?

"Hey, over here!" Tim's voice cut through Aedan's musings. They crowded around him, crouched near an overturned box, sifting through a pile of debris. Tim's hand emerged holding something delicate and frail—a photograph, its edges curled and colors faded. They huddled together, the four of them forming a tight circle as Tim smoothed it out against the dirty floor.

It was them—Tommy and Emma. They were frozen in time, their smiles wide and innocent, a stark contrast to the eerie quiet of the mill. Emma's eyes gleamed with life, while Tommy's grin held carefree ease they could scarcely imagine now.

"Look at them..." Mary said. "They had no idea..."

"Oblivious," Aedan said, staring down at the photo. The joy in their faces hit him hard, a punch to the gut. These were more than just names or mysteries; they were people once vibrant and alive, reduced to shadows in the demon's twisted narrative.

"Does this mean they were here?" Tim asked, his brow furrowed.

"Or someone wanted us to think so," Aedan replied, taking the photo gently from Tim's hands. Aedan examined it closer, turning it over. There was nothing but a date scribbled on the back—two weeks before they vanished.

"Either way," Mary said, "this is the first real connection we've found."

"Let's keep looking," Lindsey urged, determination lighting her features. "There has to be more." And so they continued, searching through the remnants of the past, the ghostly echoes of laughter and conversation replaced by the silence of a mystery slowly unfolding.

The weight of the photograph in Aedan's hands set a somber tone; he couldn't shake the feeling that they were missing something—some hidden truth that lay just beyond their grasp. They moved to leave when Lindsey and Mary paused, their attention fixed on a peculiar outline on the wall.

"Guys, look." Lindsey's voice cut through the heavy air with an edge of excitement.

There, obscured by years of neglect and shadow, was a small compartment concealed within the decaying plaster. Aedan's heart pounded in his chest as he stepped closer, the others flanking him as they eyed the anomaly.

"Who wants to do the honors?" Tim asked, a nervous chuckle escaping him.

"Here goes nothing," Aedan muttered, reaching out with fingers that betrayed a slight tremor. He traced the edges of the opening until he found a catch and pressed. With a reluctant creak, the compartment swung open, revealing its secrets to their hungry eyes. Inside lay a journal, its leather-bound cover cracked and worn, the pages yellowed with age. Aedan reached for it, half expecting it to disintegrate at his touch, but it held firm. The musty scent of old paper filled his nostrils as he carefully opened it, the others crowding around to peer over his shoulder.

"Can you make anything out?" Lindsey said, her breath warm against Aedan's ear. The scrawl was nearly illegible, but as Aedan's eyes adjusted, words began to emerge from the chaos like ghosts taking form. There were sketches too, strange symbols and drawings that made their skin crawl. But one word repeated itself over and over, weaving through the text like a dark thread: Al Ana. "Stolen souls..." Tim read aloud, his voice barely above a mumble. "What does that mean?"

"Al Ana," Aedan said, the name tasting bitter on his tongue. "She's at the heart of this. These are more than just ramblings; they're warnings."

Lindsey leaned in closer, her brown eyes scanning the pages frantically. "This is it, isn't it? This is what we've been looking for."

"Or it's what someone wants us to find," Mary countered, unable to shake the panic that clung to her like a bad omen. But despite the fear, determination surged within her—a burning need to bring the truth to light. Lindsey and Aedan exchanged a look, a silent vow passing between them.

"Let's take this with us," Aedan suggested, closing the journal with care. "There has to be someone who can help us decipher it."

"Agatha might know," Lindsey pointed out, hope flickering in her eyes. "Then it's settled." Tim nodded, his jaw set in confidence. "We keep going."

As they left the hidden room behind, the journal tucked safely under Aedan's arm, he could feel the pieces of the puzzle clicking into place. Al Ana, the stolen souls, the disappearances...they were all connected. And the group of friends were inching closer to the truth, one page at a time.

As they traversed the hallways, fear crept in. Aedan's eyes caught a glimpse of a crumpled piece of paper lying by a doorway. He bent down cautiously and picked it up, his mind racing with apprehension. He could almost taste the weight of years and secrets that hung in the air. Lindsey's hand brushed against Aedan's, her touch a silent reassurance that she was with him, that they were in this together.

Aedan studied the faded ink. A pattern emerged amidst the chaos—a sequence of trees leading toward the river, where few dared to tread. "It's a trail," Aedan said.

"Leading to what?" Tim questioned, eyebrows raising.

"Could be..." Aedan's throat felt dry, his words laced with hope. "It could lead us to where Tommy and Emma are buried. It looks like a grave marker."

"Or straight into a trap," Lindsey interjected, ever the voice of reason, even when her eyes shone with the same thrill that gripped them all.

"Only one way to find out," Aedan said folding the paper and tucking it into his pocket.

They had a new mission, a path carved out by fate or fortune—Aedan wasn't sure which. "First light tomorrow," Aedan declared, meeting their determined eyes. "We follow the trail."

"Agreed," they echoed, and with that, turned their backs on the hidden room and its dark revelations. As they stepped back into the night, the mill loomed over them, a silent sentinel guarding the secrets the four had yet to uncover. But with each step away from its shadowed embrace, Aedan felt a spark of hope flicker to life within him. Cheboygan's grim past lay threadbare before them, its mysteries unraveling with every clue they unearthed.

"Whatever's waiting for us," Aedan said to his three friends, "were ready." They nodded, and as they vanished into the darkness, leaving the abandoned mill to its ghosts, the air hummed with the promise of answers that lay just beyond the horizon.

13

Caballo (Honduran Slang)

As the sun gracefully edged toward the horizon, it masterfully painted a vast sky canvas with breathtaking hues of vibrant orange and rich purple. Aedan O'Connor zipped his backpack shut with a resolute snap. His backyard, a familiar patch of green that had hosted countless childhood games, now served as the staging ground for something far more dangerous. He turned to face Lindsey, Mary, and Tim, their backpacks bulging with an assortment of important items for the task ahead.

"Okay, this is it," Aedan said, his voice steady but betraying a hint of the adrenaline coursing through him. "We've been over this a million times, but let's run through it again. We can't afford any mistakes. Not with Al Ana lurking out there."

Lindsey nodded, her face poised and ready, her eyes scanning the tree line as if she could already see the evil awaiting them. "We stick to the trails until we hit the old mill; from there, we cut directly toward Chook River. It's less traveled, but it'll get us there faster."

"Right." Aedan's blue eyes flickered to Tim, who stood like a steadfast oak. "We've got the Holy Bible, holy water, the herbs, and the holy words to ward her off, but we're still susceptible to her evilness.

"Remember, no matter what happens, don't listen to anything that doesn't sound like one of us. Al Ana's a trickster. She'll try to deceive us with voices of loved ones, or even our own."

"Got it," Tim replied, his deep voice imbued with the kind of unshakable confidence that comes from staring down fear too many times. "And if things get hairy, we stick together. No heroics. We're stronger as a unit."

"Exactly," Aedan affirmed, stepping closer to his friends. They formed a tight circle, the gravity of the situation pulling them in like a silent pact. "We don't know exactly what we're going to encounter out there, but we know why we're doing this."

"Tonight," Mary echoed, her brown eyes fiercely determined. "Tonight," Tim agreed, his brown eyes filled with purpose.

"Then let's move out," Aedan commanded, slinging his backpack over his right shoulder.

The four friends exchanged a look that carried the weight of their shared history, and the unspoken promise that they would see this through.

The backyard gate creaked open, and the four friends stepped beyond its threshold, leaving behind the safety of the familiar. Their journey into the encroaching darkness was more than just a path through the woods. It was a march into the unknown, a testament to the courage that beats in the heart of every soul willing to face down their demons. And as the gate swung shut behind them, it felt like a final farewell to innocence, a steeling of nerves for the confrontation that lay ahead.

The woods greeted them with the hush of evening, branches stretching out like pleading hands and arms against the twilight sky. Aedan, the most timid of the group, took the lead. As he felt the familiar crunch of leaves underfoot, somewhere in that rhythmic cadence he found his veins hardening. The trails were old friends sharing secrets, and tonight, they were guiding them to a reckoning. "Keep your eyes peeled," Aedan said to Lindsey, Mary, and Tim. "Al Ana's tricks won't stop at the river."

"Got it," Lindsey replied, her voice steady as she scanned their flanks. They pressed on, the air growing cooler, the shadows stretching to meet them. Then the path threw its first challenge—a dead pine tree sprawled across their way, its trunk a barricade, downed by the last storm's fury. "Damn," Aedan said, his mind racing for a detour, but Tim was already moving toward the roadblock.

"Stand back," Tim said, his voice a low rumble of focused intent. Shedding his backpack, he mustered up all his strength and pushed, but the tree didn't budge. This was pure determination; this was a will to push through and carve a path where none existed.

He took a step back and noticed that the tree limbs were the obstacle blocking the path, and they probably could get past the rest of the tree with the limbs out of the way. Tim's hands wrapped around a thick limb, and with a grunt, he pushed again. The wood groaned as leaves made their protests, and then the limb gave way, snapping with a sound that echoed with his determination. Tim didn't stop, moving to the next branch, then the next, clearing enough of the obstruction to grant them passage.

"Nice work," Aedan said clapping him on the shoulder, admiration clear in his tone even as Tim tried to catch his breath.

"Nothing's stopping us," Tim puffed out, wiping sweat from his eyebrows, a half-smile playing on his lips.

"Nothing at all," Mary agreed, winking at Tim before stepping through the gap he created. The rest followed.

With each step, the night grew darker around them, and so did the feeling that they were walking into the jaws of a great beast. It was then that they stumbled upon it: a gaping maw in the earth, a hidden cave veiled by drapes of moss and ivy.

"Guys, look at this," Aedan said quietly, not daring to break the hush of the wood.

Lindsey approached first, caution filling her eyes but unable to resist the lure. "Could be dangerous," she warned, yet her tone held excitement more than fear.

"Or it could be exactly what we're searching for, the demon's lair," Aedan countered, feeling the pull of adventure tugging at his heartstrings.

Tim nodded; his earlier display of strength was now replaced with an eager curiosity. With a silent agreement, the four friends ducked beneath the natural curtain and entered the cavern's cool embrace.

Their flashlights sliced through the darkness, revealing the jagged contours of the cave.

And there, on the walls, were symbols of Al Ana—the ones they'd seen in the journal they pulled out of the mill compartment. They were real, etched into stone by hands long turned into skeletons.

"Al Ana." Mary breathed the name like a curse, her light trembling.

"Stay focused," Aedan urged, his pulse quickening. He fished out his notebook, the one he'd kept since this whole crazy journey began. His hand moved of its own accord, sketching the ancient script with meticulous care.

"Think you can make reason of this?" Tim asked, peering over Aedan's shoulder.

"I have to," Aedan replied, his eyes locked on the walls as if the very lines might spring to life, revealing their secrets. "These symbols... they're a piece of the puzzle. Al Ana's presence is here, carved into the very stone."

"Then let's not overstay our welcome," Lindsey suggested her words carrying the weight of wisdom.

"Agreed," Aedan murmured, snapping the notebook shut.

Together, they stepped back into the dimming light of the woods, the cave's secrets now a part of their arsenal. The cave's breath turned icy in an instant, snuffing out the beams from their flashlights like candles in a gale. Darkness surrounded them, thick and absolute, clawing at the edges of their courage with cold fingers.

"Guys—" Mary's voice quivered in the blackness, a thread of panic weaving through it.

"Wait!" Aedan fumbled through his backpack, the shapes and textures inside blurring into one frantic search. "The herbs, remember?"

"Right, right," Tim replied, heavy with forced calm.

Aedan's hands found it—small, intricately carved tokens that seemed to pulse with a silent promise of protection. The protective herbs sprang to life, their subtle hum filling the space around them, pushing back against the dark.

"Okay," Aedan exhaled, "let's keep moving."

They ventured deeper, the forest waiting beyond the mouth of the cave with a stillness that belied its secrets. Their steps were cautious, and measured, the air around them thickening with anticipation.

"Feels like we're walking into a dream," Lindsey said, her eyes wide and searching in the shadows.

"Or a nightmare," Tim added grimly.

"Either way," Aedan said, his voice cutting through the tension, "Chook River's close. I can feel it." The heaviness in the air was more than just humidity; it was charged, alive with a power that seemed to watch them, weigh them, and test their intent. It was as if the woods themselves were holding their breath, waiting for the inevitable confrontation.

"Let's find Al Ana," Mary declared, her voice brazen but carrying the weight of an oath.

And with that, they pressed on, toward the heart of the darkness and the destiny that awaited them at Chook River.

They pushed through the underbrush, their boots sinking into the soft earth with each step. The forest around them seemed to close in, pine, oak, and maple trees standing like they were on guard, noises skating across the breeze—a resonating chorus saying, *"Go back...go back now,"* urging them to retreat into the safety of sunlight. Aedan shook his head, trying to dispel the voices that slithered like serpents in his ears, their insidious message a stark contrast to the bold thrum of his heart.

"Did you hear that?" Lindsey's voice was hushed with nervousness.

"Sounds like a warning," Tim noted, his eyes scanning the dense canopy above.

Aedan paused for a moment, tilting his head as if to catch the elusive words again. "It's nothing," Aedan said. "Just the wind playing tricks." Aedan couldn't afford to let fear take root, not when they were this close. "Chook River is full of secrets," Aedan said out loud, though he kept his voice steady, "but we're not turning back."

The tangled woodland began to thin, the oppressive atmosphere lifting slightly as they neared the river. That's when Aedan saw it—a hidden shrine nestled against the trunk of an old willow, half-concealed by overgrown vines and moss. Aedan's pulse quickened as they approached, the sight of it sending a jolt of adrenaline through his veins.

"Look at this," Aedan breathed, stepping closer to examine the odd collection of items adorning a makeshift altar. There were flowers, feathers, and small crosses, each seemingly placed with deliberate care. Among them, Christian fish symbols etched into wood and stone formed a silent litany of protection.

"Someone's prayed here before...someone found this site holy," Mary muttered, tracing a finger over one of the feathers. It was familiar; it felt like a beacon calling out to those who dared to confront the darkness.

"This is it," Aedan declared, meeting his friends' eyes. "We're exactly where we need to be. This shrine...it's a sign."

"Or a last chance to turn away," Lindsey said, though her posture was clear in her facial expression.

"No," Aedan countered, feeling the certainty settle within him like an anchor. "It's a testament. We're on the right path."

They stood there for a moment longer, taking in the silent offering of courage the shrine represented. Then, together, they stepped away from the willow trees' watchful stare and made their way to the water's edge, ready to face what awaited them at Chook River.

The air thickened as they neared the river, charged with an energy that seemed to hum against their skin. Mary could hear flapping before she saw it—a frenzied dance in the sky. "Look up," Mary said, nudging Lindsey, Aedan, and Tim without taking her eyes off the spectacle.

"Oh my," replied Tim, staring at the spectacle in amazement.

"Creepy," Lindsey said, shaking her head with disbelief at what they were witnessing.

Dozens of crows darted through the air like leaves caught in a gusty wind. But one by one, they spiraled downward, their bodies thudding against the earth with sickening finality. They watched, hearts in their throats, as each bird succumbed to an invisible force and collapsed into the underbrush. "Has to be Al Ana's doing?" Tim questioned, his voice quiet, as if he was afraid to disturb the eerie silence that followed the crows' descent.

"Has to be," Aedan replied, not wanting to believe the extent of her power, even now. "She doesn't want us here."

Lindsey's hand found Aedan's, her grip firm. "We knew it wouldn't be easy," she said, her brown eyes reflecting a cocktail of emotions—fear mingled with the fiercest determination they'd ever seen.

"We're close," Aedan stated. The fallen birds were a grim reminder of what they were up against. They paused there, at the edge of the river, the soft burble of water unable to wash away the heaviness that had settled over them. Each breath they took felt like a gulp of thick air, laden with anxiety. Aedan met Tim's steady look, Lindsey's resolute stare, and Mary's alert gaze, and something unspoken passed between them—an acknowledgment of the risks, of the bond they shared, of the journey that had brought them to this brink.

"Whatever happens—" Aedan began.

Tim cut him off with a shake of his head. "We've got this, Aedan," he interjected, his voice strong despite the pall hanging over them. "We face it together."

"Like always," Lindsey added, squeezing Aedan's hand once before letting go. They drew in a collective breath, filling their lungs with the courage that seemed to emanate from the very ground beneath their feet, from the shrine they had found, from the trust they placed in each other. Then they exhaled slowly, steeling themselves for the confrontation awaiting them beyond the tree line.

"Let's do this," Aedan said, stepping forward, his friends at his side. Al Ana might have claimed these woods as her domain, but they were here to reclaim it, to stand against the darkness she spread. As they moved closer to the heart of Chook River, Aedan could feel the weight of their mission anchoring them, driving them onward.

The water swirled around them, deceptively tranquil, but nothing was comforting in its embrace. "Keep close," Aedan said quietly over Mary's shoulder, though he knew Tim and Lindsey were just paces behind.

"Feels like we're stepping into her veins," Lindsey said, a hint of awe threaded into her hushed tone.

"Then let's hope we don't end up as part of her circulatory system," Tim quipped, but the attempt at humor fell flat, swallowed by the oppressive silence that had settled over the woods.

They moved in unison, a silent pact among them that no one would be left to face the chill alone. Each sloshing step seemed to echo off the trees, the only sound in a forest that should have been alive with owls, or possums. But they too seemed to have retreated, sensing the darkness that encroached on their domain.

As Chook River's heart drew near, the air thickened to a smog. It was as if Al Ana herself was breathing down their necks, her breath a shroud of malice wrapping tighter with every inch they covered. Aedan's chest tightened, and for a moment, he had a hard time breathing. "Can you feel that?" Mary said, her voice barely above the rush of the water.

"Her presence," Lindsey confirmed, her voice sounding foreign to her ears. It wasn't fear—it couldn't be—not when so much depended on the four of them holding it together. "She knows we're here."

"Good," Tim growled with a newfound edge of defiance. "Let her know we're not scared."

Aedan glanced back at them, their faces set in a grim look, mirroring his own. This was it—the moment where legends were born or broken. "Stay sharp," he instructed, more to focus his racing thoughts than out of any doubt in their readiness. "We're in her world now."

And with that, the heart of Chook River loomed before them and not the area they'd visited before. No, this was the heart of the river, the water swirling in patterns that defied the natural flow, as if guided by an unseen hand. They exchanged glances once more, a silent agreement passing between them. There was no turning back—not when they were this close, not when they could almost taste the victory that would free Cheboygan from the grip of ancient evil.

"Al Ana," Aedan called out, his voice nervous with the pounding in his chest. "We're here...we're not scared of you." The ground shook beneath their feet, a deep rumble that seemed to shake the very soul of the earth. Trees groaned and swayed as if in agony, their branches clawing at the sky. Aedan caught Lindsey's eye—a flicker of fear there. Tim nodded once, jaw set, muscles tensed like steel cables ready to snap. Mary was shaking her head uncontrollably, seemingly stuck in an endless loop, a deeply concerning sight.

"Alright," Aedan said, the words barely audible over the crescendo of nature's upheaval. "No more games." They knew what this meant—Al Ana was throwing down the gauntlet. This tremor was no natural occurrence; it was a challenge, a dark herald announcing the proximity of evil incarnate. Their breaths mingled in white puffs, their bodies braced against the cold and the unknown.

"Let's do this," Lindsey said, her voice a blade of determination cutting through the din. "Get some," echoed Tim, his stance wide like he was ready for a cage fight, anchoring himself to the world they were fighting for.

"Fight us," mumbled Mary, as her nervousness set in.

Through the quaking forest, they forged toward the clearing, each step a declaration of war against the darkness. And then, suddenly, evil. The trees parted like curtains before a stage, revealing the heart of Chook River—the main domain of Al Ana. There she was, a silhouette against the backdrop of twisted foliage, her form undulating like smoke caught in an unfelt breeze. Shadows clung to her, caressing her edges, melding with her essence. Her presence sucked the warmth from the air, and even the bravest heart might falter in the face of such raw evil.

"Al Ana," Aedan said again, his voice sounding a little braver. They stood there frozen, four against the abyss, scared under the weight of her radiating eyes.

"Dah-dah-demon," Tim stuttered, stepping forward, still the protector but his knees shaking with fear.

"Ohhhh..." Lindsey added, her stance trembling.

"Go away!" Mary yelled, her voice brimming with nervousness-fueled horror.

Aedan drew a deep breath, tasting the electric charge of the moment. This was where their paths had led them, where the stories would be told of four friends who stood together when the shadow loomed largest. Aedan felt the pulse of the river beneath him, determined to guide them.

"Ready?" Aedan asked, though it was more a confirmation than a question. They nodded, and together, they stepped into destiny's light, their eyes never leaving the dark form of Al Ana. The battle for Cheboygan was upon them, or at least it seemed to be.

"*You dare come to me! I will take your souls. Who among you will step forward first?*" Al Ana's red hat adorned with a fern twig stood out against the blackness that consumed her. She floated forward toward the middle of the river. The water's current stopped flowing.

"You will never take my soul, demon!" Aedan shouted bravely as he stepped backward.

"*Ah, a brave one. But your efforts are worthless, you are weak. Your soul is mine, whether you like it or not,*" Al Ana replied as her dark arms reached out as if to grab them.

"We will not let you take us without—" Lindsey got cut off as she stepped backward to meet Aedan.

"*You fools underestimate my power. Your souls are already slipping away from you,*" Al Ana said as she let out a horrible laugh that echoed. Suddenly, a loud, disembodied voice cried "*Watch your back*" from behind the four friends and it got their immediate attention. All four turned to see where the voice came from, but when they turned back to face the demon, she was gone.

"Where did she go?" Aedan shouted, his voice brimming with adrenaline-fueled excitement.

"She's gone!" Tim exclaimed, his tone equally electrified but confused.

"Ran away!" Mary said with a nervous chuckle, as if she'd witnessed something hilarious.

"Wow! She vanished!" Lindsey chimed in enthusiastically.

"Let's get out of here, NOW!" Aedan shouted urgently, his voice laced with panic as he whirled around and bolted, not daring to waste another second.

"Right behind you!" Lindsey cried, her footsteps pounding the earth as she raced after him.

Tim and Mary followed suit, their hearts pounding, adrenaline surging as they fled the woods with desperate haste, driven by imminent danger.

* * *

The frantic sprint down the street toward Aedan's vacant home filled them with hope. His parents were away on vacation, visiting Eddie's family in Traverse City, and the house stood empty, safe. Aedan and Tim raced ahead, their footsteps echoing with urgency, while the girls trailed behind. Suddenly, Mary stumbled over her feet and fell, and her cry of pain pierced the air, her voice laced with distress and pain. "Ouch!" she shouted, prompting Lindsey to stop and offer aid to her fallen friend.

"Mary your knee is bleeding," Lindsey said, concerned, as she helped Mary up to her feet.

Aedan and Tim, realizing the commotion, turned back, their faces etched with fear for their friend as they rushed to help Mary up. "We gotta go now," Aedan shouted, adrenaline pumping through his body as if the demon were chasing them down the street.

They hurried toward Aedan's house, the urgency of the situation weighing heavily upon them. Al Ana's presence was still fresh in their minds. The sight of Mary's injury only added to the tension. As they entered the vacant home, the eerie silence that encircled them made them more scared. They walked into the house and Aedan found himself glancing over his shoulder, half expecting some unseen threat to emerge from the blackness in the hallway.

The encounter with the demonic entity had left them shaken to the core. Aedan rushed all over the house turning the lights on. They made their way to the kitchen, seeking solace in the familiarity of Aedan's home. "I'm hungry," Aedan said as he rummaged through the fridge, retrieving a box of leftover pizza.

"Me too," Tim said sitting down next to Aedan at the table.

Mary and Lindsey joined them, silently devouring the slices, their minds still reeling from the night's events.

Lindsey's trembling voice pierced the air, her eyes wide with fear as she clutched the leftover pizza. "I'm scared."

Aedan looked over to meet her eyes, his own burning with a fierce determination to shield her from harm. "It'll be okay, Lin," he vowed, his words a searing promise that she would be safe in his embrace. Lindsey's fingers intertwined with Aedan's, their shared look of gratitude igniting a blaze of unspoken romance.

Mary and Tim watched, transfixed, as the lovers' hands entwined. Mary's hand reached out, yearning for Tim's touch, her heart pounding with a burning desire. Tim's eyes met hers, and in that moment, he rose, his movements fueled by a primal need to protect his beloved.

"Don't worry, Mary, I'll protect you," he declared, his voice a rumbling vow that resonated deep within her core. He hugged her in a searing embrace, and Mary melted into his arms, whispering, "Thank you," her words infused with hope that this evil would soon pass.

Tim returned to his seat, his fingers curling around the last slice of pizza, a symbol of their shared hunger for life, love, and the promise of tomorrow.

The absence of Aedan's parents provided solitude, allowing them to process their thoughts without interruption. As the last slice of pizza disappeared, a heavy silence fell upon the group. Exhaustion soon took over, and one by one, they drifted off into an uneasy slumber, their heads resting on the kitchen table.

The weight of their experience had exhausted them, and they found themselves seeking refuge in the realm of dreams.

14

Small-Town Sheriff

The next day a sudden and unexpected incident occurred in the late afternoon, when a pigeon collided with the kitchen window, abruptly disrupting the restless slumber of the four friends sleeping at the kitchen table. Despite the absence of any verbal exchange, comprehension transpired among them, a tacit recognition of the shared experience that had united them the previous night. They knew they needed to report the harrowing encounter to the authorities.

Gathering their strength, they set out for the sheriff's office, determined to shed light on the darkness they had faced and seek answers to the unanswered questions that plagued their minds.

The sun's rays crept through the blinds, casting a pale orangish glow on the floor of Sheriff Ford's office. Ford's inquisitive eyes studied them, and they all knew he felt their disquiet.

"Afternoon, kids," he greeted, leaning back in his chair. "You look like you've had a rough night."

"That's putting it mildly, Sheriff," replied Aedan, his voice shaking with barely suppressed emotion. "Sheriff Ford, I need to tell you about something that happened to us yesterday at the river," he said with seriousness as he sat down on a chair across from the sheriff's desk.

"Go on, Aedan. What happened?" Sheriff Ford said, leaning forward on his desk.

"We found Al Ana, the demon, at the river yesterday. She had this chilling laughter, and her appearance was deceptively evil, with a darkness that filled in around her," Aedan said, speaking fast, nervously living the moment again.

Sheriff Ford listened intently, his expression turning grave as he absorbed the startling revelation. "Al Ana," he mumbled under his breath, fingers tapping on the worn surface of his desk.

Suddenly, the sheriff's face turned distant as he seemed to be grappling with a buried memory. "Bill," pleaded Aedan, "we need your help." He got up and leaned over the sprawl of maps and some scribbled notes. "Patterns," Aedan muttered, tracing lines between points on the map that marked the demon's appearances. "She's not random; she's strategic."

"Like a predator stalking its prey," Lindsey added, her stare flitting across the documents strewn about the desk. "We need to think like her, anticipate her moves."

"We also need to be unpredictable," Tim interjected, his eyebrows knitted in concentration. "Keep her off-balance."

Ford got up and stood by the window, watching the emptiness in the streets.

"Unpredictable, yes, but informed," he said, turning to face them. "I've been secretly tracking her movements for years. She has weak-nesses, like any creature of flesh and blood."

"Or shadow and malice," Mary corrected, a wry edge to her voice.

"Exactly," Ford agreed, sitting back down and pulling out a folder from his desk drawer filled with grainy photographs and handwritten notes. "She's clever and knows how to blend in, to become one with the darkness, but she leaves traces—patterns in her wake. We just have to know where to look."

Lindsey reached for the folder, her fingers brushing over the images of twisted demonic symbols and eerie photographs from people taking pictures of her sightings. "What kind of traces?" she asked, her voice steady despite the chill that ran down her spine.

"Disruptions in nature, for one," Ford explained, pointing to a photo of a circle of dead grass. "Where she walks, life withers. And then there are the demonic symbols and sigils: painted symbols considered to have magical powers. They're not just random marks; they're warnings, pacts, sources of her power," Sheriff Ford explained.

"Can we use them against her?" Tim asked, leaning in closer behind Aedan.

"Perhaps," Ford said. "But we must tread carefully. This is old evil, steeped in danger."

"Then our first step is clear," Aedan announced, standing up straighter. "We gather what we know, find the connections, and turn her strengths into faults."

"Knowledge is our weapon," Mary affirmed, her decision was unswayable.

"And secrecy our shield," Tim added, eyeing the door as if expecting the demon to burst through at any moment.

"Remember," Ford cautioned, his eyes dark with memories of past encounters, "Al Ana is a master of deception. She'll try to twist your mind, make you doubt your eyes, your ears...even your heart. Stay vigilant. Trust in each other."

"Trust," Aedan echoed, the word hanging heavy in the air. It was their bond, their pact against the creeping darkness that threatened their town.

"Let's start compiling everything we've got," Lindsey suggested, her hands already moving to organize the cluttered evidence.

"Agreed," Ford said. "Today, we build our arsenal. Tomorrow, we stand together against Al Ana. This is our town, our home!"

"We have an idea how to defeat her," Aedan concluded, a firm determination settling on his face as he joined Lindsey at the table, ready to forge their plan from the fragments of fear and hope that lay scattered before them. Aedan brushed a hand through his curly hair, the strands knotting between his fingers as he paced Sheriff Ford's office. "We're not just dealing with a ghost story," he said, voice tinged with a mix of excitement and trepidation. "This is real, and it's way bigger than us."

"Exactly," Mary chimed in, her petite frame taut like a bowstring. She glanced at Tim, who nodded in silent agreement.

"People could get hurt, Aedan. We could get hurt." Lindsey's brown eyes flickered to Sheriff Ford, seeking some semblance of reassurance.

Tim let out a long breath like he was trying to calm his nerves. He planted his hands on his hips, his stance wide. "And what about Cheboygan? If Al Ana's as bad as we think, the whole towns in danger."

Sheriff Ford, leaning against his desk, surveyed the group with a grave expression. The lines on his face spoke of countless nights wrestling with the secrets he'd kept and the criminals he'd faced alone. "Your fears are warranted," he acknowledged, his voice a steady undercurrent in the storm of their anxiety. "But fear can be a compass—it points us toward what we must confront." He stepped forward, a gesture that pulled their attention like a magnet. "You four have shown more courage than most adults could muster. Your unity, your determination, it's crucial now. You've got each other, and you've got me." A small smile cracked his stoic demeanor, offering them a glimmer of solidarity.

"Let's make a promise here and now," Aedan declared, stopping his pacing to stand before the sheriff. His blue eyes met Ford's, reflecting an unspoken vow. "We share everything—no secrets, no going off on our own. We face this together."

"Agreed," Lindsey said, stepping closer to link her arm with Aedan's.

"We support each other. No matter what Al Ana throws at us."

"Nothing breaks this pact," Tim added, completing the circle as he placed a heavy hand on both Aedan and Ford's shoulders.

"For Cheboygan," Mary said.

"For all of us," Sheriff Ford echoed, placing his hand atop theirs, sealing their pledge with the weight of his words. "Starting now, we fight as one."

They left the office as the once familiar streets now held a new purpose. With every step toward downtown, their resolve deepened, a chorus of silent promises echoing with each heartbeat.

"Ready?" Aedan asked, his voice sounding purposeful as they reached the threshold.

"Ready," Lindsey, Mary, Sheriff Ford, and Tim affirmed, and together, they stepped into the bond of their pact, a beacon against the encroaching, lurking evil.

* * *

Aedan, Sheriff Ford, Tim, Lindsey, and Mary moved in silence toward town. Ford led the way, his strides purposeful; he'd become more than just the sheriff tonight—he was their anchor in the storm that was coming. "Keep your eyes sharp," Sheriff Ford said as they traversed the quiet streets of Cheboygan. The words hung in the air, a reminder that Al Ana could be lurking in any shadow.

It was an unusual occurrence that caught the attention of the group. Despite the bright daylight, the streetlamps along the sidewalk in the town were illuminating one by one. "That's strange," Aedan said, looking up at a strange lighting.

"Yeah, I agree," Sheriff Ford said, gazing down the rest of the sidewalk at the other streetlamps lighting up.

"Strange," Lindsey said.

"It's broad daylight, can no one else see this?" Tim asked.

"There's no one around at all," Mary said as she looked around at the empty town.

As the group stood there, trying to understand the situation, a faint humming noise began to emanate from the lamps themselves. It was a low, almost inaudible vibration that seemed to grow louder with each passing second. Aedan instinctively took a step back, his eyes narrowing as he scanned the surroundings for any potential danger.

Sheriff Ford's hand hovered near his holster, his years of experience telling him that something wasn't quite right. Lindsey clutched Aedan's arm, her eyes darting from one lamp to the next as if expecting them to come alive at any moment. Mary, ever the pragmatic one, grabbed Tim's hand in fear and shouted, "Let's get out of here."

Just as they were about to turn and leave, a sudden burst of energy crackled through the air, causing the lamps to flicker and dim momentarily. The humming grew louder, almost deafening, and then, without warning, a blinding flash of light engulfed the entire street, forcing them to shield their eyes. When the light subsided, and they cautiously opened their eyes, the sight before them was nothing short of astonishing...

"Every corner feels like it's watching us," Lindsey said as her eyes darted to the darkened alleys they passed.

"Let it watch," Aedan replied, trying to sound braver than he felt. "We're not the ones who should be afraid."

Tim grunted his agreement, but his hand rested on the bottle of holy water at his belt—a silent testament to the fear they all shared.

As they turned onto Main Street, the wind picked up, sending a shiver down all their spines. Was it just the cool breeze, or something more sinister they thought? It felt as if the very essence of Cheboygan had changed, as though the town itself was holding its breath, awaiting the inevitable clash.

"We have to hunt her," Ford said, stopping to face them under the halo of a streetlamp. "We'll meet at dawn. No second-guessing, no hesitation. We find the demon and we end this curse."

"Agreed," Aedan replied. Lindsey, Tim, and Mary kneeled beside him, their expressions concerned. They started to part ways when a prickle of fear tickled the back of Aedan's neck. It was an instinct that something was out of place. Aedan glanced over his shoulder, peering into the darkness beyond the reach of the streetlights in an alleyway.

There, nestled between the shadows, Aedan caught the briefest glimpse of something—or someone—watching them. Two glowing embers seemed to float in the black, an evil look that knew too much. It vanished as quickly as it appeared, leaving Aedan questioning whether he'd seen anything. "Did you—" Aedan began, but the words tangled in his throat.

"See it?" Tim finished for Aedan, his eyes narrowed as he scanned the darkness. "Al Ana..." Lindsey breathed, her voice barely audible.

"What was it?" Mary said, confused as she looked around.

Ford's hand dropped to the gun at his hip, a small but definitive movement. "She's watching us. That means we're doing something right."

"Or that she's readying her next move," Aedan countered, unable to shake the chill from his bones.

"Then we'll be ready for her," Ford said with a conviction that supported their flagging spirits.

A shudder ran down Aedan's spine as the gravity of the situation settled upon them. The alleyway's shadows now seemed to conceal untold dangers, lurking threats that could strike any moment. Aedan exchanged a wordless glance with the group, their faces etched with the same apprehension that gnawed at his gut. They were no longer hunters, but the hunted, their every step dogged by the ghost of Al Ana's malice. Despite the fear coiling within him, Aedan hardened his nerves.

Aedan couldn't help but let out a nervous chuckle, breaking the tense silence. "Well, this certainly puts a damper on our plans for a leisurely afternoon stroll," he quipped, trying to lighten the mood. Lindsey shot him an unamused glare, clearly not appreciating his attempt at humor in their dire situation. Aedan held his hands in mock surrender, his lips twitching into a wry grin. "What?" A little fun never hurt anyone," he said with a shrug. "Besides, if we're going to be hunted by some nefarious foe, we might as well enjoy the thrill of the chase."

The others exchanged exasperated looks, but Aedan could see the faint glimmer of amusement in their eyes. They knew his jokes were merely a coping mechanism to mask the fear that threatened to consume them all. With a dramatic flourish, Aedan whipped out his trusty cell phone, striking a heroic pose.

"Great time for a selfie," Mary said sarcastically.

The group shuffled along the deserted sidewalk, an eerie silence hanging in the air. The sheriff's eyes darted from one darkened storefront to the next, his grip tightening on his weapon. Aedan, Tim, Mary, and Lindsey huddled close together, their faces etched with fear and uncertainty. They passed a vacant ice cream shop, its once inviting neon sign now a haunting reminder of better times. The hardware store's bay window seemed to mock them, its empty shelves a testament to the chaos that had consumed their once thriving town.

The sheriff's frustration mounted with every step, his patience wearing thin over not being able to find any signs of the demon. "I think it's time to go home, I've had enough of this day," he growled, his tone tinged with irritation that barely concealed the desperation they all felt. The weight of the unknown bore down upon them, each footstep echoing the unspoken question that lingered in their minds: Where was the demon, and when would it strike next? The group pressed on, their determination fueled by the fear that gripped their hearts. They all took the sheriff's advice and went home.

As the day ended, four friends, four lives, each with their unique challenges and battles, entered their respective homes, where the dramas of life unfolded behind closed doors.

At Tim's house, the air was thick with tension. He hesitated at the front door, bracing himself for the confrontation that awaited with his mother. As he stepped inside, the sound of raised voices echoed through the hallway. "I MISS...DAD..." Tim's sister yelled at their mom. "I know it's not fair, sweetie. Dad was taken from us too soon," Tim's mom replied compassionately. "I know you're struggling with that right now, it's okay, honey." His mom and sister were engaged in another heated grieving session, their words laced with bitterness and resentment.

Across town, Lindsey's home offered a stark contrast to Tim's. The aroma of freshly baked cookies wafted through the cozy living room where her mother sat, a soothing smile on her face. Lindsey embraced the warmth and tranquility, a welcome respite from the chaos of the day. She sat down across from her mom and stared, knowing in her heart that with perseverance and a little luck, she could weather this storm, just as she had weathered others before.

Across town, Mary's footsteps echoed on the empty driveway as she approached her house, the silence enveloping her like a heavy cloak. The curtains were shut, and the porch light remained off, a reminder of the loneliness that awaited her behind those walls. With a deep breath, she turned the key, bracing herself for another night spent in desolation. As Mary stepped inside, the stillness was almost deafening, amplifying the thoughts swirling in her mind. She couldn't help but wonder if this was how her life would always be—a constant battle against the weight of solitude. Yet, somewhere deep within, a flicker of hope burned, reminding her that even the darkest nights eventually give way to dawn.

15

The Possessed Girl

Al Ana

"Sheriff's office!" Sheriff Ford said excitedly into the phone.

"I need help now!" a chilling woman's voice demanded, dripping with panic. "What's the emergency?" the sheriff shot back, with a sharp tone.

"I'm being attacked by a suspicious-looking man in a hoodie!" she cried, her words were laced with desperation and fear.

"What's your location?" the sheriff asked as he looked down at the caller ID displaying an unknown location.

Fear gripped the sheriff as the eerie, paranormal voice crackled through the line. "I'm at the mall," she uttered, her words devoid of human emotion as she hung up. The sheriff's instincts were on high alert now—this disembodied voice bore a gloomy resemblance to a spectral entity.

Despite feeling skeptical about the mysterious nature of the call, the sheriff decided that it was important for him to investigate the situation further. "Hey, Aedan, it's Sheriff Ford. I just got a strange call from a woman in distress who sounded more like a frightened ghost than a normal human. I'm going to check on the call, so it will take me a little while to get there," the sheriff explained as he got into the police car, his tone conveying worried feelings about the distressing call.

Aedan, at home and focused on his game console, never looked up. "Okay, Sheriff," he replied with a nod. He was playing his game with a level of focus a surgeon uses during surgery.

Meanwhile, Lindsey and Mary were hanging out on the couch at Lindsey's house, flipping channels on the television when Aedan called. "Hey, Lin, the sheriff got called away to investigate a strange report. He won't be able to come over for a while," he said, relaying the message.

Lindsey brightened up at the prospect of adjusting their plans, not ready to go demon hunting again. "Alright, then, we'll make the best of it and head up to the mall while we wait for the sheriff to finish up," she suggested.

Mary was lost in the television programming guide and nodded in agreement, content to go along with whatever plan Lindsey decided on.

"Your shoes on yet?" Lindsey hollered, her impatience noticeable.

Mary, ever the lingerer, responded with a cheeky grin. "Keep your pants on, I'm ready!" Retail therapy awaited, and these two were about to paint the town...well, at least the shopping district.

Lindsey and Mary decided to walk to the mall, which was only a few blocks away from Lindsey's house. "I wonder where everyone's at," Lindsey said as she noticed there was nobody outside.

"The streets are empty," Mary replied, looking around, just as concerned.

As the mall came into view they noticed an empty parking lot. The once bustling Riverside Mall was now a haunting reminder of its former glory. As they entered the mall they saw corridors that echoed with an eerie silence, with just a few emotionless human shoppers, devoid of the lively chatter and footsteps that once filled the space. Vacant storefronts lined the walkways, their windows darkened like soulless eyes staring back at the few remaining souls wandering aimlessly.

Two women dressed in jogging outfits walked in a slow shuffling motion past Lindsey and Mary, their faces were empty of any expression, as if life had been drained from them. Their movements were slow and very mechanical, akin to the undead trapped in an endless loop.

Overhead lights flickered, casting an ominous ambiance, adding to the surreal and strange atmosphere. At a solitary perfume kiosk adorned with nothing in the protective glass cases, an attendant stood motionless, dressed in a dirty work uniform, with a vacant stare in his eyes as drool trickled down his chin. "What's happening?" Mary said with a concerned look on her face. "Yeah, it's weird. Maybe the demon?" Lindsey questioned, glancing around as they walked carefully, looking around at their surroundings. "I think so," Mary replied, shrugging in disbelief.

As they ventured deeper into the darkness of the mall, shadows danced menacingly along the walls, creating an atmosphere of terror. The air grew colder, and disembodied voices echoed around them, making their skin prickle with discomposure. *"Soul...your souls...give,"* the voices chanted repeatedly.

Outside, the sheriff arrived at the parking lot, ready to investigate the situation where the strange phone call was placed. Driving around, he noticed something odd near an old payphone sitting all alone in the corner of the parking lot, next to random plant life covering it. The sheriff drove up to the payphone, looked around, and noticed no woman present, leaving the circumstances shrouded in uncertainty and curiosity.

Sheriff Ford put the squad car in park and got out to investigate the area. He noticed a few discarded items scattered on the ground near a parking block next to a lamppost by the payphone—a crumpled tissue, an overturned purse, and what appeared to be a broken cell phone. The clues raised more questions than answers, hinting at a potential altercation.

Undeterred, the sheriff started canvassing the surrounding area, looking for any bystanders or witnesses who might have noticed any suspicious activity, but there were none. After thoroughly searching the area and finding no conclusive evidence, the sheriff proceeded into the mall to locate the security guard's office.

Upon entering the mall through a main entrance, the sheriff noticed the flickering lights and eerie emptiness inside, prompting him to take immediate caution.

He walked to the security guard's office with his hand on his gun, hoping to review the footage from the mall's cameras and piece together a clearer picture of the events leading up to the mysterious phone call.

"Hello, anyone here?" The sheriff's voice echoed with a tinge of unease as he knocked on the security guard's door. "Hello," he repeated, peeking his head inside the room, his eyebrow furrowed with concern.

"Sheriff, what can I help you with?" the security guard said as he emerged from around the corner, his sudden appearance startling the sheriff.

"Where's everyone at?" the sheriff inquired, his tone laced with worry as he scanned the seemingly deserted office.

"Everyone?" the security guard responded. "The shoppers," the sheriff said.

"Same as everywhere else, this whole town is plagued," the security guard replied sarcastically.

"I can see that," the sheriff said with his own style of sarcasm.

"The demon has its grips on this whole town, Sheriff," the security guard fired back. "Listen, I got a call from a woman saying she was being mugged in your parking lot, but when I arrived, there was nobody there, just a crumpled tissue, an overturned purse, and what appeared to be a broken cell phone next to the old payphone," the sheriff explained.

"That's strange," the security guard said as he sat down in front of a TV monitor. "Do you have security footage from outside in that parking lot?" the sheriff asked pointing to the general direction of the parking lot.

"I think so, let me check," the security guard replied as he started clicking on the computer monitor.

"You think so, huh," the sheriff said, shrugging as he watched the security guard's actions. The guard and the sheriff meticulously examined the security footage. They noticed a hooded figure lurking near the mall's entrance around the time the phone call was made. The individual appeared to be carrying a small device, potentially a burner phone used to make the anonymous call.

Determined to identify the person of interest, the sheriff enhanced the footage, zooming in on the individual's face as it briefly glanced up toward one of the cameras on the mall building. Although the image was grainy, it was clear who it was: Al Ana.

The fluorescent lights buzzed overhead as Lindsey and Mary traversed the almost empty mall. "Check out that sale at Penelope's Boutique," Mary chirped, pointing toward the window display draped in vibrant summer dresses. Mary's short, spiky red hair bounced with each step, her freckles a constellation of happiness on her face.

As Lindsey and Mary continued to explore the eerily quiet mall, their footsteps reverberated through the empty corridors. Suddenly, they heard a faint chatter coming from a nearby lotion store. Curiosity piqued, they cautiously approached the source of the mysterious sound.

Amidst the desolation, a single beacon of normalcy remained—Penelope's Boutique.

Inside, a woman sat behind the cash register, obnoxiously chewing her bubblegum, seemingly oblivious to the eerie surroundings. Her presence was a stark contrast to the lifeless figures that roamed the mall, a glimmer of hope that perhaps not all was lost in this decaying establishment.

"Mary, you're unstoppable," Lindsey said with a chuckle, her eyes bright with amusement. "Just how many dresses do you need?"

"Need is such a limiting word," Mary replied, grinning ear to ear as she made her way from rack to rack. She approached the counter where the woman was chewing her gum, creating a symphony of smacks and pops. "Can I try these on?" Mary inquired, her voice nearly drowned out by the woman's impressive bubble-blowing skills.

"It's open," the woman replied without looking up, as if stating the obvious was the pinnacle of customer service.

Mary turned to Lindsey, who was engrossed in a rack of shirts, and announced with a dramatic flair, "I'll be right back, Lin!" as if embarking on a perilous journey into the depths of the fitting room, where the true test of fashion awaited.

After trying on a few outfits and goofing around in front of the mirror, nature called. "Lindsey, hold my clothes? I'll be right back," Mary said as she left the fitting room, playfully doing the pee dance.

"Sure thing," Lindsey said as she thumbed through a rack of dresses.

Mary made her way to the restroom, the click of her shoes on the tiled floor echoing in the semi-deserted corridor. Inside, the stark white of the restroom felt sterile and cold. As Mary washed her hands, staring at her reflection, she felt someone else's presence. A shadow flickered behind her.

"Mary?" The voice was achingly familiar, heavy with emotion.

Mary whipped around, her heart stuttering. It couldn't be—yet there he stood, her father as she remembered him before a sudden and strange illness took him away, possibly at the hands of Al Ana. Same gentle eyes, the same warm smile that had comforted her through every scraped knee and broken dream.

"Dad?" Mary's voice trembled, logic warring with longing. "How is this possible?" "Shh, Mary. It's okay, sweetheart. I'm here for you." He stepped closer, his hand reaching out as if to brush away the tears that welled in her eyes.

But something gnawed at the back of her mind—a warning, an instinctual tug reminding her of the lurking evil they'd faced. Al Ana. Could this be another of her tricks?

"Mary, don't you miss me?" His voice cracked, and her resolve wavered.

"Of course I miss you, Dad." Mary's voice was low, her defenses crumbling. He looked so real, so *him*. Would it be so wrong to pretend, just for a moment, that he was truly here? He smiled, and it was like sunshine breaking through clouds. "Come here, Mary. Let me look at you."

Mary stepped forward, yearning and suspicion waging war within her. But love—love was a powerful force, and it nudged Mary ever closer to the ghost of her father. If only she could touch him, make sure he was real... "Mary, are you okay in there?" Lindsey's voice filtered through the door, distant but insistent.

"Y-yeah! I'll be right out!" Mary called back, but her focus never left the figure before her. This was her dad, wasn't it? It had to be. The mall, the normalcy of shopping, it all faded away, leaving just the two of them in a bubble of longing and impossible hope.

"Come closer," the figure commanded. Each step Mary took felt like sinking deeper into quicksand, but she was powerless to stop. Lindsey's voice, once a lifeline, now faded into the background.

"Mary?" she called again, her tone spiked with concern.

"Give me a second, Lin," Mary said, her voice sounding distant to her ears.

Something wasn't right. Her dad's eyes, once a warm, familiar brown, now flickered with a supernatural fire that resembled Al Ana's darkness. Mary wanted to run, to scream for Lindsey, but her legs refused to obey. Instead, she found herself moving closer to the figure, drawn by a force beyond her understanding.

"Who are you?" The question slipped from Mary's lips, even as part of her didn't want to know the answer. "Your father, Mary," he replied, his smile twisting into something cruel. "But you already knew that, didn't you?"

Laughter echoed off the tiled walls, chilling and hollow, and in a flash of clarity, Mary knew this was no loving reunion. This was Al Ana's deception—a trap cloaked in a dead man's face. "Get away from me!" Mary finally shrieked, stumbling backward. But it was too late; his— or its—fingers brushed against her forehead, searing like ice.

Mary's soul transcended into the physical form of her father's figure. As she was about to collapse, the demonic entity swiftly possessed her, causing her eyes to turn a glowing, ominous shade of red. This paranormal event signified a sinister transformation within Mary's being.

"*Mine,*" the demon shouted, and Mary's world spun.

Mary burst out of the bathroom, gasping for air, her heart trying to beat itself out of her chest. A woman in a zombified state turned to stare as Mary shoved past her, as if the lifeless woman knew her leader, the demon, was present.

Lindsey's heart raced as she witnessed the upsetting sight of Mary's eyes glowing an eerie shade of red, a chilling indication that something sinister might have taken possession of her friend. Trepidation washed over her, leaving her deeply troubled and fearing the worst.

Mary's mind was no longer her own—thoughts fragmented, emotions amplified to extremes she couldn't contain.

"Mary, wait up!" Lindsey's voice was a lifeline Mary could no longer grasp.

The sheriff and the mall security guard grew concerned as they heard the commotion outside of the office, so they got up, grabbed a pair of walkie-talkies to keep in touch, and spotted Mary sprinting toward the outside door. Their hearts raced and anxiety settled in the pits of their stomachs. The sheriff and security guard hurried after her, but the guard hesitated at the entrance, watching the unfolding event with fear as the sheriff continued running after her. *What could have caused such a frantic reaction?* the sheriff thought. His mind raced with worries about potential dangers or threats lurking beyond those doors as he ran to his patrol car.

Outside, the sky loomed gray and ominous, as if reflecting the storm inside Mary. She could feel Al Ana curling around her soul like smoke, her malice sinking into every pore. Panic surged, propelling her forward without direction or purpose.

"Mary, stop!" Lindsey yelled but it barely registered.

The world narrowed to a tunnel, sounds muffled, colors bleeding together. Mary's feet carried her away from the mall, away from safety, toward the busy street. Cars honked, tires screeched, but nothing made sense anymore. "Mary, look out!" Lindsey shouted.

The warning came too late. A semi-truck barreled toward her, massive and unstoppable.

For a moment, Mary stood frozen, caught in the headlights like some terrified deer.

Just as the unthinkable seemed inevitable, a breathtaking angelic figure emerged, her golden hair flowing and radiant white wings unfurled. This heavenly woman reached out, pulling Mary back from the brink of disaster, narrowly preventing an unimaginable tragedy. Lindsey's heart raced with relief, but she couldn't shake the haunting thought of how close she came to losing her friend forever.

The truck roared past, missing Mary by inches. She collapsed to the ground, shaking, tears streaming down her cheeks.

What had Mary done? Was this madness what surrendering to Al Ana meant? Lindsey wondered.

"Mary!" Lindsey screamed, reaching Mary at last, her arms wrapping around her in a fierce embrace as Mary dropped to a sitting position on the ground. "What's happening to you?"

"I don't know." Mary's voice broke into a lifeless tone. "I'm scared, Lin. I'm so, so scared."

Lindsey's heart hammered against her rib cage, a frantic drumbeat in the chaos. The semi-truck horn bellowed a warning that faded into a distant echo as Mary stumbled back from the edge of death. Lindsey clung to Mary, her fingers digging into Mary's arms, grounding her to the spot. Sitting down on the ground and holding Mary in her arms, Lindsey watched in awe as the angelic woman soared upward, her wings flapping with an electrifying burst of energy, her radiant form enveloped in dazzling white light as she ascended triumphantly back to the heavenly realms.

Lindsey could barely breathe, the air too thick, too heavy with the stench of burning rubber and her fear. "Stay with me, Mary," Lindsey pleaded, her voice cracking with emotion as the security guard watched from the mall's entrance.

The demon suddenly departed from Mary's body as a sinister dark shadow with eerie glowing eyes in a deep crimson color. It lurched menacingly toward the bushes to hide.

But another voice cut through the uproar, authoritative and sharp with concern. "What in the world—?"

Sheriff Bill Ford pulled up in his patrol car, his eyes wide with alarm as he witnessed what just happened: Mary, shaking uncontrollably on the asphalt, and Lindsey, pale as a ghost, trying to hold it together.

"Mary Thompson?" Sheriff Ford approached in a hurry, but cautiously, as if she were a wild animal that might bolt. Ford knelt beside Mary, his eyes probing. "Can you tell me what happened?"

Mary opened her mouth to speak, but no words came out—only a ragged sob. Her mind was a whirlpool, sucking down memories, thoughts, and emotions into its dark center. She couldn't form the sentences needed to explain the terror that had gripped her, the invisible force that had almost marched her into oblivion.

"Come on, let's get you off the street," Sheriff Ford said, his tone gentle but firm. His strong hands helped Mary to her feet, steadying her when the ground seemed to tilt beneath her sneakers.

"Is she going to be, okay?" Lindsey said, her voice holding a note of desperation, her hand still clutching Mary's.

"I'm going to take her to get some help at the sanatorium, and you shouldn't stay here alone. It's not safe," the sheriff replied, glancing between them. "Neither of you are not safe like this."

"Sanatorium?" The word hitched in Mary's throat, a new wave of panic cresting within her. But somehow, Lindsey knew he was right. Mary wasn't safe—not to herself, not to anyone and it was certainly not safe for her to stay there alone either.

"I'm calling my friend, I can't go with you to the sanatorium," Lindsey responded to the sheriff with anxiety.

"You can't stay here alone?" the sheriff demanded.

"Well, I'm calling my friend to come get me and I'm not going to the sanatorium," Lindsey replied firmly, yet with apprehension.

"Then I'm calling the security guard to keep an eye on you until your friends get here," the sheriff said in an authoritative tone. He looked up to see the security guard standing by the mall door. "I need you to come over here to watch Lindsey because I have to take her friend to the hospital," he said over the walkie-talkie.

"Okay I'm on the way," the security guard replied, and he started walking toward Lindsey. "Mary, listen to me." Sheriff Ford's eyes locked onto hers, searching for a flicker of understanding. "You're in a bad way right now and you need to go to the hospital to get help. We need to make sure you're protected until we can figure out what's going on."

Lindsey wanted to protest, to insist Mary was fine, but the lie wouldn't come. Lindsey knew something was wrong with her best friend, something a night at home or a pep talk wouldn't fix. So she nodded, surrendering to the truth in his words.

"Okay, take her to get help," Lindsey agreed, the weight of Mary's situation settling over her like a shroud.

"Let's go." The sheriff offered a small, reassuring smile before guiding Mary to the backseat of his cruiser.

As they pulled away from the mall, Mary turned her head, catching a glimpse of Lindsey standing on the side of the road talking on her phone, her figure growing smaller in the distance, a sentinel of their shattered normality.

The demon, seeing an opportunity, flew over to the security guard, who was walking toward Lindsey, and swiftly possessed him in a disturbing display of convulsions, which went unnoticed.

The security guard's possessed state, his body now a mere vessel for the dark force, cast a pall of angst as he stood in place, his eyes glowing yellow.

Lindsey was unaware that danger was looming toward her. The possessed security guard spotted the sheriff's patrol car departing, prompting him to take immediate and alarming action. Lindsey, engrossed in her phone ringing, stood exposed on the roadside when she looked up to see the security guard charging toward her with unnatural movements, superhuman-like speed, and ferocity. Terror gripped Lindsey, and she unleashed a piercing scream, her voice echoing the urgency of the perilous situation unfolding before her eyes.

Aedan and Tim were still engrossed in their video game session when Aedan's phone suddenly rang. Aedan snatched it up, Tim's eyes on him, his expression mirroring Aedan's concern. "Hello?"

"AHHHHHHH...AEDAN...HELP ME...AHHHHH...GET AWAY." Lindsey's voice was clipped, her words hurried as she breathed heavily, obviously running from something. "HE'S AFTER M-ME...IT'S MARY. SHE...SHERIFF FORD HAD TO TAKE HER..." The shrill tone pierced the virtual world, jolting them back to reality with an immediate urgency as Lindsey ran for her life down the side of the road.

"LINDSEY...LIN...WHAT'S WRONG...WHO'S AFTER YOU? TAKE HER? TAKE HER WHERE?" Aedan screamed as the questions caught in his throat and fear coiled tight in his stomach. "LIN...WHO'S CHASING YOU?"

Lindsey's frantic footsteps echoed on the pavement as she raced down the side of the road, clutching her cell phone tightly, her voice trembling with worry. Each breath was labored, her heart pounding with fear as she desperately tried to convey the urgency of the situation through the phone. The world around her seemed to blur, her sole focus on finding help before it was too late.

"THE sanatorium," Lindsey screamed.

Her heart pounded with panic as the security guard's footsteps grew closer, and her breath came in frantic gasps, fear gripping her as she realized she might not escape. The situation felt increasingly dire, and she couldn't help but worry about the consequences if she were caught.

Aedan and Tim scrambled to their feet, grabbing their jackets as they dashed out the door. "Where you at," Aedan said with seriousness as his face turned pale.

"OUTSIDE THE MALL," Lindsey yelled, still running in a sprint.

"I'll be over to pick you up," Aedan said sharply.

The two boys frantically leaped into Aedan's car, tires screeching as they sped off toward the mall in a desperate rush, every second counting against them.

The engine roared as he pushed the car to its limits. Tim sat in tense silence, his eyes fixed on the road ahead, bracing himself for the intense situation. Seeing an easier target, the possessed security guard stopped the chase and ran off into the gas station nearby. As they approached the mall, Aedan spotted Lindsey's familiar figure running hysterically alongside the road on the opposite side, but no one was chasing her. He slammed on the brakes, made a wheels-smoking U-turn, and caught up to Lindsey. He slammed the car into park and the boys leaped out of it, hearts pounding in their ears. Lindsey's face was streaked with tears, her body trembling uncontrollably.

"Tell us everything," Aedan demanded, his voice thick with emotion.

"THE sanatorium," she screamed. "SHE'S NOT HERSELF, Aedan," Lindsey yelled, still hyper from the chase.

"Who's chasing you, Lin?" Aedan asked, concerned, as he looked around and didn't see anyone.

"There's no one here, Lin," Tim said as he looked around with Aedan.

"The...the security...guard," Lindsey said, trying to catch her breath. "He was just here...I swear."

"We believe you," Aedan said compassionately.

"She walked into traffic—nearly got herself killed," Lindsey said, finally calming down yet still barely able to breathe.

Mary, the girl who lit up every dark corner with her laughter, confined within the cold walls of a sanatorium? It couldn't be true, Aedan thought.

"Tim," Aedan managed to choke out, turning to his friend. "We have to get to Mary.

Something's not right."

Their faces paled, the blood draining, as if Aedan had delivered a physical blow. The four of them were a unit; when one faltered, they all felt the tremor. Without a word, they knew what had to be done.

They scrambled to the car and Lindsey recounted the harrowing scene as they skidded away, each word like a dagger twisting in their hearts. "Mary, vibrant, beautiful Mary, has been consumed by a darkness I can't comprehend," Lindsey said.

Aedan's jaw tightened, his eyes burning with a fierce determination. "We're not losing her," he declared, his voice was resounding. "Not like this. Not ever."

Tim and Lindsey nodded in silent agreement, their bond forged in the fires of adversity. With renewed purpose, they sped down the road, their minds focused on a single goal: to rescue Mary from the depths of her despair.

16

Northern Woods Sanatorium

The drive to the sanatorium was a blur. All three friends were lost in their thoughts, consumed by panic. Those streets they'd traveled a thousand times before seemed alien now, twisted by the weight of their mission. When the imposing structure of the sanatorium came into view, it loomed as a harbinger of doom like never before, its windows staring blankly back at them.

"Okay, let's split up," Aedan suggested as they skidded to a halt in the parking lot. "We'll cover more ground that way."

"Right," Tim agreed, knowing his bravery wouldn't falter. He was the rock, the one who could always be counted on when the going got tough. And right now, things were as tough as they had ever been.

Lindsey nodded, her wide eyes shining with an unspoken fear that clung to her like the citizens of Salem, Massachusetts, during the Salem Witch trials. Yet beneath that, there was resolve, a fire that not even Al Ana could snuff out. "We'll find her, Aedan. We have to." "Let's move," Aedan said, and they charged through the front doors of the sanatorium, hearts pounding, ready to face whatever darkness awaited them inside.

Upon entering the sanatorium, Aedan, Tim, and Lindsey were immediately struck by the chaotic atmosphere that pervaded the corridors. The stark, institutional walls bore the scars of years gone by, the chipped paint and scuffed surfaces silent witnesses to countless stories. As they navigated the winding hallways, they encountered patients shuffling along, their movements sluggish and uncoordinated—a telltale sign of the powerful anti psychotic medication Thorazine coursing through their veins.

Some patients stared vacantly ahead, lost in their inner worlds, while others mumbled incoherently to themselves, their words a jumbled tapestry of fractured thoughts. The air was thick with the pungent aroma of disinfectant, mingling with the faint whiff of stale sweat and despair. The echoing footsteps and occasional outbursts from the patients created an eerie symphony that reverberated through the sanatorium's confines. In the common areas, patients could be seen engaging in various activities, from mindlessly rocking back and forth to bizarre, repetitive behaviors—coping mechanisms born out of their fragile mental states. They made their way to the reception area.

The sight of the receptionist, surrounded by towering stacks of files and countless papers strewn across her oversized desk, was unsettling. Her disheveled appearance, with a white overcoat around her shoulders and a nurse's hat perched atop her curly hair, gave her an eerie, witch-like demeanor.

The trio's heart raced as they approached her, the clutter and chaos giving them goosebumps. Her eyes, sunken and rimmed with dark circles, darted back and forth as if she was frantically searching for something amidst the disarray. Paranoia washed over them, and they couldn't shake the feeling that something wasn't quite right in that place. The receptionist's fingers trembled as she shuffled through the endless piles of paperwork, her movements erratic and frenzied. Lindsey cleared her throat, attempting to catch the receptionist's attention, but she seemed oblivious to Lindsey's presence, lost in her frantic world. The air felt thick with tension.

"Mary Thompson," Lindsey demanded to the receptionist, her voice echoing with more authority than she felt. "Where is she?"

"Family?" the woman behind the desk asked, peering at them suspiciously. "Close enough," Lindsey fired back. "Please, it's urgent."

She hesitated, then pointed down a poorly lit hallway. "Room 217. But you can't—" They didn't wait for permission. Room 217 called to them, the numbers etched in Aedan's brain as they sprinted down the corridor. With every step, the chilling grip of Al Ana seemed to tighten around the group's necks, a reminder of the battle they were ready for.

"Mary!" Lindsey cried out as they burst into the room, desperate to see her safe, to see her smile. But the bed was empty.

The silence of the room was an oppressive living thing—thick and suffocating. Tim stepped forward, his eyes scanning the pale walls for any sign of Mary. That's when Tim heard it—soft voices, which slithered through the air like a serpent seeking prey.

"Over there," Tim shouted, pointing to a window in a secluded corner shrouded in shadows.

They moved, their hearts pounding with a nervousness impossible to ignore. Then, like a phantom rising from the depths of despair, they all saw her—Mary, and she was outside. She was slumped over in a wheelchair with a numb look, staring off into space, her spiky red hair now a lifeless curtain around her freckled face. Beside her sat another person they recognized, equally still, equally lost—the mysterious Susan Smith, her eyes empty, her presence hollow with vacant thoughts.

The trio of friends sprinted back through the dimly lit hallways, their footsteps echoing urgently as they raced outside to the concrete playground sandwiched between the towering buildings. Their hearts pounded in their chests as they burst through the exit doors, the cool night air hitting their flushed faces. Every shadow seemed to conceal a potential threat, and the eerie silence only heightened their alertness.

"Mary!" Lindsey's voice broke the outside stillness, a tremble hidden beneath her call.

She rushed to Mary's side, hands trembling as she lifted her chin. But the eyes that met Lindsey's were voids, drained of the humor and light that defined her friend Mary.

"Hey, hey, look at me," Lindsey pleaded, her voice cracking under the weight of her fear. "It's me, Lindsey, with Aedan and Tim...Mary. You're safe now."

But Mary didn't respond. She couldn't. The Mary they knew was submerged, drowning in whatever abyss Al Ana had cast her into.

"Al Ana," Tim growled, his fists curling tight like he was ready for a fight. "She did this."

A chill racked Lindsey's body. Tim was right. The air itself seemed corrupted, tainted with a stench of malevolence that could only belong to one being. Al Ana had left her mark here, a signature written in the vacant stares of her victims.

"Look at them," Aedan said, the horror of realization dawning on them. "She's never gonna be done with Cheboygan."

Lindsey's hand found Mary's, her grip ironclad, a lifeline amidst the encroaching darkness. They stood united, four best friends facing the resurgence of evil personified, knowing now more than ever that their fight against Al Ana was far from over. And their Mary...their Mary was now the battlefield.

"We have no time to waste! We must rush back inside and determine if that vile demon has infiltrated these walls," Lindsey urged, her voice brimming with a firm amount of courage.

"I'm with you, let's move!" Aedan declared, taking the lead as they ran back into the sanatorium's depths.

"You truly believe the demon is here?" Tim inquired, his tone laced with urgency. "We cannot afford to leave any stone unturned—Mary's fate hangs in the balance," Lindsey responded, her words cutting through the air like a knife, leaving no room for hesitation.

Lindsey paced the length of the dull, white-walled corridor outside Mary's room, each step a sharp echo against the outdated tiled floor. Her mind raced faster than her feet. They had seen the hollow look in Mary's eyes—a clear sign that Al Ana was tightening her grip on Cheboygan. It was a silent declaration of war, one they couldn't ignore.

"Aedan, Tim," Lindsey said, stopping abruptly as they leaned on the wall, "we can't wait for things to get worse. Al Ana...we have to defeat her."

"We know!" Tim's voice was a low rumble of sarcasm, his frame rigid with tension. "We need a plan. A real one," Lindsey replied softly, her usually bright face drawn and pale like she was suffering from major depression. "Mary wouldn't give up on us. We owe her the same."

"Right," Aedan agreed. The three of them huddled closer, their heads bowed like knights plotting in the shadow of a dragon's lair. "Al Ana thrives on deception and fear. We beat her at her own game."

"By doing what?" Lindsey asked, the quiver in her voice failing to give a true notion or impression of the steel in her spine.

"Knowledge is power," Aedan answered, glancing between them. "I've faced her before; we know her tricks. It's time we use that against her."

"Okay, so we set up a trap?" Tim suggested, his eyebrow furrowing as he considered the idea.

"More than that," Aedan countered. "A trap implies we're waiting for her to come to us. No, we need to go after her, draw her out."

"Into the open," Lindsey chimed in, nodding slowly. "Where she's sensitive."

"Exactly." Aedan felt the flicker of hope amidst paranoia, kindling into determination. "We'll need to protect ourselves, though. Holy water, Bible, anything that can weaken her or keep us safe."

"Got it," Tim said as he cracked his knuckles. "We make her think she's winning, let her believe we're scared and unprepared. Then, when she's gloating, we strike."

"Strike hard, strike fast, and never let up until she's gone for good," Lindsey added, fire lighting in her eyes.

Aedan nodded, feeling the weight of the lead detective settle on his shoulders. "We pool our strengths. Tim, you're the muscle. Lindsey, your quick thinking has saved our behinds more times than I can count. And me..." Aedan took a deep breath. "I'll be the bait."

"No way, Aedan!" Lindsey's protest was instant, fierce. "Too dangerous."

"Which is why Al Ana will expect it the least from me," Aedan replied. "We play this smart, guys. Every move is calculated. Every risk, measured."

"Alright," Tim conceded with a grim nod.

"Then it's settled." Aedan locked eyes with them both, finding an echo of his resolve shining back at him. "We start now. Let's end this nightmare. We bring our friend back home."

"Let's get to work," Tim said, his voice a rallying cry and with that, they broke their huddle, each of them moving with newfound purpose. Their plan had begun to take shape, a glimmer of light in the darkness.

"Let's explore the depths of this sanatorium, to uncover the truth about Al Ana's whereabouts!" Aedan exclaimed, his voice resonating with an impassioned fervor.

The corridors were a snaking labyrinth, writhing with the pulse of something sinister. Their footsteps echoed like drumbeats heralding war. They moved as one entity, each of them feeding off the others' emotions. The air crackled with an electric tension, and Aedan could almost taste the metallic tang of impending confrontation.

"Remember, Al Ana's tricks are mind games," Aedan reminded

Lindsey and Tim, his voice a low mumble that cut through the thick silence. "She'll try to break us apart, but we can't let her."

"Right behind you, Aedan," Tim rumbled, his face set in determination. His fists clenched and unclenched rhythmically, ready to throw down at a moment's notice.

"Mary's counting on us," Lindsey added, her eyes flinty with a determination that matched Aedan's own. Her hand gripped Aedan's briefly, a fleeting connection that spoke volumes of shared courage.

They rounded the last corner to the basement, and there, it was unmistakable—the heart of one of Al Ana's dominions. The room stretched out, impossibly vast, shadows clinging to its edges like black paint. In the center, a vortex of darkness swirled, a visual echo of the demon's malice.

"Lives are on the line," Aedan breathed, barely audible over the thrumming power that emanated from the vortex. The words weren't just for them; they were a mantra for himself too. "Everything we love, everything we are—it all comes down to this."

"Let's light up this darkness," Lindsey said, her tone fierce with defiance. Tim nodded, his usual joviality stripped away to reveal the warrior beneath.

"Al Ana!" Aedan called out, throwing his challenge into the void. "We're here. And we're not afraid of you!"

The darkness pulsed, and an otherworldly howl filled the space. The battle lines were drawn, etching themselves into the very stone beneath their feet. This was where good would clash with evil, where the fate of their town—their home—would be decided.

"Stay sharp," Tim warned, every sense heightened to its limit. "This is it."

They stood shoulder to shoulder, a group of friends against the abyss, their wills interwoven in a tapestry of tenacity. The showdown loomed before them, fraught with peril yet imbued with a hope that refused to be extinguished.

With hearts braced and spirits ablaze, they stepped forward to meet destiny head-on.

Al Ana lurked in the corner, adorned with her eerie red fern-twig hat, and she sent chills down all their spines. Her silhouette, obscured by the hazy smoke, seemed to float ominously in the air. The aggravating laughter that echoed from her sent a wave of uncertainty through all three friends. *"Give me your souls,"* she taunted, her words laced with an ominous undertone.

"Never," Aedan said in brave defiance, but it did little to quell his growing feeling of desperation. As Al Ana advanced, her spectral form hovering ever closer, Aedan pulled out the protective herbs, which seemed like a feeble defense against the looming threat. Suddenly Al Ana retreated into the wall. Her retreat offered only momentary relief, leaving them to wonder when she might resurface, and what horrors might unfold.

The oppressive silence that followed was deafening, each second ticking by like an eternity as they remained frozen in place, hearts pounding with fear. Every shadow seemed to conceal a potential threat, every creak and groan of the old sanatorium amplified tenfold in their heightened state of alarm.

The friends huddled closer together, seeking strength in their unity, but the weight of Al Ana's lingering presence hung heavy in the air. Aedan's grip tightened around the protective herbs, their once vibrant colors now appearing dull and lifeless, as if drained of their potency by the evil force they had just faced.

Beads of sweat formed on their faces, the anticipation of what might come next more terrifying than any immediate danger. The minutes stretched on, each one more agonizing than the last, as they waited with bated breath for any sign of movement, any indication of where Al Ana might strike next.

The walls seemed to close in around them, the shadows growing longer and more menacing, until the air felt thick and suffocating. Just when they thought they could bear the suspense no longer, a faint whisper echoed through the room, chilling them to their cores. "Your souls will be mine," it hissed, the disembodied voice seeming to emanate from all corners at once, leaving them disoriented and susceptible.

"Maybe we should go home to regroup," Aedan said. The day's events had taken a toll, prompting him to propose a sensible course of action.

"Agreed," Tim and Lindsey said together, almost at the same time. They headed toward the stairway leading out of the basement when...

"Watch out!" Aedan's urgent cry pierced the air as the demon's blinking eyes emerged from the basement wall, a chilling sight. Al Ana burst forth, her presence unleashing chaos.

Aedan, Lindsey, and Tim raced up the stairs, their footsteps echoing in a frantic rhythm. Al Ana's deafening screech reverberated, sending shivers down their spines as she hovered menacingly in pursuit.

Lindsey dared a glance back, her eyes widening at the demon's rapid approach. Another bone-chilling yell ripped through the air. "She's gaining on us fast!" Her warning cut through the tension.

"Oh NO—" Tim said in a horrified utterance, only fueling their panic.

Al Ana's disembodied voice taunted, "I'm coming for you," scaring them all pale white. "Faster!" Aedan's command propelled them forward, their steps quickening as they fled the relentless demon, desperate to outrun the impending doom.

Their hearts pounded in their chests, the adrenaline coursing through their veins as they raced up the stairs, each step fueled by sheer terror. Al Ana's chilling laughter echoed behind them, taunting and mocking their futile attempts to escape her wrath. Aedan's mind raced, searching for a way to stop the demon's pursuit, but the fear of the unknown gripped him tightly.

Lindsey stumbled, her foot catching on a loose floorboard, and she let out a yelp as she tumbled forward. Tim, without hesitation, reached out and grabbed her arm, hauling her back to her feet, their momentum never faltering. As they burst through the front door, the crisp night air hit their faces, offering a brief respite from the suffocating presence of Al Ana. But the demon was relentless, her eerie howls growing louder as she closed in.

Aedan's eyes darted around, frantically searching for sanctuary, for any means of protection against the otherworldly force that pursued them. With a sudden realization, he veered sharply to the left, leading the others toward the old oak tree that stood sentinel in the yard.

"Hurry!" he cried, his voice strained with urgency. "We need to reach the tree!"

Their lungs burned as they sprinted across the overgrown lawn, the gnarled roots of the ancient oak tree looming ever closer. Al Ana's shrill laughter pierced the night, sending chills down their spines. Aedan reached the tree first, skidding to a halt and whirling around to face the others. "Quick, get out your Bibles, put them down in front of you, and form a circle!" he shouted, his voice ragged. Lindsey and Tim obeyed without question, their hands trembling as they grasped each other's arms, their Bibles lying in front of them, creating a tight ring around the oak's massive trunk.

Aedan joined them, his eyes wild with fear and determination. As the last link in the chain was forged, a crackling white light energy rippled through the air in an upward motion toward the heavens, raising the hairs on the back of their necks. Al Ana's laughter grew deafening, reverberating through the darkness like a harbinger of doom. But then, as she emerged from the shadows, her spectral form collided with the white light barrier, rippling like water against an impenetrable wall. Her shrieks of rage echoed through the night, but the light held firm, its protective magic shielding the three from her malicious grasp.

A hundred feet away in his patrol car, the sheriff observed the peculiar white light ascending into the sky. As the demon retreated upon encountering the luminous barrier, the sheriff prudently approached the circle of hand-holding youths. Aedan looked over to see the sheriff's patrol car pulling up.

"Hey, you kids alright?" the sheriff asked, his voice filled with concern as he rolled down the window, his emotions visibly frantic.

Aedan responded with a reassuring tone, "Yeah, we're good," as the group released their clasped hands, a gesture of comfort and solidarity in the face of the ordeal they just endured.

"Quick, get in now! I caught a glimpse of that demonic presence heading toward the river," the sheriff urged, his voice laced with urgency. Without a moment's hesitation, all three friends piled into the car, and the sheriff floored the accelerator, speeding toward the river with frantic determination.

17

Chook River

Chook River, a deep furrow in the landscape, presented a somber aspect that invited contemplation. Its shadowy depths seemed to harbor complex emotions, perhaps reflecting the intricate relationship between nature and human perception. The river was nothing more than a dark gash in the earth, full of malice. The eerie silence and lack of wildlife were deeply disturbing to the group of friends. Not even a single squirrel scurried across the ground, no birds chirped or took flight, and most alarmingly, there were no deer in sight. The unnatural absence of nature's creatures filled Aedan with a growing feeling of horror and concern for the well-being of the local ecosystem at the hands of the demon.

Aedan's heart pounded in his chest as he surveyed the lifeless surroundings. Why would the demon have caused such a disturbance in the natural order? Al Ana's presence seemed to have cast a spell over the entire area, rendering it devoid of any signs of life. Aedan couldn't stand the feeling that something sinister was at play, her force so evil that even the hardiest of creatures had fled for their safety. As he and his friends inched closer to the river, the air grew thicker with an ominous energy, making each breath feel like a choking.

The once babbling waters now flowed in an eerie silence, as if even the river itself had been silenced by the demon's dark influence. Aedan's hands trembled, gripped by the fear of what he might encounter next. He knew he had to press on, but the weight of the unknown bore down on him, threatening to crush his existence. Whatever lay ahead, he had to brace himself for the worst, for the demon's power seemed to know no bounds.

Aedan, Lindsey, Tim, and Sheriff Ford crept closer, their feet hesitant on the damp soil.

The moon, half-concealed by scudding clouds, cast a pale light over Chook River, where shadows seemed to squirm with a life of their own. Aedan's heart drummed a different beat, like it was trying to break free through the front lines of a war.

"Keep your eyes open," Aedan said, glancing at Lindsey. Her brown eyes were narrowed, a silent promise she wouldn't let her guard down.

Tim's hand rested on the hilt of his Bible, his face pale white. Lindsey clutched her bag of herbs in one hand, holding the Holy Bible and her vial of holy water in the other, lips moving in silent preparation for reciting the holy words. Sheriff Ford looked as ready as ever, his face brimming with determination, and his fingers kept twitching toward the gun holstered at his hip.

"Stay close," Aedan prompted. "Whatever happens, we face her together."

A sudden wind gust emerged from a silent stillness, causing a rustling sound that echoed through the trees, shaking the leaves. Then nothing; the wind stopped and the trees froze. Instant silence. A suffocating, heavy silence.

From the belly of the river, she came. Al Ana the demon. She burst from the water headfirst, her eyes glowing crimson, her red hat with a fern twig attached to it piercing the surface with urgency. The water parted around her like the Red Sea before Moses, a desperate path opening amidst the churning depths.

Aedan gasped for air, his lungs burning as he watched her break through the waves that struck without warning, parting before her as if they were trying to flee from her presence.

Lindsey's heart pounded in her ears, the rush of adrenaline coursing through her veins as she watched the demon treading water. Al Ana scanned the turbulent surface for any sign of humans.

Panic gripped Tim's chest as he realized the full peril of the situation. Sheriff Ford stood in place with his hand still on his gun belt, as if he was hypnotized by Al Ana's presence hovering above the river.

Aedan's mind raced, trying to understand what he just witnessed. How could this be real?

Lindsey felt a chill run down her spine as the demon's piercing gaze met hers. Al Ana's eyes narrowed, her metaphysical presence sending a wave of suspicion through the group. Tim's hands trembled, his instincts telling him to flee, but his feet remained rooted to the spot. Sheriff Ford's eyebrows raised so high that his forehead had wrinkles, his training failing to prepare him for an encounter of this magnitude. The air grew thick with tension, each second feeling like an eternity as they found themselves face-to-face with a force beyond their comprehension.

The air twisted around the demon, rippling as if reality recoiled from her presence. Al Ana slowly levitated toward the banks of the river near Aedan and his friends' location. Disbelief enveloped the surroundings as the once vibrant willow trees withered and shriveled, their life force drained by the sinister demon's proximity. The once lush vegetation in her vicinity rapidly decayed, leaving behind a desolate, lifeless landscape—a grim harbinger of the devastation this malicious entity was capable of unleashing.

The demon swirled her black arms around in circles, creating a shifting mass of black shadows contorting into shapes too grotesque for the group to comprehend—a nightmare made into flesh. "Scatter!" Lindsey cried as a wave of dark energy surged toward them.

Tim dove to the left, rolling behind a maple tree, while Lindsey sprinted for a cluster of bushes. Sheriff Ford crouched by a fallen log near Tim, holy water ready in his shaking hands.

A piercing shriek tore from Al Ana's lips, *"Ahhhhh,"* so loudly in Aedan's direction that he leaped aside, running away just as the ground where he'd been standing erupted, splinters of earth flying through the air like an earthquake just struck.

Stay alive, Aedan thought fiercely, scrambling for cover behind a thicket of brush next to Lindsey. Adrenaline flooded Aedan's body, and his breaths were shallow and quick. "Is that all you've got?" he yelled, more to bolster his courage than to taunt her.

Al Ana's demented laughter slithered through the night, a sound no human throat should make. *"Ha, ha, ha...You think this is a game, little one?"* she said with a disembodied voice.

Aedan clenched his fists, feeling the sting of thorns against his skin of pure fear.

Just then Al Ana unleashed an unprecedented level of evil. Shadow people emerged from the black shadows coming their way, material-izing from nothingness and transforming into near-lifelike demonic entities resembling nothing but pure evil. The air grew thick with an oppressive darkness as the demonic entities swarmed forward, their soulless eyes burning with fire and malice.

Gnarled claws four feet long extended from their shadowy forms, raking the ground and leaving deep gouges in their wake as Al Ana made it to the riverbank. A deafening screeching of inhuman shrieks and howls assaulted their consciousness, sending chills down all their spines, and making their legs shake. Time seemed to slow as the demonic horde closed in, their presence a suffocating stench of pure hostility.

Every fiber of the group's individual beings screamed to flee, but escape seemed cowardly in the face of such overwhelming evil. The battle lines were drawn, and the stakes could not be higher—the fate of humanity hung in the balance against this unholy onslaught unleashed by Al Ana's dark machinations.

"I don't think so," the sheriff said, quick to react, standing up from behind the fallen log and drawing his gun. He looked over at Tim and then opened fire on the shadow demons, but his efforts proved futile as the bullets were no match, passing through the shadows and lodging into nearby trees. Crouched behind the bushes, Aedan and Lindsey clung to each other, terror gripping them as they watched the sheriff unleash a second barrage of shots, cutting through the sinister shadow demons. Every fiber of Aedan's and Lindsey's beings screamed for immediate action, their hearts pounding with urgency as the battle raged on relentlessly before their eyes. They knew they had to help.

Undeterred, Tim wielded his vial of holy water and the herbs, holding them upright, in a desperate attempt to fend off the malicious forces approaching him as Aedan and Lindsey watched on, horrified. Tim's heart raced as the shadow demons closed in, their ethereal forms shifting and contorting in the dim light of the forest. He could feel the air growing colder, a chill seeping into his bones as the evil entities got closer. Sweat beaded on his forehead, and his hands trembled as he clutched the vial of holy water and the herbs, his only line of defense against the unholy forces that threatened to consume him. With each passing second, the shadows seemed to grow darker, more menacing, as if they were feeding off his fear and apprehension.

Tim's mind raced, desperate for a way to banish the creatures back to the depths from where they came. He knew a single misstep or a moment of hesitation could spell his doom. He watched the sheriff's bullets as they proved ineffective, and now it was up to him to wield the power of the sacred relics he carried. Tim could feel the world's weight on his shoulders, the fate of countless souls hanging in the balance. Taking a deep breath, he steadied his courage, his grip on the vial tightening as he prepared to unleash its potent force against the encroaching shadows.

Tim's holy weapons offered temporary respite, but the demons quickly adapted, their evil energy pulsating with each failed attempt to banish them. With a deafening screech, the shadow demons converged, their numbers multiplying exponentially.

Aedan's ears caught the magical swoosh of leaves, and as he turned, the heavens themselves seemed to open up. A dazzling white light, so pure and intense, descended from above like a celestial waterfall. "It's...it's beyond words!" he said, tapping Lindsey on her shoulder without taking his eyes off the angels.

"Lin...look," Aedan said with surprise, his voice trembling in wonder as he gently nudged Lindsey.

She turned "Absolutely breathtaking!" she said, her face in shock. "Is that...angels?"

Aedan replied, also in shock, "Can you believe it?" Time itself seemed to stand still in that moment of pure, unadulterated awe.

Two magnificent angels, their very presence radiating divine power, gracefully touched down within the brilliant light. Their wings folded behind their backs with an ethereal elegance. And then...their arms extended in a gesture so commanding, so powerful. A light, more radiant than a thousand suns, burst forth from their hands and enveloped Aedan in its glory.

"The chosen one," one of the angels proclaimed, their voice resonating with the weight of destiny itself. In that incredible moment, Aedan was transformed, filled with the courage of the mightiest warrior. The angels watched on like generals looking over soldiers on a battlefield.

Aedan's grip on Lindsey tightened with his newfound courage as a stray bullet whizzed past, narrowly missing them. They knew they couldn't remain hidden forever; the demons were closing in, their snarling growing louder with each passing second. Exchanging a determined look, they toughened their assurance and burst from their cover, Bibles drawn. Lindsey's arms held onto Aedan's shoulders with a fierce grip.

The sight of Aedan brandishing the Bible filled Al Ana with a fit of aggressive anger. Her four-foot-long arms flailed in his direction, unleashing a torrent of shadow demons from her army as if driven by a primal rage.

Al Ana's fury knew no bounds as she watched Aedan wield the holy book with defiance.

Her mind raced with speedy thoughts, fearing the powers it could unleash against her dark forces. She lashed out in desperation, summoning wave after wave of shadowy minions to overwhelm her adversary.

His Bible clashed against the demons' claws, each strike more powerful than the last. "STAND YOUR GROUND, AEDAN." The sheriff's booming voice echoed through the chaos, rallying them to push forward, because retreat was not an option. *It's working,* the sheriff thought as he watched Aedan blowing up every demon that got within two feet of the Bible like a balloon, letting out a black gas that disintegrated into thin air.

Aedan and Lindsey sprinted urgently to Tim's side, their hearts pounding with adrenaline. The sheriff's footsteps thundered behind them as they found themselves trapped, encircled by an ominous presence closing in from all angles. Time was running out, and every second counted in this dire situation.

"Demons closing in," Tim yelled as the situation escalated with alarming urgency.

"Quick, Aedan, over here!" The sheriff's frantic voice pierced through the chaos as a demon entity encroached.

Aedan whirled, brandishing the sacred Bible, banishing the fiend in a burst of holy light.

"Over here!" Lindsey's desperate cry rings out, another hellish abomination drawing near.

Aedan pivoted with a whirlwind of divine retribution, obliterating the foul creature.

"Over here!" Tim's panicked shout echoed, and Aedan spun once more, unleashing righteous fury upon the encroaching evil. The battle raged, each second teetering on the brink of oblivion, as they fought with unfiltered determination against the onslaught of darkness.

Suddenly Lindsey's eyes widened in fear as a towering demon loomed over her, its mouth gaping wide, ready to consume her soul. "NOOOOO," Lindsey yelled. Aedan turned and held out the Bible, extinguishing the demon, saving his love.

The air crackled with an unearthly energy as the group fought with every ounce of their strength. Tim, the sheriff, Aedan, and Lindsey stood back-to-back, their holy weapons raised in defiance, the vials of blessed water glowing with a faint, ethereal light.

"WE CAN'T LET THEM WIN!" Lindsey's voice rang out, her words laced with determination.

"We have to hold the line!" Tim yelled grimly, his grip tightening around the bundle of herbs, their pungent aroma filling the air. "We're with you, Lindsey." As the shadow demons closed in, their twisted forms writhed and contorted. "Stand your ground."

The group braced themselves for the onslaught, their hearts pounding in their chests. The demons struck with a fury unlike anything they had ever witnessed, their shadowy claws raking the air, their unearthly shrieks piercing the night. But the group stood firm, Aedan's Bible flashing in the darkness, their spirits certain in the face of overwhelming evil.

Lindsey's determination shone through as she reached into her backpack, her fingers grazing the holy words that held the key to unlocking her true potential. In that moment, she tapped into a wellspring of inner strength, a voice that soared like an angel's, pure and persistent. With each word she recited, her spirit ignited, radiating a luminous energy that transcended the ordinary. This was her moment to embrace the extraordinary, to let her authentic self shine forth, and she inspired her friends with the power of her courageous bravery.

"Seek and you shall find. I adjure you by the Father, Son, and Holy Spirit that you grow no larger but that you dry up....Cross Matthew, cross Mark, cross Luke, cross John," Lindsey sang loudly, as if she were at an opera.

Behold the power of faith and divine grace! As the sacred holy words of the Holy Bible resonated and the blessed holy water was sprinkled in the air, a miraculous transformation unfolded. The evil forces, once shrouded in darkness, were banished, each one bursting into a radiant white light, like balloons bursting forth. The demons were vanquished, and their hold over this realm shattered forever.

Aedan steadied his breathing, trying to quiet the pounding of his heart. He knew this was no game—Al Ana had tormented their town for far too long, feeding on their fear and despair.

Somewhere in the darkness, Aedan heard the clash of steel and an agonized cry. His stomach twisted, but he forced himself to focus.

They had studied the ancient texts, gathered the sacred relics, and honed their skills for this very moment. A rustling in the nearby bushes made Aedan tense, his muscles coiled like a spring. He gripped his weapon, the herbs, and holy water tightly, ready to face whatever horror Al Ana unleashed next.

"Focus," Aedan told himself. "She's strong, but we don't break easy."

And with that thought, Aedan prepared to rise, to face whatever horror Al Ana would throw at them next. Gritting his teeth, Aedan hoisted the holy water, Bible, and herbs high. His hands gripped the Holy Bible, feeling the etchings that had been worn smooth by centuries of secret keepers. With every step he took toward Al Ana, the weight of his ancestors' battles coursed through him.

"Al Ana!" Aedan bellowed, his voice cracking with both fear and fury. The demon's eyes flickered to his, a gleam of amusement in their abyssal depths. She stood there, a monument to malice, her form undulating like smoke caught in a violent storm.

"Come then, Aedan O'Connor," she hissed, a grotesque smile twisting her lips. "Show me the power of your trinket."

Aedan lunged, leading with the Bible, aiming for where her heart— if she even had one— should be. But like striking at a shadow, she dissolved into the air, reappearing a few feet away, untouched. Her laughter clawed at his ears, echoing off the twisted trees surrounding Chook River.

"Pathetic boy!" she cackled. Aedan's chest heaved; frustration and failure threatened to crush him. But Aedan couldn't let despair take hold—not now, not ever. Cheboygan needed him. Mary needed him.

That's when Aedan saw her: Lindsey, an angelic figure glowing, darting through the underbrush. Her movements were fluid, silent—a dance with danger itself. She was fire and grace, a stark contrast to the darkness that sought to suffocate them all. Lindsey caught Al Ana's eye, drawing the demon's attention like a matador taunting a bull.

"Over here, you foul beast!" Lindsey's shout pierced the night. She zigzagged across the clearing, her silhouette a blur against the moonlit fog that had settled over the river.

Al Ana snarled, distracted by the challenge. That's when Tim sprang into action. He surged forward from the shadows, a silent avenger powered by a will of steel. He threw the bag of herbs he'd spent nights studying in hope and desperation, connecting with the demon's back.

The impact sounded like thunder, a sharp, satisfying crack that split the eerie silence. Al Ana stumbled, her form wavering as if reality itself couldn't decide whether to keep her whole. "Good hit, Tim!" Aedan shouted, heart soaring. Tim had the demon on her back foot now. This was their chance, their moment. Together, they could turn the tide—they could win.

Her shriek of fury was cut short as she regained her composure, but the flicker of surprise in her eyes told them everything they needed to know. They'd struck true. They'd given themselves a fighting chance.

"Lindsey, now!" Aedan hollered, ducking a sickle-shaped claw that Al Ana threw his way. The air crackled with her anger, and dark energy swirled around her like a thunder cloud ready to burst with lightning.

Lindsey's hands danced in the air, fingers tracing symbols that glowed with an ethereal light. Again, Lindsey's holiness was a song that rose above the chaos—a promise of protection in ancient tongues long forgotten. Together, holding her Bible and reciting the poem, a shimmering dome rippled into existence, encasing them in a bubble of light that repelled Al Ana's shadowy assault.

"Got it!" Lindsey cried triumphantly as the barrier solidified, her face set in determined lines.

"Nice work," Aedan said, breathing a sigh of relief. They were safe, for the moment.

"Take your shot, Ford!" Tim bellowed from beside Aedan, his voice a rallying cry that cut through the night.

Sheriff Ford took a measured step forward, his eyes narrowed, and the vial raised. Holy water—their hope against the darkness—glinted in the moonlight. The sheriff's aim was steady, his coolness was unshakable.

The bottle roared, and the holy water streaked toward Al Ana like a comet. It hit with the force of retribution, and she howled—a sound that scratched at the very soul.

"Did we—" Lindsey began, but her words were drowned out as the demon's rage manifested into something far more tangible.

"Creatures! Incoming!" Aedan warned as twisted forms of specters, shadow people, peeled away from the shadows, their grotesque bodies a patchwork of nightmares. They surged toward them with unnatural speed, a horde sent by Al Ana to overwhelm them.

They held their ground, drawing strength from the bonds that united them. Though the odds seemed insurmountable, they refused to surrender to fear or despair. Each of them had faced trials that could have broken them, yet they emerged stronger and more resilient. With sustained courage, they met the onslaught head-on, their spirits burning brighter than ever before.

"Stand firm!" Aedan commanded, gripping his weapons—his hands tightly around the Bible and holding the holy water.

Tim and Aedan synchronized their strikes. Tim's fists were hurricanes, and Aedan's were lightning. They became a tempest, their blows landing on spectral bodies that felt like dry ice, reshaping the horrors back into the darkness they sprang from. The demons were no match for the holy water or the power of the Bible.

Lindsey worked in tandem with Aedan and Tim, their combined strengths weaving a dance of destruction. Lindsey's movements were precise, each kick and punch a sentence in the story of her defiance. Tim chanted the holy poem with Lindsey, reinforcing their barrier, their voices rising and falling in a rhythm that matched the pulsing light protecting them.

"Keep at it, keep the pressure on them!" Aedan yelled over the clash of conflict. "They can't hold against us forever!"

The battle's fury built to a crescendo, with every clash and cry etching itself into the night. Aedan's breaths came in ragged gasps, his muscles screamed, and yet, he couldn't stop— wouldn't stop. Because amidst the chaos, a pattern emerged, a sliver of hope. Al Ana, in her arrogance, became careless when she reveled in their desperation.

"Tim!" Aedan shouted, his voice barely carrying over the din. "Cover me!"

Aedan saw it again—the flicker of distraction as she conjured another vile creature. That was it. That was all he needed. With a surge of adrenaline, Aedan sprinted forward, the holy water and Bible in hand blazing with an ethereal glow. He swung with every ounce of strength, every whisper of bravery that carried him through the darkness of Chook River.

The holy water connected, a solid, resounding hit that sent tremors through the air. A howl tore from Al Ana's throat, a sound so pained, so furious, it nearly drowned out the screams of battle. She stumbled, her form wavering like a candle flame in the wind.

"Ford! Now!" Aedan cried.

Sheriff Ford didn't hesitate, didn't falter. His hands rose with the steadiness of stone, his aim true as he'd promised it would be when they first forged this unlikely alliance. The bottle of holy water—a glinting promise of heavenly justice—spiraled through the air, straight to the black heart of Al Ana.

The impact was a thing of horrific beauty. Al Ana's scream split the night, a visceral echo of agony that vibrated in Aedan's very bones. Her control slipped, her dark powers scattering like shadows at dawn. They all felt it, that fleeting moment of passivity, and it was glorious.

"Move!" Aedan shouted, the urgency in his voice as fiery as the determination in his veins.

Lindsey was a blur of motion to Aedan's left, her swift moves a dance of danger, each step luring Al Ana's focus away from him. Tim, rugged and relentless, followed through with a heavy swing of his Bible, the sound of impact a satisfying thud against the demon's shifting form.

"Keep her off-balance!" Lindsey's voice, steady and commanding, cut through the chaos as she weaved intricate gestures with her hands, the air shimmering around them with the power of ancient spells. Lindsey let out the holy words again in a heavenly song:

"Seek and you shall find. I adjure you by the Father, Son, and Holy Spirit that you grow no larger but that you dry up...Cross Matthew, cross Mark,

cross Luke, cross John." Her words weakened Al Ana further.

Aedan clutched the last vial of holy water, its contents shimmering with a light that seemed too pure for this sinister place. His heart pounded like a drumbeat of war, each pulse a reminder of what they were fighting for—their town, their lives, their friend, their very souls.

"Here goes everything," Aedan said to himself. With every ounce of courage Aedan could muster, he sprinted toward the demon, sidestepping the clawed appendages that lashed out in a frenzy.

"Al Ana!" Aedan called, his voice rising above the din. As her eyes snapped to him, malice and hatred burning in them, he saw his opportunity.

"Cheboygan is ours, not yours!" Aedan's declaration was a challenge, a call to arms.

As Aedan closed the distance, her mouth opened to release another loud shriek, but it was cut short as the vial soared from his hand and shattered upon her chest. The holy water sizzled against her skin like acid, the sacred liquid the curse to her dark existence.

The effect was instantaneous. Al Ana's scream tore through the night, a sound so raw and filled with torment it made Aedan's blood run cold. Once formidable and terrifying, her form began to crumble like ash in the wind, bright white light, souls with voices flying out of her, radiating from her disintegration. Al Ana was no more.

They all witnessed the triumph of light over darkness, as the souls, once trapped by evil forces, broke free from their tormented prison. Like radiant sparks of hope, they soared through the celestial expanse, returning to their rightful vessels—a poignant reminder that no matter how deep the shadows, the indomitable spirit will always find its way back home, igniting the eternal flame of resilience within them all.

Souls soared back into the dead red-winged blackbirds, bringing them all back to life; fluttering and flapping their wings with renewed energy and enthusiasm, they flew away majestically.

Human souls once trapped were liberated, returning to their rightful bodies—Mary, Susan Smith, Henry Gills, every soul within the sanatorium's walls, and every customer at the library, Waltz's 24s, and the mall. They rose, shedding the shackles of their afflictions, and emerged from the hospital's confines with renewed vigor and clarity. Henry Gills woke up from the spot on the sidewalk where he fell victim to Al Ana, with his first thought being to thank Aedan.

Susan Smith and Mary, strangers side-by-side, abandoned their wheelchairs as they stood tall, their voices ringing with the joy of newfound freedom. "Whoa, what happened?" Mary exclaimed, her eyes wide with excitement.

"I have no clue what just happened, but it was incredible!" Susan responded, her voice brimming with enthusiasm and a hint of bewilderment. The air crackled with energy as they tried to understand the extraordinary event that had just taken place.

"We're alive!" Mary gushed, her face flushed with adrenaline. "I'm alive!"

Susan nodded vigorously, her eyes sparkling. "My heart is still racing from the thrill of it all." She let out an exhilarated laugh. "Can you imagine explaining this to someone who wasn't here?"

Mary shook her head emphatically. "No way! They'd never believe it. I can barely believe it, and I lived it!" She bounced on her toes, buzzing with excitement. "We're so lucky to be alive"

The two new friends shared a giddy look, their minds still reeling from the incredible spectacle they had just beheld, their restored health.

Old Man Harry's peaceful evening was interrupted by an unexpected flash that caught his eye through the living room window. As he set down his book and rose from his familiar recliner, curiosity and intrigue stirred within him. With measured steps, he made his way to the front door, the darkness outside gradually giving way to an emerging light. At that moment, Harry's mind wandered, pondering the nature of this phenomenon that had disrupted the tranquility of his everyday routine. What happened beyond that threshold, waiting to be unveiled? The thoughtful old man stood at the precipice of discovery, his emotions heightened and his spirit open to the mysteries that the night might unfold.

Elara Wildheart stood in her kitchen, the sizzle of the stove punctuating the air as she diligently prepared her meal. But then her eyes were drawn to the window, where a brilliant light emerged, piercing the darkness. A triumphant smile spread across her face as she exclaimed, "Good, he did it!" Those four words carried a weight of conviction, a testament to her unmeasured belief in the success of Aedan's endeavor. In that moment, the light wasn't just a fleeting phenomenon, it was a beacon of hope, a tangible proof that their efforts had paid off. With a renewed determination, Elara knew that this was just the beginning of something extraordinary.

Aedan's parents, Eddie and Julia, were returning from their vacation on the I-75 North highway when Eddie noticed an unusual atmospheric phenomenon near their exit. As he glanced up at the sky, he observed a brilliant white light emerging from an otherwise black sky. Intrigued by this sight, Eddie remarked to his wife, "I wonder what that is," expressing his curiosity about the potential cause or nature of the occurrence.

"Heaven," Julia said as she looked up in the direction of the light, seeing the bright white aura over the woods going up toward the sky, where Aedan was miles away.

Old Man Jenkins's remarkable transformation at the Calumet Theatre was nothing short of extraordinary. When he looked up with an intense expression, it was as if a surge of vitality coursed through his veins. Instantly, his frail frame seemed to shed years of age, and a newfound vigor radiated from his being. The change was so profound, so undeniable, that it left no room for doubt—something truly remarkable had occurred. Old Man Jenkins had defied the odds and experienced a rejuvenation that could only be described as miraculous.

Back at the battle site, the darkness that had once seeped from the river, poisoning their homes with fear and nightmares, now recoiled as though wounded by the light itself.

"Look!" Lindsey's exclamation drew Aedan's attention to the river, where the cursed waters were retreating, slinking back like a defeated beast.

The group stood motionless, their breaths coming in ragged gasps, as they watched the very essence of Al Ana disintegrate before their eyes. The shadows that had clung to Cheboygan were dissipating, the weight of the dead lifted like mist at the mercy of the morning sun.

"Is it...over?" Tim asked, his voice barely audible over the sound of their victory.

Aedan looked around at his friends, their faces etched with exhaustion and awe. They had faced the abyss together and emerged on the other side. Cheboygan was free, and so were they.

"Let's go home," Aedan said, knowing the battle was won, and their journey was over. Aedan, Lindsey, and Tim stumbled toward each other, a tattered trio under the moon's watchful eye. Relief washed over them like the first breath after surfacing from underwater. Lindsey let out a laugh that was more of a sob, and in that sound, Aedan heard the release of countless nights plagued with terror.

"Guys, we did it, she's gone," Lindsey said, her voice heavy with disbelief.

"Did you ever doubt us?" Tim grinned, but his eyes couldn't hide the toll the battle had taken.

"Never," Lindsey replied, but her eyes remained fixed on where the river had once raged with malice. Her hands shook slightly, not from fear but from the adrenaline slowly ebbing away.

Sheriff Ford stepped forward, the brim of his hat casting shadows across his tired features. "I'll be damned. You kids...you're something else."

The words hung among them, a testament to their unity against the darkness. They huddled close, a ragged circle of survivors, feeling the pulse of life and the quiet strength of their camaraderie. Victory was theirs, and the weight of it was both exhilarating and humbling.

As the silence stretched, Aedan looked at each of them, these friends who had become warriors beside him. "Remember this night," Aedan said, his voice steady despite the exhaustion. "Remember how we stood together and faced what most would flee from."

"Will there be others?" Lindsey asked, a flicker of concern crossing her lively features. "Maybe," Sheriff Ford responded, holstering his weapon with a finality that spoke of battles yet to come. "But if they do show up, they won't find easy prey."

"Because we'll be ready," Lindsey added, her brown eyes gleaming with resolve. "We've learned too much, come too far to let our guard down now."

"Exactly," Aedan agreed, nodding. Aedan O'Connor wasn't just a curious and bashful teenager anymore. The mysteries he'd longed for had been darker than he could have imagined, yet here he stood, tempered by the very shadows he'd unraveled.

"Let's head back," Tim suggested, his bravado shouldering the weariness with ease. "The town needs to see that it's safe again—because of us."

"Because of us," they all echoed, a shared vow that bound them tighter than any friendship ever had before.

As they walked back through the woods, the promise of dawn kissed the horizon, and birds chirped sweet melodies banishing the last remnants of the night's horrors. They were different people than those who had entered the fray; marked by a knowledge no one else possessed, they carried it with the weight of protectors. And when the next shadow loomed, they would be the light to meet it. They embraced the warmth of the shining sun, its radiant glow a symbol of hope and renewal to them. Their path may have been marked by hardship, but it was also illuminated by an unbreakable spirit—a flame that would never be extinguished, a guiding light for generations to come.

18

Town Celebration

The town square drummed away with life, a pulsating heart of cheerfulness against Cheboygan's serene downtown atmosphere. Lanterns swayed overhead, casting warm glows on beaming faces as laughter echoed through the clinking of glasses and the rhythmic clap of hands in time with the Irish band's jubilant tunes. A banner rippled above a makeshift stage with a microphone in the center, proclaiming "Thank you: Aedan, Lindsey, Tim, and Sheriff Ford—Our Saviors" in bold letters, flanked by the flutter of red, white, and blue bunting.

Amidst the delightful aroma of charcoal delicacies coming from grills scattered all over, a heartwarming scene unfolded at one of the picnic tables. Lindsey's parents, Tim's beloved sister and mother, Mary's caring mother, and Aedan's loving parents gathered together, savoring not only mouthwatering barbecued food, sweet treats, and fruit kabobs but also precious moments of togetherness. Their shared laughter and warm embraces painted a picture of familial bonds that transcend mere blood ties, reminding them of the profound beauty found in the simple act of breaking bread with those they held dear.

"Can you believe this?" Lindsey Merritt said, nudging Aedan at a picnic table away from their parents, her brown eyes sparkling with tears of love, joy, and relief. He could only shake his head, still incredulous at the sight of their little town transformed into a bastion of celebration over them—a stark contrast to the shadow that had loomed over them mere days before.

"You...uh...you think we..." Aedan stammered, attempting to ask Lindsey out with all the smoothness of a porcupine in roller skates. But just as he was about to unleash his masterpiece of romantic eloquence, Henry swooped in like a passion-wrecking seagull.

"Hey, Aedan," Henry chirped, oblivious to the fact that he'd just karate-chopped Cupid's arrow mid-flight. Poor Aedan's love life was now as derailed as it always was, all thanks to Henry's grand entrance at the picnic table of broken dreams. "I was walking down Main Street and I found myself awakening to a new reality," Henry began, voice starting with fear and ending with gratitude. "As consciousness returned, I saw the signs of your heroic deed surrounding me, your name on every banner around town. It was then I realized that you had faced the demon head-on and came out a winner."

"I...I suppose I should explain," Aedan began softly, his eyes staring into Lindsey's.

Before he could continue, Henry gently interjected, his voice warm and conciliatory. "I wanted to thank you personally...Perhaps we could simply start over?" he offered, extending his hand with a hopeful smile. "I'd be grateful if we could put any misunderstandings behind us." His gesture hung in the air, a humble invitation for reconciliation.

Aedan paused, carefully considering his words. "I appreciate your gesture, Henry," he began, his voice measured and reflective. "There's more to discuss, but I understand your intention." He glanced at Henry's outstretched hand and started weighing the complexities of their shared history. After a moment of contemplation, Aedan reached out, grasping Henry's hand in a firm yet friendly shake. "Perhaps this is a step toward understanding," he offered, his tone conveying both caution and hope for peace.

"I agree," Henry said as he got up and walked toward another picnic table. He grabbed a hot dog off someone's plate when they weren't looking, then faded into the crowd.

* * *

Mary and Susan were strolling down Main Street, fresh from the sanatorium's confines, their steps filled with excitement as they made their way toward the town square celebration. The air was buzzing with anticipation, and they couldn't help but feel a surge of enthusiasm coursing through their veins as they got closer.

As they approached the square, the sounds of lively music and cheerful chatter grew louder. It was hard for them not to see the colorful banners with Mary's friends on them fluttering in the gentle breeze and they couldn't help but smell the aroma of freshly grilled treats blowing through the air. Mary and Susan exchanged glances, their eyes twinkling with delight at the festive atmosphere. The town's annual summer festival was always a highlight of the year, bringing together residents of all ages for a day of joy and community spirit, only this time Mary's friends were the highlighted focus.

As they entered the square, they were greeted by the sight of bustling stalls, each offering unique barbecue feasts, fresh fruit concoctions, and mouthwatering sweet delicacies. Children's laughter echoed from the nearby carousel, its vibrant lights casting a warm glow on the faces of the excited riders. Mary and Susan pondered where to begin their exploration, knowing that every corner of the celebration held the promise of new experiences, and cherished memories, and Mary couldn't wait to be reunited with familiar faces. The day stretched before them, full of possibilities and the simple pleasure of sharing it with friends.

"Hey...Mary?" Tim Spencer's voice boomed over the noise, his excited nature cutting through the festivities like a torpedo getting ready to strike.

Mary spun around, her eyes lighting up as she spotted Tim waving enthusiastically from across the street. Susan smiled at the sight of her new friend's face breaking into a radiant smile. "Tim! Over here!" Mary called out, beckoning him over with an eager wave of her hand.

The two friends waited, bouncing with excitement as Tim navigated through the bustling crowd, weaving in and out of groups of people. "Can you believe this turnout?" Mary exclaimed, her eyes sparkling as she took in the vibrant decorations and lively atmosphere.

"The food smells so good," Susan said, eager to get some delicious food for once, especially after such a long wait.

"The town square has never looked more alive!" Mary mentioned, her stare fixed on Tim as he drew nearer.

The enthusiastic expression and boyish grin on his face was unmis-takable, even after she had temporarily lost her mind. The unexpected encounter stirred a mix of emotions within her— surprise, nostalgia, and a hint of nervousness and love. As Tim approached, the sounds of the party seemed to fade into the background. Mary found herself transported back to their shared past, memories flooding her mind. She took a deep breath, composing herself for the impending conversation, wondering what she would say to him, and what this chance meeting might mean for both of them.

"It's going to be an unforgettable night; I can feel it!" Mary declared to Susan, her voice brimming with anticipation.

As Tim finally reached them, he exchanged a sentimental hug with Mary. "I'm so relieved...I'm so happy to see you safe, Mary," Tim said, his voice filled with warmth and concern as he embraced her even tighter. "I can't imagine how frightening this was for you," he added, offering romantic empathy.

"Honestly, I don't remember what happened," Mary replied, her voice trembling with the weight of her ordeal.

"But you're here now, and that's what matters most," Tim reassured her, his compassionate tone conveying unrelenting support during her distress. "Susan, I'm relieved to see you looking well and restored to health. The situation you've been through must have been incredibly difficult, but your resilience is truly inspiring. Please know that you're in a safe place now, surrounded by people who care deeply about your well-being," he said, his voice filled with genuine relief to see her healthy.

"Yeah, I'm not sure what happened, and how do you know who I am?" Susan replied, her eyes wide with anxious curiosity to unravel the truth.

"Well, let's just say your story helped motivate us to solve the riddle of what was plaguing this town," Tim responded, his tone resolute and confident, driven by a sincere desire to uncover the truth and protect the innocent.

With the promise of a night filled with laughter, music, and cherished memories, they linked arms and plunged into the heart of the celebration, their spirits soaring higher than the twinkling lights adorning the town square.

"Yo, Aedan!" Tim yelled enthusiastically, waving his arms to catch Aedan's and Lindsey's attention. "Come over here, buddy! Mary and I are hanging out, and you've got to join us!" His voice was brimming with excitement, inviting Aedan and Lindsey to share in the fun and camaraderie.

"Attention!" The microphone amplified Mayor Johnson's voice, and it sliced through the merriment. The crowd settled into an expectant hush, turning toward the makeshift stage where the mayor stood front and center, his smile as wide as the horizon.

"Today, we honor four individuals whose courage knew no bounds," he began, his eyes sweeping over them. Aedan and Lindsey straightened, soldiers ready to receive their commendation. Sheriff Bill Ford, usually the picture of apathetic authority, allowed a rare grin to grace his features. Tim, usually so brash and bold, shuffled his feet, bashful under the spotlight. Mary and Susan stood aside, their expressions reflecting a sincere demeanor as the joyous celebration carried on around them. At that moment, they were just observers, taking in the scene with an earnest appreciation for the occasion and the emotions it evoked.

"Without Aedan, Lindsey, Tim, and Sheriff Ford, Cheboygan would be at the mercy of darkness," the mayor continued, his voice swelling with pride. "Their selflessness, bravery, and determination have saved us all."

The square erupted into applause, a roaring cascade that made the air vibrate with admiration. Hats flew into the sky, and whistles pierced the evening as the townspeople expressed their gratitude in a symphony of celebration.

The mayor's words hung heavy in the air, a solemn reminder of the sacrifices made to protect their small town. As Aedan looked around at the gathered crowd, he could see the deep gratitude etched into every face.

Aedan felt his own flush with a mix of humility and pride, an odd sensation that tethered him to the ground while his heart soared. Lindsey reached for Aedan's hand, squeezing it in silent compassion, her touch grounding him. Beside Aedan, Tim's chest puffed out, his eyes shining with unspoken emotions, while Sheriff Ford tipped his hat in acknowledgment, the gesture encompassing both thanks and a rekindled hope for their community.

"Let's hear it once more for our brave friends!" Mayor Johnson prompted, and again the cheers washed over them, as potent as the waves of the river that had borne witness to their trials. Aedan, Lindsey, Mary, Tim, and Sheriff Ford stood together as a group, not just as friends, but as defenders of Cheboygan, bonded forever by the adventure that had changed their lives—and their town—for good.

As the last of the applause faded into the cool evening air, Aedan slipped away from the crowd's embrace. The echo of their cheers still buzzed in his ears as he found a secluded bench under the shadow of an old oak tree. The town square, still alive with fluttering banners and the warm glow of bright lights, felt like another world from this quiet corner.

Aedan leaned back, closing his eyes for a moment, letting the weight of everything that had happened wash over him. He'd faced down fears that would chill the soul, stood toe-to-toe with darkness itself...and he'd won.

"Brave"—the word echoed mockingly in Aedan's mind. *Was I?* he thought. Sure, the townspeople saw Aedan that way, but within, he knew the truth was more complex. He wasn't the same kid who used to chase shadows for the thrill or get bullied in school; these were real demons, and the stakes were life itself. There was no denying it; he had grown, changed even. The reflection looking back at him from the river's surface bore the same bright blue eyes, yet they held a new depth—a pearl of wisdom earned through fire and fear.

"Son?"

The sound of that voice—worn, but warm—cut through Aedan's reverie like sunlight through a mist. Aedan opened his eyes to see him, Eddie O'Connor, his dad, standing there as if he'd materialized from his thoughts. Eddie's face, once marred by Al Ana's dark influence, was now just tired and lined with concern...for Aedan.

"Hey, Dad," Aedan said, his voice ecstatic, suddenly unsure of how to bridge the gap Al Ana had carved between them. Aedan took a step closer, hesitated, then closed the distance in a few determined strides.

The embrace they shared was one of survivors, of father and son, of two souls who had been to hell and back again. Relief poured from Eddie in a shuddering breath as Aedan clung to him, feeling the steady breath against his own.

"Damn, Aedan, I was so scared I'd lost you," he said with enthusiasm into Aedan's hair, his voice thick with emotion.

"Me too, Dad. Me too," Aedan managed to say, his throat tightening, trying to get the words out. But here they were, together, safe. The nightmare was over, and the dawn promised a fresh start, a chance to rebuild what had been broken.

They pulled apart slightly, just enough to share a look that said more than words could. It was a silent promise, a vow to use this second chance wisely, to cherish every moment given back to them.

"I think you have a future in paranormal investigations, son," Eddie said, his words filled with warmth and belief in his child's potential.

"Maybe, Dad, maybe," Aedan replied jokingly, yet there was an underlying appreciation for his father's tireless support and encouragement. In that moment, their bond transcended mere words, forging a connection built on empathy, understanding, and a shared journey of growth.

"Come on," Aedan said finally, "let's go back. They'll be wondering where we've disappeared to." He put his arm over his dad's shoulders.

"Lead the way, son," Eddie replied, a proud smile touching his face. He put his own arm over Aedan's and onto his shoulder, guiding him gently toward the light and laughter of the celebration. Together, they walked back into the heart of Cheboygan, a town that had seen darkness but now basked in the light of victory and hope—a light that, thanks to its brave defenders, burned all the brighter.

The town's beating heart pulsed with renewed vigor in the warm smiles exchanged between neighbors, the laughter of children playing once again, and people dancing to the tunes. Though the scars of the townspeople's struggles remained, they served as reminders of the strength and courage that had carried them through the darkest of times. With each step, the people of Cheboygan reclaimed their town, their homes, and their lives, united in the knowledge that they had survived adversity head-on and emerged victorious.

Lindsey Merritt and Mary Thompson leaned against the trunk of a maple tree that had stood sentinel in Cheboygan's town square for longer than anyone could remember. She watched as Aedan and his father walked back to the celebration, her brown eyes reflecting a mixture of pride and contemplation. The festive lights woven through the branches above her flickered like stars coming down to celebrate. "Hey, Lin and Mary." Tim's voice broke through her daydream as he approached, his broad shoulders casting a shadow in the glow of the celebration lights.

"Tim," Mary said, offering him a loving smile. "Can you believe it? After everything..." He shrugged, a boyish grin on his face. "We did good, didn't we?"

"More than good," Sheriff Ford chimed in as he walked up, joining their little circle. His once stoic demeanor was softened by the trials they'd faced together. "You kids—you've shown this town what real courage looks like."

Lindsey felt herself blush at the praise. "We had a great example," she said, nodding toward Ford.

The sheriff chuckled, tipping his hat back slightly. "Well, I learned a thing or two myself.

Trusting in others...that's been my biggest takeaway from all of this."

"Speaking of trust." Lindsey turned to look at Aedan, who was now making his way over to them. "I never would've thought—"

"That he'd be the one leading us out of the dark?" Tim completed her sentence with a knowing look of sarcasm.

"Exactly," Lindsey agreed, her bright eyes meeting Aedan's as he joined them.

"Hey," Aedan breathed out, a hint of vulnerability beneath his newfound confidence. The way he looked at her, with admiration, was so different from before; it was because he realized he truly loved her—she was not just the girl he grew up with, but the person she'd become in all her true potential.

"Hey, yourself," Lindsey replied, her heart skipping a beat, but she smiled ear to ear. "Look at us," Aedan said, his blue eyes bright with emotion, "the ragtag team that saved Cheboygan."

"Ragtag?" Tim scoffed playfully. "Speak for yourself, O'Connor."

A ripple of genuine laughter passed between them, binding them tighter than any shared danger ever could. They gathered closer, their shadows merging into one.

"Here's to defeating Al Ana, to saving our town..." Aedan raised an imaginary glass.

"...and to find family in unexpected places," Mary added, her voice thick with emotion.

"To become stronger than we ever thought possible," Tim interjected with a nod.

Sheriff Ford, eyes glistening, tipped his hat once more. "And to new beginnings—for everyone."

They stood there in a huddle, each lost in their reflections of the harrowing journey behind them, yet united in the profound transformation it had wrought.

"Thank you," Aedan said quietly, his words laced with the gravity of their shared experiences. "For everything."

"Always," Tim replied, his protective nature still at the forefront.

"Forever," Lindsey echoed, realizing at that moment how deeply their lives were intertwined.

"Family doesn't always mean blood," Sheriff Ford stated, the wisdom in his voice grounding them all.

"Yes," Mary agreed, looking around at the faces of her friends. "Family."

In that simple affirmation, the past and the present melded into a promise of sustained support, of adventures yet to come, and of a unity that would stand against whatever future threats loomed over the horizon.

Aedan stepped onto the weathered stones lining the bank of the river, his eyes tracing the gentle flow of water that just days ago was a torrent of chaos. In a nearby bush, the banshee lurked, her presence undetected as she eavesdropped on Aedan and his unsuspecting friends.

Time was of the essence as she absorbed every word, every whisper, every secret shared between them.

The afternoon sun cast dappled light through the leaves, creating a mosaic of shadows and brilliance on the surface. It seemed impossible that this cheerful scene was the final act of their harrowing adventure. "Hard to believe it was all real, isn't it?" Mary's voice broke the hush, her presence beside him both grounding and invigorating.

Aedan turned to look at her, noting how the ordeal had etched a new depth into her brown eyes. "Yeah, like waking from a nightmare into a dream," Aedan replied, tossing a pebble into the river. The ripples spread, carrying away the last vestiges of dread.

"Except we can't wake up from this," Lindsey said softly, watching the water smooth over again. "We've come out stronger, haven't we?"

"Definitely," Aedan agreed, feeling the weight of their experiences solidify into something unbreakable within him. "You know, Lin, I never thought I'd see the day when Cheboygan would be peaceful again."

"Me neither," she confessed, tucking a strand of wavy black hair behind her ear. "But here we are." She hesitated before adding, "And here we'll stay."

"Stay?" He caught the significance of her words, an affirmation that reached beyond the river, beyond the town itself.

"Stay," she confirmed with a nod. "There's more to life than escaping from what scares us." Her gaze met Aedan's, steady and determined. "Thanks to you, I've learned that facing our fears, together, is where true courage lies."

Aedan felt a warmth spread throughout himself, one that had nothing to do with the sunlight filtering through the trees. "Together," he repeated, the word feeling like a promise.

"Hey, how about that movie now?" Lindsey exclaimed, her eyes sparkling with excitement as she flashed a mischievous grin at Aedan. The mere suggestion ignited a fire within her, a burning desire to share this moment with him.

"Um, I'd like that," Aedan responded, his cheeks flushing red as a wave of bashful endearment washed over him. In that instant, their hearts raced with the thrill of possibility, a passionate connection that promised an unforgettable adventure.

"Speaking of the future," Lindsey continued, her tone shifting toward the practical yet laced with a hint of excitement, "we've got college applications coming up. Any idea where you want to go?"

"Wherever I go, preferably the University of Michigan, I want to study something that makes a difference. Maybe paranormal studies or criminal justice," Aedan shared, his mind filled with visions of solving puzzles, protecting people, and even preventing evils like Al Ana from retaking root ever again.

Lindsey smiled; her approval was evident. "I was thinking about environmental science or biology at the same school. After everything, I feel like giving back to nature, you know? I've always wanted to be a Wolverine."

"Sounds like you," Aedan said, returning her smile. There was a comfort in knowing that their paths, while diverging, would always be connected by the bond they shared. "Whatever comes our way, we'll handle it. Just like we did with Al Ana."

"Exactly," Lindsey agreed, with determination. "With the strength we've found in each other, there's nothing we can't face."

They stood side by side, two young warriors forever altered by the battle they'd fought, ready for whatever lay ahead. In the reflection of the water, they saw not just themselves but also the future—a tapestry of challenges and triumphs interlaced with the threads of their indomitable spirit.

A thoughtful pause hung between them before Aedan responded, his voice resolute, "Let's go to the cemetery and say something to our gone-but-not-forgotten friends," Aedan said, glancing at Lindsey, Tim, and Mary, who nodded, understanding the unspoken need to honor those they couldn't bring back.

The walk to the cemetery was silent, each footstep a drumbeat of remembrance. They arrived at the modest gravestones of Tommy Canfeld and Emma Taylor, nestled under the shade of an old willow tree. Aedan felt a chill despite the warmth of the afternoon sun.

"Hey, Tommy...Emma," Aedan began, his voice empathetic. "I wish you could've seen what happened the other day. The town...your town is healing. You both should've been there, laughing and hugging your families."

Aedan knelt, placing a hand on the small gravestone. "I promise you, right here, right now, I'll do whatever it takes...Your stories won't just be cautionary tales—they'll be reminders of the strength we found because of you."

The breeze carried away the weight of his words, and somewhere in the rustling leaves, Aedan heard their quiet acceptance. He rose, his resolve solidifying like the earth beneath his Feet. "Come on," Aedan said, turning to his friends. "We've got a future to build—and dates to go on."

"Damn right," Tim chimed in, clapping Aedan on his back.

"Hey, we're like...like a melody that finally found its harmony," Mary said, her eyes twinkling.

"And that's something worth protecting," Lindsey added, her voice a low rumble amidst the swell of conversation. They all fell into contemplative silence, the kind that speaks volumes without uttering a single word. It was a moment of recognition—for the paths they had walked, the fears they had faced, and the growth they had experienced.

"Look at us," Aedan said with confidence. "We started as fragments, pieces scattered by the wind. And now..." His voice trailed off as he surveyed the faces around him, seeing not just friends, but a family forged in fire.

"Better, stronger, closer," Lindsey said, her hand finding Aedan's and giving it a reassuring squeeze.

"Each of us came into this with our very own demons," Tim reflected, his face distant yet clear. "And look at us now, standing here, not just survivors, but conquerors."

"Conquerors with a cause," Mary quipped, eliciting chuckles from the group.

The festivities had dwindled, the night claiming the square with its starlit shroud. Aedan stood at the fringes of the gathering, his friends beside him, their figures casting long shadows in the glow of the remaining lanterns.

"Feels like we've just closed a book we've been living in," Aedan mused aloud, his voice tinged with a quiet reverence for all the appreciation.

"Only to find there are more chapters ahead," Lindsey countered softly, her eyes reflecting the promise of countless tomorrows.

"Chapters filled with unknowns," Tim added, a grin spreading across his face. "But, hey, that's what makes life an adventure, right?"

"An adventure we're ready for," Mary chimed in, her optimism infectious as she squeezed Tim's shoulder reassuringly.

As the group began to disperse, Aedan wandered back toward the river alone, the gentle babble of water a soothing epilogue to the cacophony of celebration. He crouched down, his fingers curling around a small stone, its surface cool and smooth—a stark contrast to the heated battles they had endured.

"Here's to peace, to those we've lost, and to my future with Lindsey," he said, his words carried away by the breeze. With a flick of his wrist, he sent another stone arching through the air. It kissed the surface of the river, sending ripples cascading outward in concentric circles.

In the dance of ripples, Aedan saw the final defeat of Al Ana—the restoration of peace to Cheboygan. But beyond that, in the ever-expanding rings, he recognized the echoes of their courage, reaching into the unknown, into the adventures yet to come.

With a deep breath, Aedan turned back to join his friends, the stone's entry point now indistinguishable from the rest of the river, as if Al Ana had never disturbed its calm. Birds chirped their thanks as the wildlife went back to normal and with that, their journey was over; they all simply awaited the next sunrise. And with that knowledge held close to their hearts, they faced the dawning of a new day in Cheboygan, ready for whatever lay ahead.

THE END

19

Abandoned Lumber Mill Poem

Start where all things lost yearn to be found,
  Where echoes of the past still swirl amidst the silence around.
  At the old lumber mill by Chook River, where memories reside,
  An ancient place where secrets sleep and time cannot hide.
  In deep shadows, a curse embraces,
  Where evil dwells, in hidden spaces.
  Within forsaken walls, she hides,
  In the darkness where the sorrow lies.
  Beware the room no light can touch,
  Where sounds echo, haunting way too much.
  A place of secrets, long submerged,
  In ancient halls where spirits emerged.
  But remember, in the darkest room,
  There lies a tale of woe and doom.
  For some places hold a curse,
  Where an evil demon dwelt, now in reverse...

— Jerome McGinn

20

Al Ana the Soul Stealer Poem

Al Ana's Curse

Through dark shadows, where secrets hide,
   Al Ana roams with sinister strides.
   With a chilling fear, they start to disappear,
   She's stealing souls, chasing after all your tears.
   With eyes that burn like embers' glow,
   She watches, and waits, as disembodied whispers flow.
   Her dark silhouette dances like deadly mist,

Invading minds, such a bitter twist.
She hunts the vulnerable, the weary soul, the lost and alone,
Whose confidence begins to let go.
With icy breath, she draws them in,
Their cries of anguish drowned from within.
The forest paths, become treacherous mazes,
Where Al Ana's presence casts a deathly haze.
Each step a dance with fear and dread,
As the demon's shadow lingers overhead.
The night conceals her wicked game,
As victims fall, losing their names.
Their souls depart, a stolen flight,
Leaving only silence, void of life.
But hope persists, a flickering flame,
Defying darkness, whispering a name.
A whispered prayer, a holy mist,
Guiding lost souls from the demon's grips.
So tread with care, when night descends,
Because Al Ana lurks, her evil never ends.
May light prevail, drive back the shade,
And souls escape the demon's raid.

— Jerome McGinn

About the Author

A compassionate wanderer, Jerome McGinn's spirit roams far beyond Michigan's borders. From ancient Mayan ruins to the untamed wilderness, his curious mind forever seeks the extraordinary. Whether crafting spine-tingling tales or edge-of-your-seat thrillers, this modern-day Renaissance man embraces life's richness with insatiable zeal. Behold the boundless imagination of a storyteller born to inspire awe.

You can connect with me on:

- https://www.jeromemcginn.com
- https://www.facebook.com/jeromemcginnauthor
- https://www.instagram.com/jerome__mcginn
- https://www.linkedin.com/in/jeromemcginn
- https://www.amazon.com/author/jeromemcginn